damaged

ALSO BY AMY REED

BEAUTIFUL

CLEAN

CRAZY

OVER YOU

damaged

Amy Reed

SIMON PULSE

NEW YORK LONDON TORONTO SYDNEY NEW DELHI

This book is a work of fiction. Any references to historical events, real people,
or real places are used fictitiously. Other names, characters, places, and events are products
of the author's imagination, and any resemblance to actual events or places or persons,
living or dead, is entirely coincidental.

SIMON PULSE

An imprint of Simon & Schuster Children's Publishing Division

1230 Avenue of the Americas, New York, NY 10020

First Simon Pulse hardcover edition October 2014

Text copyright © 2014 by Amy Reed

Jacket photographs copyright © 2014 by Michael Frost

For information about special discounts for bulk purchases, please contact Simon & Schuster
Special Sales at 1-866-506-1949 or business@simonandschuster.com.

The Simon & Schuster Speakers Bureau can bring authors to your live event.

For more information or to book an event contact the Simon & Schuster Speakers Bureau
at 1-866-248-3049 or visit our website at www.simonspeakers.com.

Jacket designed by Russell Gordon

Interior designed by Mike Rosamilia

The text of this book was set in Adobe Garamond Pro.

Manufactured in the United States of America

2 4 6 8 10 9 7 5 3 1

Library of Congress Cataloging-in-Publication Data

Reed, Amy Lynn.

Damaged / Amy Reed. — First Simon Pulse hardcover edition.

p. cm.

Summary: Numb after the death of her best friend, Camille, Kinsey starts to shut down, but Hunter,
Camille's mysterious boyfriend, has other ideas and whisks Kinsey off on a multistate road trip
to forget the ghosts of their pasts and their own fears.

[1. Death—Fiction. 2. Grief—Fiction. 3. Best friends—Fiction.
4. Friendship—Fiction. 5. Automobile travel—Fiction.] I. Title.

PZ7.R2462Dam 2014

[Fic]—dc23

2014002657

ISBN 978-1-4424-5699-0 (hc)

ISBN 978-1-4424-5701-0 (eBook)

For Elouise, my heart in the wild

ONE

It's morning again, and I'm waiting for the school bus like a loser. It has now been two months of mornings without Camille pulling up, stereo blaring, in her hand-me-down Ford Taurus. Lately, since she started dating Hunter Collins, the music had changed from soulless pop to moody indie bands neither she nor I had ever heard of, which, quite frankly, seemed a little ridiculous in contrast to her windswept deep brown hair, wholesome cherubic face, and homecoming queen status. Equally ridiculous was loud music on a country road at seven thirty in the morning, pulling up in front of a barn-turned-house-turned-pottery-studio-slash-showroom.

Now there is no ride. I must walk the quarter mile to

Grandma's house on the other end of the property, where the school bus picks me up because that is technically my address. I could have told the driver to pick me up where I actually live—"the slave quarters," as Mom likes to call it—but I couldn't bear to burden him with the knowledge that not only did my best friend die two months ago in a horrible car accident during which I was driving, but I am also poor and living with a crazy "artist" in a glorified shack owned by a grumpy old lady who wants nothing to do with either of us. That's too much bad fortune for most people to bear. People like you to think they care, that they're endless pits of compassion, but in reality, information like this makes them start sweating and getting all squinty, and all they want to do is get as far away from you as possible before they catch whatever you have.

So I keep quiet and let people think the more pleasant stuff about me: straight A student, soccer star, full athletic scholarship to the University of Michigan in the fall. That makes them happy. People love to hear about the kid with the great future ahead of her. I don't tell them how that shining future has dimmed about 50 percent. I don't tell them that Camille was supposed to be my roommate, that we had already secured our dorm room for next year. I don't tell them about our plans, the life stories we'd been writing together since we were little kids, how we were going to be together for the rest of our lives.

ONE FREE PACK OF ANY MARKTEN® CARTRIDGES

| MANUFACTURER'S COUPON | EXPIRES 4/30/2015 |

Consumer: Limit one coupon per purchase of specified product per store visit. Limited to tobacco consumers of legal age to purchase. Valid in face-to-face transactions only. Not to be transferred, sold, or reproduced. Any other use constitutes fraud. Participation in this promotion at discretion of the retailer. Offer good only in U.S.A. **Retailer:** We will reimburse your normal retail price plus sales tax, plus postage and 8¢ handling, provided you have complied with the terms of the Nu Mark LLC Coupon Redemption Policy. Void when submitted by unauthorized agent. We reserve the right to request and verify retailer's purchases and sales of our products. VOID WHERE PROHIBITED. Cash value 1/20¢. Redeem by mailing to: Nu Mark LLC, CMS Box 97100, 1 Fawcett Drive, Del Rio, TX 78840. This is not a Nu Mark LLC mailing address. My normal retail price per pack of MarkTen® e-vapor cartridges, plus sales tax, is $_____.

© 2015 Nu Mark LLC F3846
MARKTEN and related design marks are trademarks of Nu Mark LLC.

1970114809177523

5 97100 20501 0

0097100-126708

01-571896

Enjoy this offer.

For more MarkTen® e-vapor offers, call 1-855-MARKTEN.

FREE

Pack of cartridges for your MarkTen® rechargeable e-vapor device.

■ Classic *or* Menthol ■

~2.5% nicotine by weight at time of manufacture. For more information visit MarkTen.com

We were going to move to San Francisco after we graduated, get an apartment together, be maid of honor at each other's wedding, have kids at the same time and raise them like siblings, buy houses on the same block, and after our husbands died we'd become roommates again, sharing an apartment in some hip retirement community where we'd race each other in our motorized wheelchairs. I don't tell anyone about how we were supposed to be together. Forever. Always.

But enough about that. There is no use whining about what could and should have been. Camille is dead and I am not. What I need to do is focus on the future, when I can leave this place and all of its history behind, when all of this will fall away, when everything and everyone will be new and fresh, when I will be new and fresh, and the world will be full of possibility again.

It's been two months since Camille died, and I haven't cried yet.

In theory, I know this is supposed to be the saddest I've ever been in my whole life. But in practice, I feel nothing. You may wonder how this is possible. You may think *something is wrong with this girl*. But no—I am in fact handling this in the most logical and efficient way possible. Focused. Unsentimental. These are good things. They are signs of a successful, determined individual. Mom, however, disagrees. But she is not a successful, determined individual. She is a mentally unstable, failed artist on food stamps who sells tourists pottery out of a shed in Middle of Nowhere, Michigan.

Mom takes twisted pride in the belief that her apocalyptic mood swings make her some sort of authority on feelings. On the day of Camille's funeral, she held my wrist in her fingers, and after a few seconds said, "Good, a pulse." I just shrugged and started walking without her to Grandma's for a ride, because (1) it was time to leave for the funeral, (2) I don't have a car, (3) Grandma does, (4) I haven't been too into driving after the accident, (5) Mom never got her license, and (6) even though she hates us and wants to spend as little time with us as possible, Grandma was still, like everyone in the next three counties, going to the funeral, and knew it would be way too evil, even for her, to refuse us a ride.

So Mom grabbed her purse and followed me out the door in her way-too-red-for-a-funeral dress and said, "Kiddo, if I wasn't there to see you come out of my vagina, I'd think you were a robot." She says I didn't cry as a baby; I would just frown and make a forceful yet passionless squawk to make my requests known.

I didn't cry then and I didn't cry at the funeral. I per-formed my duty, went to the church, hugged Camille's par-ents, hugged her/our friends, hugged a bunch of people I barely knew, sat somber as the priest and various people spoke about how great she was. I watched the casket being lowered into the ground, but I knew she wasn't really in there. It was just her body, just her bag of bones, not her soul. That flew away the moment her head smashed in. It could still be flying around, lost on its way to wherever souls go when their bodies fail them. Camille could still be around here somewhere, invisible, looking for a new home.

While everyone cried, I remember wondering who mows the grass at the cemetery. How long does it take to mow all that grass? When the mower guy is finished, does he have to go back to the beginning and start all over again? How does he feel driving over graves, with the blades chopping mere feet above skeletons? These are the things I thought instead of crying.

If Camille were here, she'd tell me I'm being crazy, that I'm in denial about my feelings. She'd have some great explanation for why crying is good, something about the great landscape of human emotion, the importance of catharsis, how holding back feelings is the cause of psychic distress and even physical illness. She was a big fan of feelings, and she could be very convincing. She was a lot smarter than anyone knew.

Camille would tell me to snap out of whatever this is that I'm doing, and for her, maybe I would actually try. She'd look at me with her big brown eyes and I'd know I could tell her anything. I'd let her fill me full of ice cream and show me those horrible rom-coms she loved, and maybe I'd actually laugh at the parts that were supposed to be funny, and we'd fall asleep on her parents' big couch with popcorn stuck in our hair, feeling safer and saner than I've ever felt anywhere. Her mom would come in on her way to bed and remind us to brush our teeth, as she has done almost every Friday night since we were old enough for sleepovers. Camille would chase me around the bathroom growling, with rabies toothpaste foam all over her face, and I'd forget what I was pretending to not be so upset about.

It sounds cheesy and sentimental, and I hate that just about as much as I hate crying, but I would be lying if I said Camille didn't make me a better person. Ask anyone who knew us, and they'd tell you the same thing, except probably not as nicely. She calmed me. She helped me breathe. Just being near her, just hearing her voice, made it easier for me to rein in the sadistic drill sergeant part of myself. But now that she's not here, that part of myself seems like the only thing I have left. That demanding voice is the only one I can hear in the space where hers once was. So I listen. It's better than the alternatives. It's better than silence.

But enough thinking about Camille. The more I think

about her, the closer I am to slipping into crying territory, and that is not an option. I have work to do. I have the rest of my life to figure out now that she's not in it.

As sad as this all is, the truth is that tears don't change anything. Tears don't bring Camille back. But no one else seems to have gotten that memo. People for miles around, people who never even met Camille, have shed gallons of tears for the beautiful, kind, and smart homecoming queen whose life was cut too short. I know they cry for me too—the best friend, the driver of the car. Poor girl, they think. I must feel so responsible, they think. They Dr. Phil their way into a diagnosis—PTSD, survivor's guilt. "It wasn't your fault," everyone reminds me—teachers, classmates, the school psychologist, the freaking mailman. I was driving the car, yes, but I was 100 percent sober. And the driver of the oncoming truck wasn't. And his truck was so much bigger than the car I was driving. And he had the yield sign, not me. And I had my hands at ten and two. And I aced driver's ed. They say all these things, petting me like I'm some fragile thing, praying they won't be the one who finally breaks me. They have a vague sense of obligation to comfort me, to ask me how I'm doing, but no one really wants the truth. No one wants me to actually take them up on their offer—"Anything you need, honey. Anytime." Their sighs of relief are audible when I tell them I'm fine. They're off the hook, I'm not their responsibility, they can go back to their lives and forget all about me. But they still get to feel proud of themselves because they "made the effort." They still get to be the hero even though they didn't do any actual work.

Who knows, maybe I am part robot like Mom says. Maybe that's the part I got from my father. Maybe that's the big secret— my father was a robot—and that's why Mom refuses to tell me anything about him except (1) we left him when I was two (she says "we" as if I had a choice in the matter) and (2) he's dead now.

But, whatever. Enough about the Man Who Shall Not Be Spoken Of. I see the school bus chugging itself in my direction as I swat mosquitoes in front of Grandma's house. "House" is actually an understatement. It's a mansion. It has a fancy historical registry sign in front of it because it was built in 1868. A few times a year, cars full of stuffy old Historical Society of Michigan board members and big donors show up for Grandma's catered soirees (which Mom and I are never invited to). She lives in there alone with eight unused bedrooms and six unused bathrooms. I stopped asking Mom a long time ago why we don't live with her, when the house has so much extra space and is so much nicer than our place. She has never given me a good answer. She always says something like, "I lived in that museum for seventeen years and barely made it out alive. Trust me, you do not want to live in there with that woman.

She'd crush us with darkness. We're much better out here in the slave quarters."

I feel all eyes on me as the bus pulls up. I'm still something of a fascination for the underclassmen who don't know enough to try to act cool and not stare. I'm the only senior riding the bus besides Jack "Booger" Bowers and two special ed kids. Just one and a half more weeks of this, I tell myself as I make my way down the narrow aisle to the back of the bus. Just six more school days and one weekend until I'm free from all these peoples' memories. I look out the window and try not to think for the rest of the bus ride. I add up the address numbers in my head. I make up equations with the numbers I see on passing license plates. Numbers are clean. Numbers don't have feelings.

I can't get off the bus fast enough as it pulls up at Wellspring High School. I don't enter the school through the front door anymore. I don't want to walk past all those huddles of people, all the cliques in their usual places. There are some I want to avoid more than others, the various gradations of friends and half friends. I don't want to see their sad, expectant eyes. I don't want to have to make another excuse for why I'm not stopping to talk.

So I go around to the side entrance where all the computer geeks congregate. They are all so wrapped up in their various handheld devices that no one even notices me. I make a quick trip to my locker, arrive to class early, and take my seat in the empty classroom. I take out my book and homework and set it on my desk. I open the novel I'm reading and shove my face in it—the universal sign for "Leave me alone."

Two months is long enough for most people to stop feeling the need to hug me, which is a huge relief. Camille was always the hugger, not me. It's been long enough for teachers to stop offering me extensions on assignments, which I never took anyway. Coach Richards stopped bugging me about my quitting track and field weeks ago, after there were no more races left to run. Classrooms no longer turn silent when I enter. People have more or less gotten used to this half version of me, the Kinsey-without-Camille, the girl with the dead best friend. They keep their distance accordingly, as if death is contagious.

One by one, our friends have taken my hands in theirs, looked into my eyes, and, oh so earnestly, said something to the effect of "Kinsey, we already lost Camille. We don't want to lose you, too." For a couple of weeks, I went through the motions of caring. I sat at our lunch table pretending to eat while they talked about everything except the fact that they had already spread out to fill in Camille's usual spot.

They had always been Camille's friends more than mine. I'm not like her, not the social butterfly who considers dozens of people "friends." Truthfully, I only ever had one friend. The rest were acquaintances, people I could take or leave, people I don't miss now that they've given up trying to keep me in their circle. They have filled in my space at the lunch table now too. It's like we were never even there.

I've started bringing my own sad lunch to school so I can avoid the cafeteria—PB and J or leftovers of whatever I can find in the kitchen. I've never liked crowds in general, but now the lunchroom is completely unbearable. The seniors seem even more manic than in years past, as if the upcoming graduation means leaving more than just high school. It means shedding the heavy tragedy that still poisons the air despite everyone's crazed attempts at cheerfulness. They can shake off Camille's death when they throw their caps in the air at graduation in two weeks. That will be the real goodbye, more so than the candlelight vigil, the assembly at school, the standing-room-only funeral, the interviews with news reporters who came all the way from Grand Rapids and even Chicago. In only a handful of days, high school will be over. Everyone will finally have permission to forget.

I eat outside behind the gym, even though it's humid and pushing ninety already, even though the mosquitoes have come early and the news has been warning that the Midwest is on track to have the hottest summer on record this year. "Global warming!" my mother always wails when it's hot. That's when almost anyone else around here would mutter "Damn hippie" under their breath. This is the part of the country where science is called liberal propaganda.

But I'll take the company of the mosquitoes over the cafeteria any day. At least I can breathe. At least I don't have a couple hundred people looking at me and whispering, waiting for me to cry.

I'm the only one out here except for the burnouts under the bleachers. I can see their heads bobbing through the slats, the cloud of smoke hovering in the heavy, wet air. If I was someone else, I might want to join them. I might want to deal with Camille's death by getting lost in that cloud of smoke, by simply trading in this world for another.

But that is not my way. I am not weak like them. I will stay in this world and I will follow my plan no matter what. I am stronger than sadness and loss and tragedy. You have to be if you want to succeed. At the end of the day, that's what matters: Strength. Endurance. Perseverance. Moving on in spite of everything.

One more day, done. Just five more school days until the end of high school forever.

The bus is loud on the ride home. Everyone is giddy with

their upcoming escape. I stare out the window and try to tune them out as I watch the world go by. We drive through town before heading onto the rural roads. A few tourists wander the sidewalk like zombies, looking for things to buy. People vacation here for the lake and the dunes, but they always end up in town at least once. When they realize there's nothing for them but a grocery store, a couple of crappy antiques shops, and a working-class town trying to survive, they head back to their vacation homes. I think they're shocked that real people actually live here, that we're not all on vacation like them, that most of us can't even afford most of the stuff they do here. Except for maybe Hunter Collins's family and their Midwestern empire of crappy chain diners called Kountry Kitchens.

And now, as if the thought conjured him out of thin air, there he is: Hunter. Camille's boyfriend. On the sidewalk. Riding his skateboard with a paper bag in his hand. It's the first time I've seen him since the accident. I'd heard rumors that he'd gone off the deep end, stopped going to school, started drinking a lot. The bag in his hand is crumpled around the shape of a bottle.

He has the blue eyes, tan skin, and chiseled cheekbones of an all-American boy, the star quarterback, the homecoming king. There's a sense that he could have been any of these things if it weren't for the slouch in his posture; the permanent scowl; the greasy, chin-length hair hanging in front of his eyes, so greasy I can't tell if it's brown or wet blond; the cloud in his eyes, the mix of sadness and anger. It's like he's a good design that somehow got mangled; somewhere on the assembly line, a piece of him went missing.

Camille always accused me of secretly looking down on her for being popular, for being homecoming queen, for loving horses, for genuinely liking her family and her life. But the truth is I was in awe that anyone could be that happy; her capacity for joy was superhuman. There's no wondering what Hunter saw in her. Everyone loved Camille. She was beautiful, yes, but that's too obvious. She was one of those rare popular girls who was also incredibly kind. Not *nice*—that's different than kind; that's just acting. Camille was a genuinely good person, and genuinely cared about pretty much everyone and everything she met. She cared about me. For some mysterious reason, she loved me best out of everyone who loved her.

I look at Hunter now and everything about him is the opposite of that girl I remember, the darkness to her light. What did she see in him? Was he something for her to fix? To shine and make pretty? Something to make her feel serious, to give her depth? Or was her desire something as shallow as the good girl wanting to take a spin with the bad boy, senior year, a few months before college, slumming it before growing up?

But she said she loved him. She didn't tell me much, but she said that. She only ever said that. And maybe that's the reason she didn't tell me anything else, because when she looked me in the eye and said, "Kinsey, I think I'm in love with Hunter Collins," with the most serious, earnest look I'd ever seen in our fourteen years of friendship, I laughed in her face. Because the first thing I said was, "You can't be serious. Not that loser."

Looking at him now, at this brooding, half-drunk boy across the street, I still have no idea what she could have loved. Something inside me squeezes tight, pushes the air out of my lungs. My heart caves in, stops beating, at the realization that there are things I didn't know about Camille, huge expanses of her insides that she never showed me, a secret life where she was capable of loving this feral creature on the sidewalk, where her love of him meant she must have loved me less. And I hate him for it.

I close my eyes to make him go away. I count to ten. This is the closest I've ever gotten to remembering Camille since she died. *Really* remembering her. She is suddenly more than a name, more than a timeline and empty facts. I have gone beneath the surface, something I promised myself I wouldn't do. I let this feeling get too far; I didn't stop it soon enough. It takes all my concentration to push it away, to clean my mind, to empty myself of these useless feelings.

But when I open my eyes, Hunter seems suddenly closer.

His eyes meet mine like magnets.

I am colder than I've ever been.

I can't look away.

The world falls away and there is only us.

He is standing on the sidewalk with his skateboard in his hand, with the same look on his face I must have on mine, one of surprised terror. The cloud in his eyes is gone. It has been replaced by something even sharper than fear.

Something has shifted, started, some kind of ticking, a timer; where there once was stillness there is now vibration, tiny unravelings. I have become a time bomb. Something inevitable is going to happen. The bus starts moving and our heads turn, synchronized, our eyes holding on to each other. He starts walking, then running as the bus picks up speed, but he can't keep up. He jumps on his skateboard but it is too late. The bus turns the corner and he is gone, as easy as I conjured him.

When he is out of sight, I can breathe again. My body goes back to normal. I have no idea what that feeling was, but it's over now. Hunter is gone, out of my life. There will be no more surprise rushes of feeling, no more losing control.

I look up to find a sea of beady eyes staring at me. He was not my apparition. They all saw him too. They saw me see him. They saw him running after the bus. There will be talk, people will speculate about what this means, but I don't care. These people, this world, will be out of my life soon. They can go on thinking whatever they like while I move on and leave them behind.

Everyone for miles around knows the story of the accident. Most probably assume we're some kind of unit now—Kinsey Cole and Hunter Collins, the best friend and the boyfriend. The survivors. But the truth is, that night was the first and only time I ever met Hunter Collins. Being present at the same death did not turn us into friends, did not automatically create a connection where there was none to begin with. It was simply an unfortunate coincidence that we crossed paths at that particular moment. Then our paths went in different directions. End of story. Until now, I suppose. But that was a fluke, never to be repeated.

It shocks people to discover that Hunter and I are not in touch, that we haven't latched onto each other for comfort, that we haven't established some sort of support group where we relive the accident over and over and cry in each other's arms about how much we miss Camille. Until now, I haven't seen him since that night and I don't plan to. Why would either of us make the effort to connect when all it would do is remind us about the one tragic thing we have in common? The logical thing for both of us is to move on and try to forget.

But I can't help remembering the night they met. I can't help thinking I could have done something to stop it. It started out a party like every other party Camille dragged me to so I could be more "social." She had dressed me up in some of her clothes, none of which looked right. She had been complaining about how sick she was of the boys at our school, how she had known them all since kindergarten, how boring they all were, how shallow. I was trying to be useful, telling her to wait for college. But she was never good at waiting.

I remember the moment she saw Hunter across the room. I saw the look in her eyes that said she had just made up her mind about something. I looked where she was looking, saw the long-haired, heavy-lidded guy with the beer in his hand leaning against the wall, looking both cooler and more dangerous than any of the guys at school. We both knew who he was. Word gets around when someone new and mysterious shows up. I knew as much about him as she did: recent relocation from Chicago, senior at the high school the next town over, rich, rumors of drug selling, a possible criminal record, a drinking problem, maybe even a violent streak.

All I did was say, "Camille, no." But she started walking in his direction. I did not follow, did not grab her arm, did not make up some excuse for why we had to leave. As soon as I saw her plastic cup greet his in its muted cheers, I turned around, left the party, and walked the three miles home.

But I don't want to think about that. I don't want to think about Hunter. I don't want to think about Camille, but no matter how hard I resist, she keeps trying to come back, even after I took all the pictures of her down from my wall, even after I put away all the things she ever gave me or let me borrow, even after I stopped doing all the things we used to do together, even after I stopped returning her mom's phone calls. It should be easier to forget. It should be easier to wipe my mind clean. I've been able to handle it until now, until Hunter showed up and made his messy appearance in my tidy life. I've always been able to fight off the memories before they solidified, but now it feels like a barrier's been broken, a wall has come crumbling down, and I am suddenly exposed, vulnerable. How could seeing someone I barely know for a few seconds do this? Maybe I'm tired. Or maybe the memories are getting stronger than me.

The bus drives out of town and into the cornfields. I try to forget how much Camille changed in the three short months they were dating, how she waited so long to introduce us, how suddenly she had secrets. I try to forget how little Hunter tried to win me over the night we finally officially met, how he didn't seem to care what I thought of him at all. Everyone talked about how he wasn't at the funeral, just like they talked about how I didn't cry. I shove all of this out of my mind as the bus pulls up in front of Grandma's house and I get off. As I walk the quarter mile to my house, I ready myself for another game of avoidance.

There's a rental car parked in front of the PEACE DOVE POTTERY sign (I can tell it's a rental because no one actually drives white midsize sedans by choice). Mom has customers. I practice a smile in preparation.

The bells on the door jingle as I open it and for a moment I feel like a visitor in my own house. I have to act different when there are customers around—friendly—and, quite frankly, I don't have the energy right now. I want to run through the showroom to the kitchen, shove my face full of cereal, and peacefully study for my last round of tests before it's time to leave for work.

As I enter, I am attacked by something fast, white, furry, and yapping. I feel a sting in my ankle as the creature latches onto my pant leg, so I do the only thing any sane person would do in this situation—I kick. The thing goes flying across the room and lands at the feet of a severely obese woman standing next to an equally obese man.

"Kinsey!" my mom yells.

"Snowflake!" the fat woman cries.

I pull up my pant leg to see two small beads of blood, like the bite of a baby vampire.

The woman lifts the dog off the floor and starts babbling at it in a baby voice. Mom glares at me, like it's my fault I was attacked.

"Sorry," I say. "Is it okay?"

"Snowflake is not an *it*," the woman says. "Snowflake is a *she*. Aren't you, baby?" She nuzzles her chubby face into the evil puffball's neck.

"Sorry," I say again.

Mom smiles her winning smile and pats the woman's shoulder. Only I know how much she really hates these people. "It's all right," she coos. "I think everyone just got a little startled. Isn't that right, Snowflake?" Snowflake doesn't answer. "Kinsey, why don't you go in the back and do your homework, okay? I'll start wrapping these up. The berry bowl and the two mugs, right?"

The woman narrows her eyes like she's being tricked. "Yes," the man finally says, pulling out his wallet, no doubt wanting to get this over with as quickly as possible.

The door to the kitchen is behind the counter where they're all standing, so I have to maneuver awkwardly around them.

Mom taps away at her calculator, even though she knows this equation by heart. These are her two best sellers: fifty dollars for a bowl with holes in the bottom; twenty dollars each for coffee mugs with her cheesy dove logo on the side. Hippies love it because it's the sign of peace. Conservatives love it because it supposedly has something to do with Jesus. Mom loves it because it's an easy twenty dollars for something that takes her no time to make.

I grab a bowl of cereal and pour some soy milk on top, then plop down on the couch in the big open space that is our combination kitchen/dining room/living room. Mom declared our household vegan two years ago, very much against my will. "But I'm an athlete!" I protested. "I'm a growing teenager. I need protein." Beans and tofu have protein, she said. Tempeh. Seitan. So I supplement my diet of whole grains and organic vegetables with milk shakes and chili cheese dogs at work. Sometimes I eat up to four hot dogs a night. It's disgusting.

"Fucking tourists," Mom says as she enters the kitchen. I can hear their white car crunching away on the gravel.

"The season's just starting," I say. "You can't be burned-out already."

"Like those two even eat berries," she says. "That bowl is going to end up holding candy or potato chips or whatever it is those pigs eat."

"Be nice," I say. Among other things, my mom is a food snob. This is a strange thing to be when you're on food stamps and living in rural western Michigan, where most people's idea of fine cuisine is fried perch or some kind of casserole doused in cream of mushroom soup. She refuses to make anything resembling a casserole. Instead, she experiments with things like massaged kale, toasted quinoa, acai berries, and various other ingredients she has to convince the grocery store in town to order even though she's the only one who will ever buy them. It's been sixteen years since she lived in San Francisco; you'd think she would have gotten over it by now.

"How was school today?" she says in a sarcastic voice. She's not one for parental conventions like caring how your kid's day is. She's standing at her stage behind the kitchen island where she concocts her culinary experiments, like the rest of the room is the audience to her cooking show. The studio is where she makes and displays her pottery, but the kitchen is where she does a different kind of art with food. With all her creativity, it's pretty remarkable that I got none at all. And she never fails to remind me how much this disgusts and disappoints her.

"Fine," I answer.

"Don't 'fine' me."

"Don't 'how was school today' me."

She throws some roots and vegetables onto the counter. "I think I'm going to make a stew in the slow cooker. It should be ready in about four hours."

"I'm working tonight," I say, drinking the slimy sweet sludge from the bottom of my cereal bowl.

"Do you really need to work this much?"

"Mom, you know I'm saving for next year. I'm going to have expenses."

"You and your planning," she sighs, chopping a purple potato from the garden. "You're so stuck in the future all the time. Always preparing for the worst. It's a self-fulfilling prophecy, you know? If you expect something bad to happen, it will."

"Somebody's got to think about the future," I mumble just loud enough for her to hear. I walk over and put my bowl in the sink. She chops vegetables violently as I walk away.

It's 4:41 p.m. when I get on my bike to ride to work for my shift that starts at five. I can usually get there in eighteen minutes if I haul ass, with one minute left to put on my apron and wash my hands. Like many things, I have this down to a science.

I ride a few miles through farmland, then a patch of what's left of the forest that used to cover this entire area, hearing nothing but the buzz of bugs and the crunch of my tires on the road. In these moments, with my lungs and legs burning, with nothing and no one in sight but road and trees, I can pretend for a moment that I'm somewhere else, somewhere forested and exotic like the Pacific Northwest or Costa Rica. This road could be leading anywhere. I could be an explorer. I could be on my way to discover something no one's seen before. But then the fantasy is inevitably shattered by the homemade sign for SHERI'S HAIR STUDIO tilting precariously in front of a bubblegum-pink double-wide trailer. Half a mile farther is a sign for BOB'S COMPUTER REPAIR at the end of a long weedy driveway. There's nothing exotic in the middle of all these trees, just regular people trying to make a living. Camille and I never had a problem making fun of these roadside businesses and how embarrassingly country they all are, regardless of the fact that my mom's studio and her parents' horse-boarding business are in the same category. This was the only time Camille would come close to showing any meanness—she loved her parents and she loved horses, but she wanted out, same as me. Neither of us was rich. Neither of us was worldly. We were both country girls who desperately wanted to be something else. When things like pizza delivery, high-speed mass transit, corner stores, or ice cream trucks would show on TV, we'd both get quiet, yearning for these urban things as if the tragic lack of them made our lives incomplete.

Our disdain was always strongest on the way to the beach, when we had to pass through Tourist Hell to get to the part of the lake only the locals know about. We'd hold our breath when we turned right on Lakefront Road, when the forest opened into Sunset Village, which is basically just a string of cheap motels, RV parks, and crappy restaurants lining the shore of Lake Michigan. In Camille's car, we felt at least somewhat impenetrable, but on my bike I have to dodge ATVs and mothers yelling at screaming children running across the road. This strip serves a very different tourist from the ones in town nearly fifteen miles away. Sometimes these tourists wander that way, unaware of the unspoken segregation, but mostly they stay here. Somehow they know town is for a different kind of clientele, people who do not stay in RV parks or overcrowded campgrounds or motels boasting free breakfast buffets. South of here, it is like a completely different lake, with no public beaches for miles. Instead, there are dunes and forest dotted with vacation cottages, either owned by their occupants or rented for hundreds or even thousands of dollars per night. The word "cottage" is a misnomer, a strange part of Midwestern vocabulary that has never made sense to me. "Cottage" makes me think of something tiny and quaint, like a life-size version of a gingerbread house. But here it means any vacation home, ones with satellite dishes and hot tubs and tennis courts and three-car garages, ones that are ten times bigger than the shack I live in and used only on weekends for a third of the year. As soon as the leaves start turning, all those miles are abandoned, all those beautiful houses locked up, empty until the sun shines again.

The tourists in Sunset Village will never own cottages. They are lucky to share this cramped, dirty beach with a bunch of other people who will never own cottages. Instead of fine wine, they drink cheap beer in cans softened by beer cozies that read "Beautiful Lake Michigan," even though their section of it is muddy, oily with speedboat exhaust and sunscreen, and dotted with the occasional floating Band-Aid or lost toy. Instead of drifting along the coast in private sailboats, they rent dune buggies to take out their aggression on the sand. Instead of golfing on perfectly manicured courses, they play miniature golf at Art's Arcade & Holes. Then, sunburned and beer-tired, they come to my work demanding hot dogs and milk shakes.

As I coast into the parking lot of Gabby's Snack Shack, I feel a momentary shock of guilt for looking down on these people. It's my mother's judgmental voice in my head, not mine. For someone who's still technically living with her mother and barely making enough money to feed her daughter, she still manages to be a snob about a lot of things. Whenever the topic of Sunset Village tourists comes up, she always gets a disgusted look on her face. She refers to them as "those people." When I tell her she's being elitist, she refuses to believe me, as if her liberal beliefs automatically trump her actual behavior. Sometimes she's just as bad as Grandma.

I lock up my bike and fall through the door of Gabby's Snack Shack at exactly 4:56 p.m., a new record. Contrary to the name, there is no Gabby. My boss, Bill, bought the place eight years ago from a guy named Kevin. He didn't know who Gabby was either.

"Ahoy there, matey!" Bill says from the cash register, where he is ringing up a very sunburned family.

"Hi, Bill," I say. As much as I hate serving tourists, I always feel a strange sense of relief when I hear Bill's welcome. Especially lately, work has become one of the four things I look forward to, besides running, sleeping, and eating. Bill never tries to talk to me about Camille. The tourists don't even know she ever existed. Here, I can be totally anonymous, someone besides the girl whose best friend died. Here, I'm expected to just do my job, eat as much free food as I want, and listen to Bill's bad jokes.

"Don't sweat on the food," Bill says. The customers don't find it as funny as he does. They follow me with their eyes as I throw my bag under the counter, tie my apron around my waist, and wash my hands.

"How's tricks?" Bill says.

"Meh," I respond. Bill is one of those jolly old guys who it's impossible not to like. And what's crazier, he genuinely seems to like people, *all* people, even the most demanding and ungrateful and untipping of tourists. It's impossible to not cheer up at least a little when you're around him, which is part of why I actually like my job, despite the horrible clientele, terrible pay, and the fact that I go home smelling like grease after every shift. It's nice to be around someone who always seems so genuinely happy to see me. Sometimes I feel like Bill's the only person in western Michigan who isn't waiting to see me cry.

"Have I got a surprise for you!" Bill says. He often speaks with exclamation points.

"A raise?"

"Even better!" he says, then calls over to the back of the restaurant, "Hey, Jessie, come over here. I want you to meet Kinsey."

From behind the soft-serve machine emerges a mousy girl I think I recognize from school. "Hi," she squeaks. She squints as she stares at me. "You're Kinsey Cole."

"Yes," I say. "I know."

"Oh my god!" She covers her mouth with her hands and her eyes grow wide. "Is this Camille Hart's job? Did I take Camille Hart's old job? Oh my god."

There is nothing I can say to make this not suck. Bill swoops in to save the day. "No, no, honey," he says. "Camille didn't work here." He catches my eye and blinks an apology. "In fact," he continues, his voice so upbeat I can tell this Jessie girl is already forgetting what she was upset about, "it's just been me and Kinsey the last couple years. But this summer's going to be busy, I can feel it! And that's where you come in, Jessie. You're going to save the day!"

Since when do we need someone to save the day? Why didn't Bill tell me he was hiring someone new? Did he actually think I'd be happy about it? All this means is I have to share my meager tips with someone else. And now I have one less thing in my life that doesn't suck.

If Bill thought hiring someone new would mean less work for me, he was sadly mistaken. Not only did I have to run the register while he was in the back cooking, I also had to train the incompetent Jessie and run interference all night to try to prevent her from knocking things over. For someone so small, it's pretty amazing how much damage she can do.

I ride my bike home in twilight, sticky with four-hour-old sweat and French fry grease. My shorts are slimed pink with the remains of a double-scoop strawberry ice cream cone Jessie seemed to have flung across the restaurant at me in an epileptic fit. I have no idea how many times she said "I'm sorry" to me over the course of the night, but I would estimate it to be in the hundreds.

If I ride fast enough, I can't smell myself. So I tear through the night, fueled by three hot dogs, two bags of potato chips, a root beer float, and frustration. Bats dance their creepy silhouette against the darkening sky. Something about them makes my heart clench tight with an impending memory, but I push it away before it has a chance to solidify, an action that has become so automatic I barely notice it anymore. In my head, I cross off "work" from the short list of things I enjoy.

In a few minutes, I will be home. Mom will be working in her studio, one of the few times she doesn't feel the need to talk to me. I will take a shower, brush my teeth, crawl into bed, and drift away to a place where things are still as they should be.

Forest. Night. You call bats flying vermin. You are trying to make a joke. But I can't laugh. Not tonight. I am stone, my jaw cement. I am trying to punish you.

You say, "Say something, Kinsey."

I say, "Something."

"Very funny."

The lightning bugs are early. You want to stop and catch them but I keep driving. This is not a time for diversions. The night is unsalvageable. You are the only one laughing. You laugh harder to fill up the silence, to make up for me, to make up for him, to make up for the fact that neither of us is trying.

We should have known. The bats and the lightning bugs making ominous promises, all their dashing and blinking, their violent silence screaming a warning.

"Kinsey," you say, but you are not talking to the girl in the car. You are talking to the sleeping girl, the watching girl, the Kinsey of now, the Kinsey outside this memory. I am driving but I am not driving. We are here but we are not here. We are only visitors, tourists. You are taking me on a trip. You are my tour guide. Making me remember.

"What, Camille?" I say, my voice slicing the dark.

This is where you take me. The night, dark. The party, painful. Hunter and me, lost in our own silences. He has too much to drink. I stay too sober. I insist on driving. You say I always want to drive when I can't fix things.

This is how we cope: You laugh when you get nervous. You laugh when you are scared of the dark. A shadow in the shape of Hunter is slumped in the backseat, nothing more than a mannequin for this memory, a placeholder. He knows so many ways to sleep. I hold on to the steering wheel tight. The whiter my knuckles, the safer I feel.

"Kinsey, the next part is going to suck." This is not what you said then, but it is what you say now.

"We can stop it," I say.

"No we can't," you tell me. "It already happened." Then you laugh. "And you're supposed to be the smart one."

"We just have to try."

"But, Kinsey," I hear your voice say inside my head. "You can't fix everything. Some things you just have to let happen. Some things you just have to let go."

TWO

Camille.

It is dark. I can't breathe. I am hot and sweaty and tangled.

Someone tied these sheets around me while I was sleeping.

Camille.

You were here.

Was it you who tied me up like this?

I can still hear your voice. I can hear you saying my name.

I feel the seat belt across my chest.

The night in my hair.

The bugs in my ears.

My hands squeezing tight.

The night, ready to explode.

No. This is my room. I blink. I pull my arm out of the sheet and turn on the lamp. Everything is where I put it. This corner, that corner. The ceiling, the floor. All hard, sturdy, real. Everything where it belongs. The shadows blur the edges, but they are not dark enough for you to hide in.

Camille. I was sitting right next to you. I could have reached my hand over and touched you. But I couldn't even look. It was my last chance to look at you.

No. It was a dream. Just my brain firing synapses. Just electricity, just chemistry. Just something made out of nothing.

Camille is dead, there's nothing I can do about it, and I have a history test to study for.

Mom walks into the living room in her bathrobe and slippers, and I'm already showered, dressed for school, and hours into studying for a test I know I'm going to ace.

"Didn't you get the memo?" she says as she puts a kettle on the stove for tea. "You're graduating in a few days. It's kind of a rule that you don't have to study for your last tests."

"I don't want to mess up my 4.0," I say, and even though I'm not looking at her, I can tell she's rolling her eyes.

"You got accepted to college months ago," she sighs. "They're not going to unaccept you because you get a B on one test."

I have the only mother on earth who wants her kid to work less hard at school. She'd rather I run off and join the circus. Good grades are my twisted form of rebellion.

"What are you going to do when you have nothing left to study for?" she says.

I open my mouth for a witty response, but nothing comes. What *am* I going to do? My stomach drops at the thought of a whole summer with only work to kill my time. What am I supposed to do with the rest of the hours of the day?

"Are you going to have any fun this summer?" she says. "You're *eighteen*, Kinsey. Do you have any idea what that means?"

It means I'm technically an adult. It means I'm going to college in the fall. It means I'm getting away from you and this town for good. It means I'm going to be free.

I collect my things and stuff them in my backpack. "I have to go to school," I say, not answering her question.

Mom sighs like I am the world's greatest disappointment. "How is it possible that I raised such a little Republican?"

The test is easy and I finish long before everyone else. I spend the rest of class alternating between trying not to fall asleep and obsessing about the fact that I have nothing left to study for. I only got about four hours of sleep last night, and it's hard to keep my eyes open, but ever since my conversation with Mom this morning, I can't stop thinking about the summer, dreading the endless hours of waiting for my life to start.

As I'm walking to my last class of the day, one of our old friends, Heather, stops me in the hall.

"Kinsey!" she says, and throws her arms around me. I try to hug back, but it's never been something I'm good at. "How are you?" she says. Maybe it's because I'm so tired, maybe it's because I've accidentally caught some end-of-school nostalgia, but something inside me softens and I find that I actually don't hate talking to her.

"I'm okay," I say. "Just trying to make it through these last days of school."

"Yeah, tell me about it. It's torture, isn't it?"

I nod, not knowing what else to say.

"Do you have any plans for this summer?" she says, the conversation quickly confirming itself as small talk, which most conversations inevitably are, which is one of the main reasons I try to avoid talking to people.

"Working, I guess. Getting ready for college. What about you?"

"Same. Hopefully spending a lot of time at the beach. That's what I wanted to talk to you about. A bunch of us are going to the beach after school. Will you come, Kinsey? You can ride with me. Please? I miss you. We all miss you."

I don't even have time to think of a good excuse before "Yes" comes sputtering out of my mouth. Where did that come from? My hand flies to my lips in surprise, as if I just swore in church or accidentally blurted out a big secret. I did not mean to say yes. I do not want to go to the beach with Heather. I do not want to hang out with old half-friends. I do not want to be in the sun and around people laughing.

"Really?" Heather says, as surprised as I am at my response. "Oh my god, that makes me so happy! I'll meet you in front after school, okay?"

"Okay," I say because I can't think of a way to get out of this.

"We're going to have so much fun!" Heather waves and skips away and I mope my way down the hall to my last class of the day, dreading what I just agreed to.

We're driving to the beach in Heather's old Ford Fiesta, windows down and excruciating boy-band music blaring. According to Camille, who learned from the trusty source of her other best friend, the Internet, you're not really supposed to keep listening to this kind of music after about age thirteen. But here in the country, I guess we're a little bit slow.

I'm crammed in the backseat with Erin and Lacey, two

girls who, even after all these years going to the same school, I still have a hard time telling apart. No one's even vaguely trying to include me in the conversation, which centers around figuring out whose parents are going to be out of town when during the summer, and who they can get to buy booze for the parties. I stick my head out the window, trying to get some relief from the suffocating heat. The road buzzes by below me, and for a moment I feel turned upside down, like I'm no longer inside the car or touching the seat.

I'm floating. I'm hurtling through space.

I'm falling.

I close my eyes. I hold my breath.

I brace myself for impact.

But nothing. I feel the seat, my feet on the floor, and my hand on the door. I open my eyes. I'm still in a car with these girls. They're still planning their summer full of parties. I'm not quite sure what just happened, but I know I need some sleep.

We take the shortcut to avoid Tourist Hell and reach the turnout to the secret beach. Technically this is state park land and should be accessible to everyone, but some brilliant soul put up a PRIVATE PROPERTY NO TRESPASSING sign on the dirt road to this beach a few years back, and no one wants to remove it. Only locals know the sign is a fake, and we plan to keep it that way. Families with kids usually clear out by the late afternoon because everyone knows that's when the teenagers come. And the good kids leave before it gets dark, because that's when trouble—or fun, depending how you look at it—starts.

Like at school, the beach is separated into cliques. Everyone knows the crowd I'm with gets the spot under the big tree closest to the water. There are already a few people over there with blankets and towels spread out. Other groups dot the beach with umbrellas and chairs they stash permanently in the back of their cars all summer. Heather and the other girls chat in front of me as I follow them to the tree, a feeling of dread spreading in my stomach. What did I get myself into? I'm nearly ten miles from home, with no car and no bike. Even if I wanted to walk home, I'm wearing flip-flops and carrying a bag full of books.

The people on the blankets smile at me and say hi with high-pitched, overexcited voices, unable to hide their surprise. I never understood what Camille saw in these people. They're nice enough, but so incredibly boring. After the football season's over, the guys don't do much but get drunk and talk about the football season. And the girls don't do much else besides talk about each other and hang out with the boys. I think Camille was starting to figure this out toward the end, when she was dating Hunter, because she stopped hanging out with them so much. But then again, she also stopped hanging out so much with me. Who knows what she was really thinking?

If Camille were here, she'd tell me I'm being judgmental, that I'm looking for differences in people instead of similarities, that I am setting myself up for alienation. She loved words like that—"alienation." She'd deliver this diagnosis with a straight face, totally serious, and it would be impossible for me to say something cynical and snarky in response. She cared so much, I had to take her seriously. I couldn't shrug her off like I did everything else.

The thing is, she truly believed people are good. All of them. She believed we are all born with good hearts, but sometimes the world beats people into acting against their nature. Even mass murderers. Even rapists and baby killers. Even my mother. Camille believed my mother loves me and is proud of me, but she's so sick and badly medicated that she doesn't know how to show it. Camille could convince me of a lot of things, but she never got very far with this particular theory.

Camille was going to study psychology at U of M. She wanted to be a therapist. She would have been a great therapist. She could have helped so many people.

Stop it. What am I doing? What is wrong with me the last

couple of days? I can't let these thoughts in. I can't let the sadness of missing her slither its way into my consciousness and make me lose focus. If I let it in, it will push everything out. If I let it in, it will take over and never leave.

"Want a beer?" one of the boys asks me.

"No thanks."

That's the longest conversation I've had in about half an hour.

I sit in the shade and watch the girls pull their shirts off. When it gets hot, girls here wear bikinis to school underneath their clothes. I have a feeling this doesn't happen in most parts of the country.

"You're not wearing a suit?" either Erin or Lacey asks me.

"I didn't know I was going to the beach when I was getting dressed this morning."

Camille always said I have a way of making everything sound bitchy.

While the people around me talk, pop open beer cans, and lather sunscreen on each other, I look around the beach. Despite the heat, despite the sunshine, there is something gloomy in the air. The trees seem closer, more towering, leaning in as if to smother us. The end-of-the-year excitement has a sinister tinge to it. But everyone is smiling and laughing like they don't even notice, and maybe it is all in my head. Maybe everyone really is as happy as they seem. Maybe the sun is shining just to shine, with no ulterior motive.

I look around at the other huddles of people. Some of them are going off to college in the fall like me. Some are moving to Grand Rapids or Traverse City or even Chicago right away, eager to accept the first minimum-wage job they can find. Many are sticking around here and going to the local community college. Some will work for their family's farm or business in town, getting ready to take it over someday. Still some haven't even thought that far ahead. I don't know how anyone could consider staying here or, even worse, not think about it at all. How can anyone just let life happen to them like that? How can anyone stand not being in control? That's how you get trapped. That's how you wake up thirty years later and realize you haven't gone anywhere or done anything. That's how you get to the end of your life and realize you've wasted the whole thing.

"It's good to see you here," one of the girls says. Everyone's staring at me.

"Thanks?"

They look away, as if I failed some important test. I was supposed to say something else.

The lake shimmers as a speedboat goes by. A dog barks. I follow the noise to a group of guys on the other side of the beach, dressed in dark, definitely not-beach clothes, huddled in a tiny puddle of shade under a sickly looking tree, circled by a collection of empty beer cans. The dog, a pit bull, is pulling against the leash, trying to get at the boat, which, by now, is probably a mile away. All but one of the guys laughs, but I can't see his face because his back is turned. They look vaguely familiar, but they definitely don't go to my school. Kids from the neighboring town don't usually come to our beach. It's a different kind of town, with a different kind of people. Many of them have their own waterfront property. If not, their families belong to the country club, which has a private, pristine beach much larger than this one.

This beach is small and shaped in a C like an amphitheater, so you can pretty much hear anyone's conversation if you listen hard enough. "Dude, why did you make us come here?" one of the boys says to one whose back is facing me. He doesn't answer. The dog licks his hand, and he pets his head with what seems like extraordinary tenderness. The other guy shrugs and turns to talk to the others. The dog rests his head on the quiet one's knee. Then the mysterious figure turns and stares straight at me, like he knew exactly where I was, like he knew I was staring.

Hunter.

I lose my breath and for a moment, the feeling of falling

from earlier in the car comes back. I should not be here. I pick up my bag and start walking without saying good-bye. I hear a sharp laugh. I hear someone say, "Nice try, Heather." I hear Heather call, "Hey, Kinsey, wait!" but no one makes any real effort to make me stay. I walk, looking straight ahead, trying not to trip on my sandals collecting sand, trying not to look toward Hunter even though I feel his presence pulling at me. I walk and I walk, down the dirt road and through the swarms of mosquitoes hiding in the shade, trying not to feel my shoulders already aching from the weight of my backpack. I hear a car behind me. I move over to let it pass. It slows. An automatic window buzzes down. "Hey!" someone says. I turn. Hunter.

"Are you following me?" I stay, still walking, trying not to flinch from the sharp pieces of gravel stuck in my sandal.

"That's rather presumptuous, don't you think?" he says, driving slowly beside me as I walk.

"Why were you at this beach? Why were you in town yesterday?"

"Maybe *you're* following *me*." He grins, and he transforms for half a second into someone shockingly handsome. Camille always talked about that grin. It made her stupid.

"Where are you going?" he says.

"Home."

"Don't you live, like, really far away?"

"How do you know where I live?"

"Because I was in the car when Camille picked you up that night. Jesus, you're paranoid."

That night. He said "that night."

"Let me give you a ride," he says, like we are having a normal conversation, like he didn't just bring up the main thing I refuse to talk about.

"I can walk."

"I'm sure you can, but I don't see why you'd want to when you have a perfectly good offer of a ride."

I stop walking. My feet and shoulders hurt and I haven't even walked a mile yet. "Are you drunk?" I say.

"Depends on how you define drunk."

"Is that supposed to be funny?"

He shrugs, smirking, as if I am the pathetic one for asking such a question. "You were drunk yesterday," I say. "When I saw you in town. You were drinking out of a paper bag."

"That was yesterday. Maybe today I am a new man."

I squint and inspect his face. He does the grin again, and for a moment I think I see what Camille saw when she looked at him and forgot anything else existed. My shoulders sag under the weight of my backpack and I imagine for a brief moment walking the ten miles home in these flip-flops, which are already rubbing a blister between my toes.

"Okay, fine." I open the door and get in. Leather seats, air-conditioning, buttons and touch screens and lights everywhere. "Nice car," I say, but I know it comes out sounding like a criticism.

"I know it's a little ostentatious," he says. "But the stereo's killer."

"This is your car?"

"Technically, it's my dad's. But he usually drives the Porsche in the summer."

"Is that supposed to impress me?"

He laughs. "No, I think it's as ridiculous as you do. I was hoping to get a laugh."

"Do you know how to get to my house from here?" I say, all business.

"You know I'm on your side, right?"

I turn and look at him. "What?"

"You don't have to treat me like an enemy."

"I'm not treating you like an enemy."

"Oh yeah, this is how you treat everyone."

"What is that supposed to mean?"

"You don't have to push me away, you know."

"You don't know anything about me."

"It's not going to hurt you for us to be friends."

"I don't want to be your friend."

"Ouch." He looks away and for a moment I think I might have really hurt his feelings. But I don't care.

I sit in the cushy leather seat, looking straight ahead, gritting my teeth. Part of me wants to jump out of the car right now, but the part of me that wins is the one that wants a ride home. We turn onto the road that goes to my house. I am almost there. After I slam the door behind me, I will never have to talk to Hunter Collins again.

"Why are you wearing long sleeves?" I say.

"Are you the fashion police?"

"It's like a million degrees outside. You're the only person in western Michigan who's wearing long sleeves right now."

"Is it weird being in a car with me?" he says, like we're having two completely different conversations.

"When you assume things about me and try to pretend there's a friendship where there is none—yes."

"This is the same road," he says. "Just a couple miles up is where the accident happened. You can still find glass and little pieces of metal. Have you seen it? The big white cross on the side of the road someone put up? The pile of wilted flowers and ratty old teddy bears?"

I don't say anything. I don't want to say anything. I don't want either of us to say anything. I want him to stop talking.

"Say something," he says. He doesn't get it. What is wrong with him?

"Why are you talking about it?"

"Why aren't you?"

"Just take me home."

We drive in silence for the next two miles, in the opposite direction of where the accident happened. I push him out of my mind. I keep my eyes on the road, adding up the numbers on mailboxes in my head. When he pulls up outside my house, I grab my bag and get out without saying anything. When I slam the car door, it's not as loud as I hoped it would be.

"I have created a masterpiece!" Mom declares when I enter the kitchen. The counter is covered with cutting boards and the rejected parts of vegetables. The smell of something baking fills the room and I am suddenly grateful.

"What is it?"

"Eggplant, heirloom tomato, basil, and zucchini tart, with a dollop of cashew cream and toasted almonds. You're just in time."

I set my bag down and wash my hands, get plates and silverware and glasses out.

"To what do I owe this honor?" Mom says.

"I'm hungry."

We eat and I listen to Mom rattle on about her day. She

manages not to say anything mean for the whole meal. I'm glad she's in a self-absorbed mood tonight. She doesn't want anything from me. After dinner, she says she's going to paint.

"But you haven't painted in forever," I say.

"I know, isn't it wonderful!" For now it is. But I know what this mood inevitably leads to. I know it is only temporary.

Alone in the house while Mom's in her studio, I can't figure out what to do with myself. I call Grandma to see if I can use her computer, but she comes up with some excuse why her whole house has to be off-limits because she's tired and doesn't want company. I watch TV until boredom morphs into exhaustion. Alone in the dark house, my sleepiness gets the best of me, and I start imagining the walls are closer than normal, the ceiling lower, like they are slowly closing in on me, moving when I blink. Strange sounds seem to emanate from the corners, from places just out of sight—a soft knocking here, a muted creak there. I decide that hallucinations are probably a good indicator that I need to go to sleep. So I read in bed until I can't keep my eyes open. I turn out the light, relieved this stupid day will be over as soon as I fall asleep.

In the place between awake and sleeping, the thought drifts through my mind—is life nothing more than this? Just killing time with distractions until it's over?

"Kinsey, you didn't have to be so mean to him."

I am holding the car together with my hands. My muscles tense as I keep it from flying apart. It is up to me to keep everything together. Always.

"He's a good guy. Really. Give him a chance."

The mannequin of Hunter is in the backseat—lifeless, stiff plastic. He cannot help me. The thin metal in my hands buckles.

"Slow down, Camille!" I say. "The wind is too strong."

But I know you can't do that.

"Just try. You're not even trying."

This is how fast we were going. This is how fast we will always go.

"Wait!" I say. "I was the one driving. This is not how it happened. Let me drive."

But you know I will try to change things that cannot be changed.

"Camille!"

The lights. Like two holes in the night. I lose my grip and the ceiling goes flying, the metal like wings. Hunter flies away with it. My hands are bleeding. More parts fall away until there is no car left, until it is just you and me and wind and light.

"Who's driving?" I scream.

No one.

"Step on the brakes!" I scream.

There are no brakes.

Just light and wind and me screaming, me thrashing about. I am running through space to nowhere. I am always running. I run but I don't move. The light comes closer until it is all that is. The light and the screams and the wind and the metal. Then the crash and the float and the flying away.

"I should have been the one driving," your voice says into the light. I cannot see you. I cannot see anything.

"You were drunk," I say.

"But still. You killed me."

THREE

From white to black, like smashing into a wall.

Flying through infinity, then cold and hard and way too still.

I am a lump of gravity.

I suck in air.

My muscles tense, full of needles.

I have been running. I am running. I need to run.

Shadows everywhere. Outlines of furniture. Stationary things.

Something in the corner.

A shadow in the shape of a body.

A shadow that could be solid.

The figure moves. An arm goes up. Reaching for me.

Everything in my body is ice.

"Camille?" I whisper.

Wind blows through the open window, curtains flutter, and the figure is gone.

My eyes adjust to the dark. My water glass and lamp are knocked off the table. Broken glass swims on the floor. Like the aftermath of a fight.

"Fuck this."

I jump out of bed. I pull on shorts and a sports bra and T-shirt and running shoes. The clock reads 3:52 a.m.

Don't drink water. Don't eat. Don't stretch. Don't think.

Just start running. Just move. Just go.

It is already warm in the darkness. The lightning bugs blink on and off. My feet crunch the gravelly pavement. I close my eyes and feel the mechanics of my body. My bones and muscles are the only things I can trust.

Run. Just run. If you run fast enough, nothing can catch you. If you run long enough, everyone else will give up.

Mom is sitting at the kitchen table when I get home. I am drenched with sweat, panting hard. She is stirring soy milk into her tea. She raises an eyebrow at me. Keeps stirring.

"Do we have any canned beans?" I pant. I need protein and that's the closest I can get in this house.

"Sometimes I wish you were just a pothead," she says. "That I could understand."

"Mom, do we have any beans? Or some of that fake taco meat maybe?"

"You're so pedestrian, Kinsey. I named you after a sex doctor and this is what I get."

She's in one of her moods. I knew it was coming. I have to eat fast to get out of here as soon as possible. I grab a box of cereal, the least healthy thing I can find that still says "organic" so Mom will allow it in the house. I fill a mixing bowl with nearly half the box.

"Are you anorexic?" she says.

"You're asking me this as I'm about to eat five servings of cereal?"

"How long were you running?"

"I don't know. What time is it?"

"Almost seven."

"I guess about three hours."

"Three hours! Are you insane?"

"I walked part of the time and I stretched in the middle. Calm down." I fill a huge glass full of water and gulp it down. I fill it again.

She sighs and shakes her head. "You run too much. It's like an addiction. It's a sign of mental illness."

Over the years, I've developed a thick skin to protect me from her judgments. Usually they just roll right off me; at worst, they're a mild irritation. But right now, I'm raw and jagged and unprepared, like my protective walls have crumbled. Maybe it's lack of sleep. Maybe it's the long run with no food or water. Maybe I'm losing my mind.

Instead of ignoring her and walking away like I always do, I want to fight. Anger mixes with adrenaline from the run and fills me with a dark electricity. I slam my glass down on the table. "Seriously, Mom? You ran out of things to judge me about, so you picked practically the healthiest things a person can do for their body? Are you really that desperate to bring me down to your level?"

A wicked grin spreads across her face, like she's thrilled I'm finally playing her game. "My level?" she says. "I'm an artist living on my own terms in a society that breeds nothing but sheep."

"You live in a shack, Mom. You don't even have a job."

"Somehow I raised a sheep."

"You're being a bitch."

"Baa, *baaaa*."

"Very funny."

"You're running on a treadmill."

"I run to feel free."

"A sheep and a hamster."

"Mom, stop."

"What are you running from, Kinsey?"

"Shut up."

"What are you running from?"

"Shut up!" I pick the glass up and throw it on the ground. I want a crash, I want shards of glass flying, I want her to bleed. But it doesn't break, just lands with a sad thud and rolls around in its puddle.

"Pathetic," Mom says. She starts laughing, cackling like a cartoon witch. I grab the cereal bowl and take it to my room. My head pounds with anger and dehydration. My eyes sting with what could be the beginning of tears. It's been so long since I cried, I don't remember what it feels like. I get to my room, slam my door, and sit on my bed. Close my eyes. Take deep breaths. Force the pain back in. Force my eyes to dry. She won't get any tears from me today. No one will. Ever.

By the time I get to school, I feel almost normal, except for a headache and a slight cramp in my left quad. Today's Friday. Only Monday, Tuesday, and Wednesday of next week left, which are unofficially optional for seniors, then high school is over for the rest of my life. I hand in my final English paper, which I finished days ago. And that's it. No more papers.

No more tests. Everyone else is giddy, swept up in the ritual of graduation like every year before them. Sheep, my mom would say. But I wish I felt as they did, wish I could find the motivation to smile and hug and sign yearbooks. But I feel strangely empty and lost, like something has been taken from me, like I'm mourning the loss of homework assignments and studying, like all of a sudden I have nothing left in the world.

I have one class left, but I leave school early. I've never cut class in my life. But I'm not the only one today; cars full of seniors pour out of the parking lot, on their way to the beach, on their way to get ready for parties I will not go to. For a moment, I panic. I don't have a shift at work tonight. Bill said three in a row was no good, especially since I'm working all day Saturday and Sunday. He insisted I have Friday off, so I could "have fun with my friends." Little does he know.

I use the pay phone at the gas station across the street to call Grandma. She answers in her usual exasperated tone. I tell her I'm coming over to use the computer. She lectures me about my manners but ultimately agrees when I lie and say I need to do research for a final paper that counts for half my grade. "Fine," she sighs. "At least you're doing something with your life." She may be an old bitch, but at least she has some of her priorities straight.

When I get onto the country road, I stick out my thumb.

The first car stops to give me a ride. I am very aware that in the real world, this particular form of transportation is considered dangerous. But this is not the real world. This is a place where nothing happens. The driver is an old lady who lives a half mile down the road from me. She babbles about her grandkids while I stare out the window.

I knock on Grandma's door. She doesn't like it when we enter without knocking. We don't even have keys. I think she's secretly afraid Mom will steal her stuff and try to sell it. Grandma doesn't even bother to come to the door and greet me. I just hear her gruff voice from somewhere inside call, "Come in."

I open the heavy front door and enter. Somehow it's about twenty degrees cooler inside. The blinds are all drawn and everywhere I look it's dark wood and velvety colors Grandma describes as "merlot" and "indigo." Even though a house cleaner comes every week, it still seems dusty, like the air is thick with years of accumulated boredom and repressed feelings. I don't know how she lives in here alone. It's the most depressing place I've ever been.

"Hi, Grandma!" I say, attempting to sound somewhat cheerful. I figure I owe her that much for letting me enter her dungeon. I hear a grunt of acknowledgment from somewhere deep in the house, but nothing more. I walk up the creaky grand staircase to the computer room. Sickly red light streams in through stained glass windows and paints my skin. All the angles and dimensions of this place seem somehow off, and I feel dizzy for a moment, unstable, like the staircase is rippling beneath my feet, like everywhere I look are fun house mirrors that warp the world into twisted versions of itself.

The feeling passes as quickly as it came on; I take a deep breath and remind myself that lack of sleep can bring on impaired balance. I look around to reacquaint myself with reality, but even though the world has stopped spinning I am still in the same haunted house. It's still cold and dark and full of whispers. I can't believe my mom grew up here. No wonder she's so crazy.

The computer room doesn't fit with the rest of the house, which is why I like it. It's a small room with a big window, which I open wide to let as much air and sunlight in as possible. The walls are plain white instead of covered with ornate wallpaper, and the shiny laptop and printer sit on the desk like they could actually belong to someone in this century. The browser is still open to the same thing I was looking at the last time I was here, something about extracurricular activities at the University of Michigan. I click in the upper right hand corner and start typing:

how to stop nightmares

Dr. Phil's site says something about dreams reflecting unfinished business from your life, how repeating traumatic events is normal. Thanks a lot, Dr. Phil. He says talk about it with someone. Not going to happen. Next.

Everywhere I look says basically the same thing: anxiety, stress, emotional issues, traumatic experience. All the suggestions seem so stupid: avoid eating close to bedtime, don't drink caffeine or alcohol, don't watch scary movies, spend time in nature, think happy thoughts, try to take charge in the nightmare and turn it into a happy dream, and if none of that works, see a therapist. The longer I search, the weirder the websites get. It's astounding how many people claim to be certified dream interpreters. What kind of school issues these certifications? I also come across quite a few magic spells. Who are these quacks? I want step-by-step instructions that have been endorsed by major medical schools. I want something certain. I want something scientific. But there's nothing like that. No one has a real answer. The Internet is full of people claiming to know things they don't actually know.

I close the laptop and feel a sudden gust of cold wind. I look out the window but the leaves on the trees are still; there isn't even the slightest breeze. I rub my eyes and realize suddenly how exhausted I am, and apparently so out of it that now I'm hallucinating temperatures and air movement. But a little tiredness I can deal with. Sleep is something I can control. And that's when it comes to me:

The only real way to avoid nightmares is to not sleep at all.

"Someone called for you," Mom says when I get home. *"A boy."*

"Who?" I say, even though I already know who it is, though I have no idea how he got my number.

"He didn't say. But he had a low voice. Very manly. Sounded cute."

"How does someone *sound* cute?"

"Same way someone *sounds* like a bitch," she says. "For example."

I open the fridge and say nothing.

"Oh, and Camille's mom called," Mom says. "Again."

My throat closes up and guilt spreads through me like poison.

"What is that woman's problem?" Mom says, her voice sour. "Can't she take a hint? How many times does she have to invite you over for dinner before she realizes you're never coming? Her kid dies, and now she's trying to adopt you? It's creepy."

It takes all of my strength not to jump across the room and strangle her.

"I'm going out tonight," Mom says. "Don't wait up."

"Whatever."

"What are you doing?"

"I don't know."

"You're not working?"

"Nope."

"It's the last Friday night of high school, and you don't have plans?"

I pull a jar of peanut butter and an apple from the fridge.

"God, Kinsey, why don't you just kill yourself right now?"

Before I have time to even realize what's happening, my arm retracts and my shoulder shifts back, like some kind of involuntary muscle memory left over from when I used to play softball. I throw the apple and it barely misses her head. It thuds against the wall behind her.

For a moment there is complete silence while Mom's eyes grow big and her mouth drops open. I freeze. I make a quick mental note of where the kitchen knives are in case I have to defend myself from her attack. I wait for surprise to morph into fury, but instead her body relaxes and her face opens into a big cruel grin, and she erupts into her cackling laugh she reserves especially for me when she thinks I'm a big joke.

"You think you scare me?" She picks up the half-smashed apple from the floor and tosses it back to me. I catch it. "You were going to eat that, weren't you?"

I say nothing. I feel the wet pulp in my hands.

"It's still half-good," she says. "You don't want to waste food, do you?" She walks over and pulls it out of my hand, holds it up to my face. "Here," she says. "Eat it." She pushes it against my lips.

I back away. "No," I say.

"Come on," she says, getting closer, pushing the apple even harder against my teeth. My face is wet with it. The sweet smell makes me sick. "Eat it."

"No!" I shove her and she stumbles a few steps back. She smirks and tosses the apple at my feet.

"Nice to see you're not a total wimp."

Neither of us moves. Neither of us is willing to be the first to look away. My eyes burn into her and I can hear nothing but the fire in my head growling *I hate you I hate you I hate you.*

Finally, she looks away, breaking the spell. She walks in slow motion to the kitchen table and picks up her purse. "I'll wait for my ride outside," she says, then struts out the door. Her moves are exaggerated, like she has to remind herself how to walk.

I can't be certain, but I think I just won that round.

I am watching TV. I am trying to stay awake. I start getting drowsy as soon as I get bored, which is always. I click through channel after channel, not staying on anything too long. The longer I sit here, the more like a zombie I feel. I can sense myself getting stupider with every reality show I linger on too long. It seems like every other channel has a version of the same show about ridiculous, irresponsible rich people. Why are there so many of these shows? Why do we allow these horrible people to be famous? Is it because of people like me, bored idiots sitting on their couches for hours on end, needing desperately to be entertained? People who, despite their better judgments and taste, can't help but be fascinated by how this different species lives, these people who are so far removed from the real world the rest of us live in.

What would it be like to never have to worry about money? To be so rich you don't even have to care about how you treat people because you know there will be more lined up to follow you around and be your "friend"? What if you felt entitled to anything you wanted, entitled to having your own TV show, entitled to hundreds of thousands of people fascinated by watching you shop and talk on the phone. What if you could get away with anything? Would that power automatically corrupt the best of us? If you gave a saint a billion-dollar trust fund, would he turn into an asshole overnight?

No matter how fast I change the channels, my eyelids start to feel heavy. I make a pot of very strong coffee. Agave syrup will never taste as good to me as good old-fashioned white sugar, but it's better than nothing. I sip the sweet concoction as I watch a series of commercials: dating hotlines for lonely people, two-year technical colleges, drug rehab, something about Jesus, weight-loss systems, at-home electrolysis kits. They assume I am one of the lost and ugly who watches late-night TV on a Friday, and they are right. The marketing companies are speaking to me. They are saying, "Get a life."

I return to a show about rich people. An orange-skinned, leathery-faced woman gets Botox. Someone's toy poodle catches a lizard by the pool, and they all have to talk about it for ten minutes while drinking margaritas.

This tiny blender will change my life, and it comes with a free knife that's sharp enough to cut tin cans! This man found the Lord, Hallelujah! This woman lost 133 pounds and now she's perfect!

Mom's still not home.

This pillow is soft.

My eyes are heavy.

Heavy.

So heavy.

Motionless. The air is like paper. Thin and sterile. Blank. We sit on a log on the side of the road, watching the show.

"Why can't I feel the fire?" I say.

"This is what it's like to be a ghost."

"I'm not a ghost," I say. "I'm dreaming."

"Same thing."

A fireball lights up the trees. Shadows dance across every-thing solid. Red and black and red and black. There is your car, becoming a skeleton. The world is melting in front of us.

A semi truck is tipped over, cradled by a wall of trees. The driver is out, eyes wide with flames, a phone to his ear, petrified, his only movement his wet mouth: "Oh god oh god oh god oh god," he says, such useless words against fire.

I close my eyes. So many lives are over.

"Kinsey, look!" you say.

"No," I say.

"You have no choice."

Hunter is no longer a mannequin. He is a live, breathing thing. He is all movement. His skin is charred. He is made of fire. He is pulling me out of the burning car. "Are you watching?" you say. He sets me down on the side of the road, in a grassy spot away from danger.

"Do you see how he cushions your head with his hand?" you narrate. "How gentle?"

"I didn't know he did that." My voice is small. "Why'd he get me first? Why didn't he get you?"

"Oh, you'll see."

Sirens in the distance. The night getting bigger.

Hunter carries your body in his arms. You are covered with blood. You are roasted. Your face is completely gone, like someone shoved it inside your head. Your arm hangs limply at an unnatural angle. You are nothing but a bag of meat and bones.

"Oh god oh god oh god." I don't know who is speaking.

The approaching fire truck lights the trees a strobing red. On off, on off. Like a pulse. Like the forest's heartbeat. The car on fire, consuming itself.

I try to run. But Hunter's burning arms are around me now, holding me too tight. I thrash and buck, but he is too strong.

I try to close my eyes, but he's holding them too, pulling them open, forcing me to see. "Let me go!" I say. But he cannot hear the cries of a ghost.

"Oh god oh god," I say; "Oh god," says the truck driver; "Oh god," says Hunter, all of us singing in harmony with the light. Our prayers, pulsing in the dark.

FOUR

I wake up screaming.

My legs run but I am going nowhere.

The world is hard and dark and close around me.

A stranger's chipper voice calls from somewhere.

Is this hell?

Strange canned music.

Is this the waiting room for hell?

No. I am on the floor. My foot kicks the couch. My forearm is sore where it must have hit the table. My cup is smashed on the floor in a puddle of cold coffee.

"No!" I scream. I punch the couch until my hand throbs with the memory of the dream. "No!" I scream until my hand is bruised, like some small amount of violence can pound out this feeling. An infomercial for an exercise machine is on TV. The announcer chirps his empty promises. How dare he try to sell me something so useless at a time like this? How dare he, when Camille is dead?

The room wobbles around me. Something is off. Something is tilted. All the angles of the walls seem askew. Things are not in the right places. It's like someone came in and moved everything an inch to the right. I am dizzy. I close my eyes. I go back to black, back to zero. But the world is slanted even there.

The only solution is moving. You can't sleep when you are moving. Nightmares can't chase someone who's running.

So I run. I was asleep for barely an hour, but I run. My stomach feels sick and empty, I am dizzy with exhaustion and adrenaline, but I run. The trees are black like they should be. No red. No light pulsing. The trees are not breathing. The only breath is mine, harder than normal. My body is weak. My legs feel like noodles. But I keep going. I will push through this. I will run through this weakness. It is all I can do.

This is the forest but it is a different forest. This is not where she left me. This is not where she was taken. That was somewhere else. Miles away. Still charred by the explosion. The stupid white cross someone stuck in the ground. The wreath of fake flowers. The teddy bears and candles and notes from people who barely knew her. But that is not here. The trees here are still standing, still fresh, still green behind the darkness. This road has not been cursed.

Run. Run. Breathe. Breathe. Run.

Light. In the distance.

Two eyes blinking.

The trees shift, become feathered tentacles, grasping for me.

I run faster. I run from everything chasing me.

The night stirs. The light grows. The ground shakes.

She is coming to replace me.

It was not Camille who was supposed to die.

Pure white. Blindness.

Some force pulls me off the road, like arms made out of wind.

I am lying in a coffin, the roots and vines tying me in, taking me under.

A sharp pain shoots up my leg.

Death starts at the feet and moves upward.

The brain is the last to go, to make sure you remember every last detail.

The light fades.

White then red then nothing at all.

Like a flashlight losing batteries.

But I am not gone.

It is dark again and I am in a ditch. Dirt sticks to the sweat on my skin. I am not dead. This is not heaven or hell. That was just a car driving in the night. I breathe. My heart pounds in my chest, testing itself. I sit up. My head aches. All I've had to drink in the last eight hours is coffee.

I shift my weight to my legs and stand up. Fire burns a trail through my leg. I steady myself on my right foot and tap the ground with my left. Pain throbs with the pressure. The pain sobers me, makes the night stop moving.

It is the middle of the night.

I am standing in the road in running shoes and ripped pajamas, and I just twisted my ankle.

My best friend is dead instead of me.

As I limp home, I can't stop replaying the dream in my head. I can't stop seeing Camille with no face. I squeeze my eyes tight, but she's still there, an empty hole, gone forever. I try to remember what she looked like before—her eyes, her nose, her lips—but it's like that's all been erased, like my whole life's worth of memories is gone, and now she's nothing but her absence, nothing but a big gaping wound.

I force myself not to think about her. I count my steps. I count the trees. Whenever I feel the sting of emotion coming on, I find something else to count. Numbers have no feelings.

Numbers don't miss people. I count everything I can find until I get home. I count ice cubes into a plastic bag. I count five Advil into my mouth. I count how many times the Ace bandage wraps around my ankle. I sit back down on the couch and count the channels until it's time to get ready for work. Whenever I get sleepy, I press my left foot against something hard so the pain will wake me up.

Mom still isn't home when I leave to open the restaurant for lunch, which is more than fine with me. I don't have to hear her making fun of me as I attempt to ride my bike the eight miles to work with a twisted ankle. I don't have to listen to her calling me stupid for going running in the middle of the night. I don't need reminding. Every time my left foot pushes on the pedal the pain reminds me how dumb I am.

When I get to work, I feel dizzy. I nearly run into a family crossing the street for their morning shift at the beach. As soon as I walk in, Bill notices something wrong. "Had a little too much fun last night?" he kids.

"Totally," I say, wishing it were true, wishing I could blame how I feel on something normal like a hangover.

The new girl, Jessie, peeks out from behind a freezer and smiles timidly. I don't bother saying hi.

People are already lined up outside the door by the time we open at eleven. Bill's excited and talking too loud, cracking stupid jokes that make my headache worse. All I want to do is prepare food so I don't have to talk to anyone, but Bill says Jessie needs practice on the soft-serve machine. What kind of idiot needs practice on the soft-serve machine? This is who I have to share my tips with?

Not that I'm making any tips today. I can't stop myself from being rude to pretty much every person I serve. I keep getting orders wrong. I ring up someone's hot dog and sundae and it somehow comes out to $127.83. At one point, I totally zone out while taking an order. I just blank for I don't know how long, looking out into space, like my brain shut off for a minute. I come back to the customer saying, "Hello? Hello? Anybody there?"

As she walks away, I hear the lady say to her husband, "I heard about there being a lot of problems out here with kids and prescription drugs. They call it hillbilly heroin. It's just so sad to see it in person."

I want to scream at her, "I'm not a hillbilly, you redneck!" but before I have a chance Bill comes over with a concerned look on his face that almost makes me start crying. He puts his hand on my shoulder and says in a soft voice, "Kinsey, are you okay?" and for a second I want to tell him everything. I want to tell him how Camille won't leave me alone, how I'm afraid to sleep, how I think I'm going crazy, how it should be me who's dead and not her. But then I see Jessie not even try-ing to hide the fact that she's eavesdropping, and the lady who thinks I'm a hillbilly drug addict staring at me while she chews her disgusting meal, and I will not give them the satisfaction of seeing me fall apart.

"I'm okay," I say, and try to smile as convincingly as possible.

"Are you limping?" Bill says.

"It's no big deal. Just twisted my ankle a little, running. Happens all the time. It'll be fine in a couple days."

"Maybe you shouldn't be on your feet."

"I'm fine," I say, my smile shaking no matter how hard I try to maintain it. "I promise."

"Okay," he says. "But maybe you should switch jobs with Jessie for a while."

I pretend I am an assembly line. I pretend I am a machine. I put hot dogs in buns. I put ice cream in cones. I put yellow goop on stale corn chips. I tune out all the chatter around me. I start to feel all right. The Advil's doing a good job with my ankle. I have a lot of things to count.

But then I turn around, and all of a sudden the sun is shining on the freezer in a way that makes it look like fire. The chrome reflects the light and turns everything orange.

I try to breathe but nothing comes.

I am only my muddy reflection in orange chrome.

I am the absence of a face.

I am just a hole.

I look away, toward the door and the sea of people. I try to settle my eyes on something. The door opens and someone walks in, someone so familiar I can sense it all the way over here.

My eyes find her face. It's Camille.

She looks at me and smirks. Her eyes crinkle the way they do when she thinks something's funny. But different. With an edge.

I hear her voice in my head: *You can't outrun me, Kinsey.*

I hide behind the hot dog machine. I am crouched on the floor between it and the wall. Greasy dust bunnies collect at my feet, threatening to bury me. The world is wobbling and I feel cold, so cold.

Jessie's face pops around the corner and I shudder backward. But there is nowhere left to go.

"Are you okay?" she says, but the look on her face says she already knows the answer.

"Yes," I snap.

She walks away and I hear her talking. "Um, Bill," she squeaks. "Um, I think Kinsey is . . . I think she's having some problems."

Screw you, Jessie. What do you know? I am fine. Look, I'm standing up. I'm brushing myself off. I'm walking like a normal person over to resume my position at the soft-serve machine. "Kinsey?" Bill says behind me, and as I turn around my right arm somehow comes with me, outstretched, and I don't even feel it as it knocks over the cone dispenser. But I watch the fall in slow motion, the cones flying through the air and smashing to the floor. I hear Camille's laugh echoing out of the air vents. As I fall to the ground, I can sense everyone in the restaurant come to see what the commotion's about, crowding around the counter, looking at me on the floor. I can hear the hillbilly heroin lady saying, "See what I mean? So sad." My arms move but they seem to be making a worse mess. I don't know if I am breathing.

Bill comes over and kneels down. I am shoving smashed cones back into the dispenser. He puts a hand on my shoulder and says my name. I don't respond. I can't. I have to keep cleaning. I have to keep moving. I'm afraid of what will happen if I let myself be still.

"Honey, stop," Bill says. He grabs my hands, both of them, and I am immobilized. A sound comes out of my mouth like something deflating. Not words. I am incapable of words.

"I think you should go home for the day," Bill says.

"I'm fine," I say, but my voice sounds thin, like paper.

"You need a rest." He smiles, and I know he's trying to pretend it's not a big deal. But I know he knows it is. "You need to rest your ankle so it gets better. Jessie and I can handle the rest of the day."

I nod because I'm too tired to speak. I am too tired to fight anymore.

He helps me up. I scan the room and all the customers look away. They scuttle back to their seats, embarrassed for me.

"You don't have to come in tomorrow if it still hurts, okay? Just give me a call later and let me know how you're feeling."

I can't tell if this is pity or kindness. I don't know how to tell the difference. All I know is it hurts and I want Bill to stop looking at me like this, stop talking in this tone of voice. I just want out of here.

I take off my apron and grab my backpack from under the counter. The restaurant is silent. Jessie's sweeping up the smashed cones. Customers pretend to eat their meals, but their eyes keep darting over to the show behind the counter.

"Do you want me to call Annie?" Bill says. "I bet she'd come by with the truck and give you a ride home."

I shake my head no and walk outside before he can protest. A wall of heat greets me as soon as I leave the air-conditioned building. I am vaguely aware that I should be feeling something. Humiliation, maybe. Shame. Fear. But I feel nothing. I am too tired and too empty to care.

Camille, is this what it's like to be a ghost?

I get on my bike and start pedaling. I am not going home. I am not ready to be inside that house again, not ready to possibly face my mother. I just go and go until the forest opens to fields and the fields turn into neighborhoods and the sidewalks lead into town. I park my bike at the library. I am covered in sweat and my ponytail is only half-intact. I enter the library looking like a crazy person. I sit at a free computer and don't even care who sees what I look up:

how to do exorcisms

Unfortunately, most sites say the first step is to be full of the Holy Spirit. Since the only time I set foot inside a church was at Camille's funeral, I think that's going to be pretty unlikely. I'm not sure Camille's going to take me seriously when I tell her to be quiet in the name of Jesus. Most sites recommend hiring a professional exorcist. One says I should definitely wear purple. One says that demonic possessions are often mistaken for mental illnesses, but prescription medications will only make the demons sleepy. The further I look, the more I'm convinced I'm hopeless.

"What are you trying to exorcise?" says a voice behind me. I scream, and the sound reverberates around the quiet library.

I turn around and see Hunter. The handful of people scattered around the library stare at us. The librarian glares at me sternly.

"Sorry," I mumble to the librarian. I turn to Hunter. "You *are* following me," I growl.

"That's kind of conceited, don't you think?" He smiles his lazy smile. How can it be so easy for him to smile?

"What are you doing in my town?"

"*Your* town?"

"You know what I mean."

"Wellspring has a fine library. My town does not."

"What do you want with the library?"

"If you haven't noticed, along with computers with which people can look up how to do exorcisms, libraries also have these things called books, which I coincidentally like to read."

My slow brain tries to formulate something cruel about being surprised that a loser like Hunter even knows how to read, but before I can say anything, a loud "Shush" comes from the direction of the librarian.

"Did you call me yesterday?" I whisper.

"Yes."

"Why?"

"When I saw you the other day at the beach, I got the impression you needed a friend."

Something inside me cracks a little, sends a lump to my

throat that I have to swallow down. "I have plenty of friends," I say, but even I know it sounds like a lie.

"Okay," he says.

"Excuse me." The librarian coughs from her desk. "Will you kindly take your conversation outside?"

"Yes, ma'am," Hunter says with a smile. He gives her a military salute, and a tween girl by the magazine racks giggles. I grab my backpack and follow him outside.

"Seriously, why were you looking up exorcisms?" he says as the door closes behind us.

"I wasn't," I lie. "I mean, I just sort of ended up there. You know how that happens. You start off doing something on the Internet and then somehow you end up in some weird place."

I am acutely aware of how messy my hair is, how my clothes are stiff with dried sweat and sticky with spilled ice cream, how I must smell like hot dogs. Even though I hated him a moment ago, I am hit with a sudden need to not leave, to stay with Hunter, like despite my lack of sleep over the last few days and the nightmares and hallucinations, I suddenly feel safer than I have in a long time. I start to panic. My chest tightens at the thought of him walking away, of being left to ride home, alone, with my demons.

But just as I recognize that I'm not breathing, Hunter says nonchalantly, "Want a coffee? I'm buying."

Air enters my lungs, and the pressure on my chest loosens. I nod my agreement, trying not to look too grateful. We walk in silence over to the coffee shop. I try to focus on my steps. I count them instead of thinking about how this was one of Camille's and my favorite places to go, how I haven't set foot in it since she died.

The familiar smell of the café makes me nauseous. I have never been here without Camille. It looks different—less glamorous, more dingy—without her in it.

I order a quadruple iced espresso.

"Whoa, killer!" Hunter says. "That's some serious caffeine."

"I'm a serious person."

"Yes." He laughs. "You are a very serious person."

We sit at a table in the back. I am grateful Hunter didn't pick Camille's usual table by the front window. She loved being able to see everyone coming and going. She loved everyone being able to see her. Just one of the million ways we were different.

I try to focus on the community bulletin board behind Hunter's head. I count all the flyers I recognize from my mom's weird friends offering massage, acupuncture, private yoga classes, something called Reiki. I feel all eyes in the café on us.

"How do you like being famous?" Hunter says.

"Ugh."

He laughs.

"You seem okay with it," I say.

"Why do you say that?" He takes a sip of his hot chocolate. What kind of guy orders hot chocolate with extra whipped cream?

My mouth opens before I have a chance to think about what's going to come out. "Why do you seem so . . . okay?" I hear myself say, and suddenly the air seems so thin, like all the fog that's accumulated over the last few days gets cleared out. All the people in the café disappear and the crappy music fades away, and it is only me and Hunter at this table. I relax and it feels like melting, it feels like losing five hundred pounds, and all I want to do is keep letting go. I don't want to fight anymore.

"I'm a mess," I whisper, and it feels like I've never said anything truer in my life.

He looks at me from behind the wall of his hair, and there's something in his eyes that goes way deeper than his cool and brooding affect, deeper than his reputation, something sad and old and achingly familiar. He nods but says nothing, and for a second, I feel like I'm looking at him as Camille must have, like she's inside me looking at him through my eyes, and I'm filled with so much warmth all of a sudden, like gratitude that he's looking at me with those eyes, that somehow him seeing me makes me a better person, like how Camille made me better. "I'm a mess," I say again, and my voice breaks, and for a second I think I'm going to finally lose it, I'm going to break down right here in front of all these people, in this coffee shop, with this sound track of cheesy pop ballads, and I just can't do it, I can't. So I tighten myself up again. I zip up my armor. The air thickens back around us and makes me impenetrable.

"Me too," he finally says. My mouth can't open in response, so we sit in silence for a while. But it's not an uncomfortable silence like so many others. It's like we're floating. Like we're meant to be here.

"I started drinking like crazy after she died," he continues. "It was too easy, you know? It always has been. I'm a waiter part-time at one of my dad's restaurants, and I just steal bottles of booze from the bar and of course no one does anything because I'm the son of the guy who pays their wages. And I just drink and drink so I don't have to feel anything." He takes a sip of his hot chocolate. "But it never really goes away. No matter how hard I try to run from it."

The silence returns. I'm afraid to look up. I'm afraid of seeing my reflection in his glassy eyes.

"Do you think it's possible to die from sadness?" he finally says.

I feel something growing inside me, something warm and solid. Maybe it's gratitude, but that's not strong enough a word. The feeling is fiercer than that. It's like I want to grab myself by the shoulders and shake me. I want to scream at myself, *Why did you wait so long for this?*

"I don't know," I say so softly I can barely hear my own voice. "Sometimes I feel like I'm drowning. I try to move but that just makes it worse. Like it gets thicker and tighter and heavier the more I try to fight it."

"It," Hunter says.

"Her," I say.

"Yes."

I look into his eyes. They are deep blue pools I could drown in. "I can't say her name out loud."

"You don't have to."

I look down and suck out the last of my coffee. The sound is shockingly loud. It breaks the spell, returns us back to the café. I feel some magic slip away. I want to hold on to that place where we were floating, removed and above all of this, in the silence that was just ours. But it's gone.

"So now what?" I say.

"I don't know," Hunter says. "Just life, I guess."

"I don't have one," I say, shocked by the words as soon as they come out of my mouth. What is it about Hunter that is making me talk like this?

Hunter gives a sad smile. "We can be friends, you know?"

I nod weakly, so wanting that to be true. Maybe we can. Maybe this is a beginning. All the disdain I felt for him, all the judgment, has morphed into something new. I've always thought he was such a loser, not good enough for Camille, somehow beneath us for being so obviously broken. But now, it is those same things that make me want to trust him, that make me think that maybe I don't have to be alone in all this. Because now I am broken too.

"Want to go do something?" he says.

"No," I say, and I only half mean it. "I need to go home. I need to sleep. I haven't been sleeping." Something aches in me, wanting to tell him the whole story. But it is not time for that. It may never be time for that.

"Yeah," he says. "You look like you could use some sleep. No offense."

"None taken."

"Do you want a ride?"

"I have my bike."

"I have a really big backseat. You could fit like ten bikes back there."

"But won't it mess up the leather interior or something?"

"Do I seem like the kind of guy who gives a shit about leather interior?"

I smile, and I swear I hear my cheeks creak from disuse.

"She smiles!" Hunter exclaims.

"I bet you're very proud of yourself."

"Absolutely."

We go back to the library to get my bike. The grumpy librarian is hiding behind a tree smoking a cigarette. Hunter lifts my bike into the back of his car no problem. We don't say much on the ride home, but it isn't awkward. The seat is so comfortable, I catch myself nodding off a couple times.

"Give me your phone," he says when we pull up to my house. "I'm going to put my number in it."

"I don't have a cell phone." For the first time ever, I'm not embarrassed saying it.

He leans over me and gets a pen out of the glove compartment. His arm brushes against my chest. He smells good, clean, like expensive soap, so different from how I saw him days ago in town on his skateboard, with greasy unwashed hair and the bottle of liquor in a paper bag.

"Give me your hand," he says. His hand is warm around mine. It is soft and strong at the same time. He writes his number on my palm.

When I get out of the car, it feels like part of me stays inside with him.

I can tell Mom's home because her purse is on the kitchen table, her shoes are on the floor, and her jacket's hanging off the couch. The house is silent and the door to her room is closed. She is sleeping off whatever she did last night.

I am nauseous with exhaustion and too much coffee. My ankle is throbbing. I swallow a few more Advil and eat a piece of toast. The walls wobble around me.

I know I can't stay up forever. As much as I hate to admit it, my body will always be stronger than my mind. It needs sleep. If I don't let it, it will figure out a way to make me.

Maybe I can just decide to face it. Maybe I can just lie down and close my eyes and wait for whatever happens. Maybe I can let the darkness come and trust that it won't last forever. Maybe I can come to believe that maybe, possibly, things are going to be okay.

We are here in this place where it is always sunset. Not the pretty kind you see on Lake Michigan, not the ones that light up the sky like fireworks. This is a place where everything is blank; it would be white if not for the faint stain of blood.

The nothingness goes on forever. The flatness of the earth turns into an equally flat horizon. There is a line in the distance where below stops and above starts, but no matter how long I walk I can never get there. This is an empty place. A nothing place. A place for waiting.

"Is this heaven?" I say.

"No," you say.

"Is it hell?"

"No."

"Where is it?"

"This is nowhere. This is where I live now."

"I'm scared," I say.

"You should be."

I stop walking. I look at you. It is you but it is not you. It is a ghost in the shape of you. It is a body made out of smoke. It is wearing a sheet painted like you, with eyeholes cut out. When I look into the holes where eyes should be, there is nothing.

"Camille?" I say.

The wind shifts and turns hot. The sheet flutters and is gone. I am looking into a nothingness that may or may not be you. The wind whips itself into a wall of fire. I turn around and start running. My heels burn. I follow the horizon. I run to infinity.

"Camille, I'm scared!" I scream. The world is on fire and I can't outrun it. I keep running and going nowhere. This world is a giant treadmill.

"Maybe you need to do something scary," your voice coos inside my head.

"I don't know what to do," I say.

"I'll show you," you say.

"But where are you? I can't see you. How can I follow you if I can't see you?"

Your ghost softens around me. I am effortless. I am your puppet. I am running in air. White space. Infinity. I am held in the space between nothing and everything.

"You can't get away from me," you whisper inside me. "You can never get away."

FIVE

I wake up crying. I'm not surprised. I'm not scared. Light streams through the window and I know exactly where I am. I know exactly where I've been. This is the way it is now. This is the way I sleep.

I don't bother jumping out of bed. I don't thrash around and try to fix it. I don't do anything but cry.

Strange how it is so easy, how the tears know exactly how to flow, despite so long being dry.

Strange how there are things the body remembers despite the mind trying so hard to forget.

Strange how I don't try to stop it, how I don't squeeze the tears back in, how I give myself to the pain, how I let it win.

Strange how I no longer care about winning. There is no prize for not feeling.

There's nothing I can do. The horizon is out of reach. The sky is up and the earth is down and I will never get to the place where they connect.

I can't stop crying. I cry years' worth of tears. I cry for Camille and I cry for me. I cry for everything and everyone I never cried for. I will fill up the nowhere place with my liquid sorrow until it floats us all away.

Camille, why aren't you here? You are supposed to be here. You are the only one who's ever been allowed to see me cry.

I can almost feel my head in your lap, your fingers in my hair, telling me to breathe. I don't breathe now that you're gone. I only suck at air. My lungs only barely lift.

Camille, I don't know how to do any of this without you.

"Kinsey?" Mom's voice from the hall. "Kinsey, are you okay?"

This is the other her, the mom I get only sometimes. "Mom," I blubber. I don't care that I sound like a child.

She enters my room and comes over to the bed. She sits on the edge and pulls me to her lap. She holds me while I cry, rocking back and forth, saying nothing but an occasional "Let it out" and "Everything's going to be okay." I don't believe her, but I keep crying. I close my eyes and pretend she's Camille.

The longer I cry, the more the world solidifies around me. It is not tilted like before, not out of focus and strange. I don't know how long we're there, but it is somehow long enough for me to run out of tears.

Mom squeezes me after my last sniffle. I sit up, surprised that my head doesn't ache and I don't feel dizzy. I look at her and see the woman I love who rarely shows up anymore. "What do you need?" she says.

"I'm hungry," I say.

I lie on the couch and watch her make breakfast. She's so graceful in her movements, natural in a way I never feel except when I'm running or playing soccer. But there's a sadness today, a weight to her limbs, a dullness in her eyes. This is the way it usually happens—in pairs; her kindness and sadness are inseparable. She may hug me for the next few days, but I will have to listen to her cry through the thin walls.

I sit down to the elaborate breakfast—tofu scramble, blue cornmeal pancakes, and fresh fruit salad. My mouth waters.

"Coffee?" she asks, and I feel my stomach lurch.

I shake my head dramatically, passionately no.

I stuff my face with food while Mom picks at hers. She looks up occasionally from her plate and studies me, but she says nothing. I don't look up because I know her sadness is waiting for me and I don't want to deal with it right now.

This is the mood that precedes her bouts of apologizing, of rehashing every hurtful thing she's done in the last few weeks. It's more for her than it is for me. She wants to punish herself by remembering. But she doesn't understand that it punishes me, too.

I eat about a pound of tofu scramble, four pancakes, and a heaping bowl of fruit salad. My stomach is full and my eyes are empty and this is the closest to okay I've felt in a while. But I can sense her over there brimming with emotion, wanting me to join her. Didn't she notice that I'm cried out? Doesn't she understand that I've reached my quota for sadness?

I can't let her talk; I know I must speak first. How does a person make conversation with their mother? How do normal families talk?

"How was your date last night?" I say.

"That was two nights ago," Mom sighs. "It's Sunday today." It's like it pains her to speak, like she can barely manage these short sentences.

"Oh," I say. I wonder how long she's been like this. Did she shift during the date? The morning after? This morning? I wonder how much longer I have with this version of her.

"Let's not talk about me. I'm so sick of talking about me." She stands up, shuffles around the table, and kisses me on the top of my head. She walks to her bedroom, her body moving as if possessed by someone twice her age. She closes the door quietly behind her.

I clean up the dishes and put the leftovers in the fridge. I hum loudly and out of tune to fill up the silence, in case she cries.

I fill up the bathtub with hot water, add some of Mom's handmade lavender bubble bath. I step the foot of my twisted ankle in and feel the warmth enter my muscles, my tendons, my bones, healing me from the inside. I start to lower myself down, anticipating being enveloped by the water, but then I stop, panicked. I stand up, get out quickly from the water. I hold my breath and look at the palm of my hand.

It's still there. Just barely. Hunter's number. Half-wet and starting to shiver, I find a lip pencil and write the number on a tampon box. I get back in the tub, savoring it. Warmth feels so much better the colder you are.

I don't get out until I'm so hot I can't imagine ever being cold again. I wrap myself in a towel and grab the tampon box. I am drowsy with warmth and food, but I know if I don't do it now I may never do it. Camille said do something scary. Do something scary and maybe I won't be so scared.

The living room is quiet and empty as I dial his number on our landline. It only rings once before he answers.

"Hey," he says, like he was expecting me.

"Hey," I say, suddenly aware of how naked I am.

Camille, is this okay?

I wait outside for Hunter to pick me up. The sign for Peace Dove Pottery has been flipped to closed all weekend, even though Saturday and Sunday are when Mom makes most of her sales. I figured out a long time ago that I would need a job to make my own money if I was to have any sense of security. Before working at Bill's, I babysat and mowed lawns and cleaned houses, anything to put some money in the bank. Camille always called me stingy because I never wanted to spend any of it, but she didn't have to worry about money as much as me. Her parents weren't rich, but at least they were stable. I have nine thousand dollars saved up, and I'm working as much as I can this summer to build it up even more.

Wait, do I have a job? Was that yesterday I fell apart at work? The last few days are a blur, but I can remember Bill sending me home. I remember hiding behind the hot dog machine. What was I hiding from? Camille? Was I hallucinating Camille? I was supposed to call Bill last night to tell him if I was coming in today. It's after three now. It's too late.

I should be worried. I should be running into the house

to call him and apologize and beg to keep my job. But I feel a strange sense of relief, like one less thing is tying me here, like I am that much closer to freedom.

Hunter rolls up in his fancy black car with the tinted windows and I can't help but chuckle. "What's so funny?" he asks when I get in.

"Your car," I say. "It doesn't suit you at all."

"I know," he says. "I should be a banker or in the mafia or something."

"Or a chauffeur."

"You look better today," he says as he pulls out of the driveway.

"Thanks," I say. "I think I slept for like a whole day."

"You must have needed it."

"You have no idea."

We wander around town for a while, looking in the windows of the tourist shops. I forgot to take any Advil this morning, and there's a dull pain still in my ankle whenever I step on my left foot.

"I can't believe people buy this crap," Hunter says, looking in a window of overpriced house wares.

"Yeah," I say.

"My mom buys this crap."

"Really?"

"I think she likes to keep pretending this is our summer home she's decorating, not where we actually live now."

I knew Hunter was from Chicago originally, but Camille never told me the details. I don't really blame her, though. I made it pretty clear I wasn't interested whenever she tried to talk to me about Hunter.

"She doesn't like living here?"

"No. I don't know. Maybe she could like it eventually, if she made some friends or had some kind of life. Or if we were here for a reason besides being banished."

"Banished?"

"My dad pretty much still lives in Chicago. Sometimes he comes by on the weekends. But it's obvious he sent us here to get rid of us."

I don't know what to say. I barely know Hunter, but he's telling me the kind of thing I wouldn't tell anyone. It's like if I told him about my mom's mood swings, about how mean she can be sometimes, about how sad. I only ever told Camille that stuff, and only late at night, in the dark. But I can tell Hunter wants to talk. For some reason, he wants me to know these secrets. "Why would he do that?" I ask.

"He's a sociopath," Hunter says flatly.

"Oh," is all I can think to say.

"He's a control freak. And he doesn't want us interfering

with his glamorous life. So he hides us away in the middle of nowhere so he won't be bothered. So he can have his affairs in peace and he won't be reminded every day that his son is a worthless piece of crap."

There is fire in Hunter's voice. His hands are fists. He is walking fast and I have to jog a little to keep up. I'm suddenly embarrassed for my town, for how small it is, for how little there is to do here.

"This place must be pretty awful compared to Chicago," I say. He doesn't say anything. "I always hoped I'd end up somewhere like Chicago one day. San Francisco, actually. A real city."

He stops walking and looks at me so intensely I start to feel a little uncomfortable. "San Francisco?" he says.

"Yeah, it seems like such a cool place. So much culture and history." I don't say anything about Camille's and my plan to move there together after college.

I don't understand the way Hunter is looking at me, like he's thinking hard, like he's figuring things out, like something very important is happening inside his head.

"I want to talk to you about something," he finally says.

Uh-oh. Isn't that the kind of thing someone says before they break your heart?

"Okay?"

"It's weird," he continues. "I was debating whether or not I was going to bring it up. But then you said San Francisco just now. So, I don't know, maybe it's a sign."

"A sign for what?"

"I'm going to San Francisco. I've always wanted to, but it was always kind of a dream I didn't take too seriously. But after everything that happened, the last couple months, I've been really thinking about it, planning it. I've had my bags packed for three weeks, but something has kept me from leaving yet. Something told me to wait." He pauses and looks at me as I try to comprehend what he is saying. "Maybe I was supposed to wait for you."

Images flicker through my head: the Golden Gate Bridge, young hip artists and musicians, bustling sidewalks, palm trees and sunshine and colorful house-studded hills. A whole new world. A whole new life.

There's an electricity in Hunter's eyes. "We could leave anytime," he says. "We could leave tonight."

This is crazy. He's crazy. This whole idea is crazy. But something I've realized in the last few days is I'm crazy too. Maybe I always have been, but I've spent so much energy keeping it inside, keeping it hidden. I've always relied on my intricate lists and plans to keep me sane, everything predictable and in control. But what if I did something unpredictable for a change? What if doing something crazy is the sanest thing I can do?

"I assumed I'd go alone," he says. "Because there was no one else. No one who understood what I had to get away from. But you get it. You *know*. You're the only one who does."

I am holding my breath. If I breathe, I might blow him away.

"This town, this county, this state. This whole . . ." He sweeps his hands around the sad town full of dusty, abandoned things. "Everything. All of it. It's like it's . . ."

"Haunted," I say.

"Exactly," he says. I nod. I feel my heart pumping in my chest. I want to run. I want to run all the way out of here. But I think I want to take him with me.

"I have to get out of here," he says.

"Yes," I say. Adrenaline and hope and fear burn in my chest.

"Yes?"

"Yes," I say. "I want to go. I want to go with you. I want to go to San Francisco."

I can hear Camille, somewhere far away, laughing.

SIX

When I open my eyes, I am not screaming. I am not crying or shaking. I am not scared. Even though it takes me more than a few moments to realize where I am. Even though I still don't really know.

I am in a car. Hunter's car. The air is thick and stuffy with our breath. He is next to me, in the driver's seat, eyes closed, breathing deeply. The windows are filmy wet with condensation, glowing with pale morning.

I open the door as quietly as possible, but the sound is still jarring. Hunter shifts in his seat but does not wake up. I step out and enter the day. The air is fresh and cool and I breathe it in as deeply as I can. I can't remember the last time I took a really good breath. It seems like forever since I haven't had the weight of anxiety pressing on my lungs.

We are in an empty parking lot. A small building sits at one edge, surrounded by perfectly maintained flower beds. Everything sparkles with morning dew. It is quiet except for the cheerful chirping of birds and the occasional car driving at freeway speed somewhere close but out of sight.

I walk toward the building and read the sign: VISITOR CENTER. It opens at seven thirty. I have no idea what time it is. I buy a Coke from the vending machine by the door, sit on a picnic bench, and crack it open. The cold, sweet bubbles make me feel brand-new.

I'm somewhere I've never been before. I fell asleep and awoke and, just like that, I have a brand-new life. I remember packing hurriedly, not even bothering to be quiet. Mom was asleep in her room, probably with the aid of a serious prescription. And even if she woke up, I knew she wouldn't try to stop me from going. This is just the kind of thing she'd want me to do. I scribbled a note for her, something about needing to get out of town for a while to figure things out. I said I'd call her. I said don't worry. I signed it "Love, Kinsey."

I remember leaving the house at midnight, sitting on my duffel bag on the side of the road. The bugs were singing their usual symphony, but it seemed louder somehow, more dramatic, like it was announcing my escape, trying to give me away. The moon was empty and the night was black. All the lights were off in the house. I sat in the dark, waiting. I could hear the trees shivering even though there was no breeze. I waited for Hunter. I waited for Camille. I waited for whoever would get to me first.

I filled the darkness with plans. I filled in the empty spaces with details. I turned the enormity of San Francisco into items on a to-do list. Systematic. Methodical. Not scary. I would do these things and I would do them perfectly:

1) Arrive in San Francisco

2) Stay at a youth hostel or other inexpensive temporary housing

3) Find a job with a flexible schedule (probably waitressing)

4) Find a room in an apartment with (serious and responsible) students

5) Take BA prerequisites at a community college. Get 4.0 (obviously)

6) Establish California residency after a year so UC tuition will be cheaper

7) Transfer to UC Berkeley (hopefully with another soccer scholarship, or possibly some kind of scholarship for abandoned children of crazy women)

8) Start my real life

This plan made sense. This plan made me safe. There were no holes for uncertainty to slip through.

I don't know how long I waited for Hunter to arrive. But when he did, after I threw my bag next to his and a bunch of camping gear, a cooler, and what appeared to be a case of liquor in the trunk, after I got in and buckled my seat belt, he looked at me strangely, like he was inspecting me, and asked if I had been sleeping out there. He said my eyes had been closed; I had been sitting completely still.

"Maybe I was meditating," I said.

"Were you?"

"No."

We didn't speak after that. I never asked where we were going. He put on some kind of instrumental rock, beautiful but sad, like the sound of so many instruments crying. I snuck looks at him occasionally, but I had to look away quickly. I didn't like what I saw. He was scared too.

I don't remember falling asleep. I remember looking out the window and seeing nothing but waves of dark pattern. I remember the sad sound track. I don't remember dreaming. When I fell asleep, it's like I disappeared. And now, I am reborn in this new, unknown place, the air somehow clearer than it ever was back home.

I have found it—the cure, the secret for getting rid of

Camille. As long as I keep moving, the ghosts cannot catch me.

Across the parking lot, Hunter's door swings open. He stands up and stretches as he looks around, catches my eye, and smiles. He starts walking over and some little voice inside tries to remind me that I don't even know him, that this is crazy, but I don't listen.

"How are you feeling?" he says as he sits down next to me.

"Actually, kind of great. How long was I out?"

"About four hours until I pulled over. I wanted to go farther, but I couldn't keep my eyes open, and I had a feeling I shouldn't wake you. I think we've been here for about four hours."

"That's like a full night's sleep."

"Yeah," he says, reaching over and pulling the Coke out of my hand, taking a sip. "You don't have crazy eyes anymore."

"I had crazy eyes?" I say, grabbing the can back.

"Um, yeah," he says sarcastically. "Like psychotic crazy eyes. Like the worst I've ever seen. And I've been around some really high people in my life."

A minivan turns in to the parking lot. It is somehow shocking to see something suddenly moving in this stillness. We watch it as it crosses the empty lot and pulls into the parking space right in front of our picnic table. A jolly-looking old man steps out the driver's side while his female counterpart steps out the passenger's side. "Good morning!" they chirp in unison, breaking the magic of the quiet morning.

"Wait five minutes," the old man says. "We'll be open in a jiffy." They scuttle into the building.

"In a jiffy," Hunter says.

"I need to brush my teeth."

As I walk back to the car to get my toothbrush, I notice how stiff my body is. My ankle is still a little sore, but not nearly as bad as it has been. Maybe this trip will be good for it, all this sitting in the car.

Inside the building are racks full of brochures and displays of taxidermied animals. The man and woman sit behind a counter with a sign that says ASK US ANYTHING! I splash water on my face in the bathroom and brush my teeth. It's the first good look I've had at myself in a mirror for a while, and I'm shocked by how gaunt I look, how skeletal. I have dark bags under my eyes and my hair is a mess. I wet it down and try to wrangle it into a tighter ponytail. Maybe I should just let myself go completely. Maybe I should let my hair turn into dreadlocks. What is the uniform for someone on the run?

When I get out of the bathroom, Hunter is standing in front of a giant map of Michigan. I stand by him and find our tiny towns, tucked away against the lake, far from any cities.

Then it hits me—I have no idea where I am. I scour the map for some clue, follow the thick line of a freeway north until it comes to a red YOU ARE HERE sticker on the other side of the Mackinac Bridge.

"We're in the Upper Peninsula?" I cry, much louder than necessary.

"Yeah," Hunter says, looking at me like I'm crazy, like it should have been obvious somehow.

"Why are we in the UP?" I am suddenly angry. I am furious.

"Why not?" Hunter says, obviously not understanding the severity of the situation.

"It's, it's—" Nothing comes.

"You have something against the Upper Peninsula?"

"Yes. I mean, no. I mean, it's ridiculous to go this way. There's nothing up here. It'll take way longer."

"I didn't realize we were on a deadline." He's making fun of me.

"It just doesn't make sense." The more I say, the more he seems to find me amusing.

"I've never been to the UP before, have you?"

"No."

"We've lived a few hours away from it our whole lives, but we've never gone. Isn't that unfortunate? There's like this big wild world just a few hours away, but we've never explored it."

I don't say anything. I know whatever comes out of my mouth will sound stupid.

"We're on an adventure, Kinsey. Now's as good a time as any to discover what our great state has to offer. Look at all these marvelous brochures!" He fans out the stack of glossy pamphlets in his hand.

"But it's not efficient!" I cry, cringing immediately at the whine in my voice.

"Who said we were trying to be efficient?"

"I . . . it just seems . . . it would make more sense if . . ."

"For fuck's sake, Kinsey, you just ran away from home. This seems like an opportune time for you to practice making less sense."

I don't say anything. It takes me a while to absorb "you just ran away from home."

Hunter's laugh sounds like a chain saw. "Camille told me all about your love of efficiency."

"What?" My stomach drops at the sound of her name. "She talked about me? What did she say?"

"Just that you had an incredible . . . *enthusiasm* for order."

"She said that? What else did she say?"

"It doesn't matter," he says, not laughing anymore.

"It does matter. Tell me! What was the context of her saying that? Was she talking about something in particular?" I know my voice is rising but I don't care. Bells jingle welcome as a loud, multi-kid family enters. It is suddenly too crowded in here. I need air. I hurry toward the door, vaguely aware of the info desk couple calling, "Have a nice trip!" in unison.

Hunter follows me out the door. "Jesus, calm down," he says. "It's not that big of a deal."

"It is a big deal!" I scream, then spin around and, before I have a chance to know what I'm doing, punch him hard in the shoulder.

Time stops. His eyes narrow. The birds stop chirping. "Did you just *hit* me?" he says slowly, his voice low, snarling.

"Oh my god, I'm sorry. I didn't mean to. I just . . . I don't know what happened."

"Dude, it is *not* okay to hit people." I can tell by the way he looks at me that this is about way more than us, way more than here. He's looking at me like I'm someone else, someone worse. No one's ever looked at me like this, not even close. Even Mom in all her cruelty never looked at me with so much hate, so much pain. Hunter is not looking at me. He sees someone else. Someone who broke his heart bad.

"I'm sorry," I whisper. I know it means nothing.

He looks away, toward a break in the trees that opens up to blue sky. When he looks back, it's me again in front of him.

"Want to see the bridge?" he says, tired.

"The Mackinac? Is it close?"

"It's right over there."

We walk in silence across the parking lot, behind a building, and through another smaller parking lot. The trees open on our right to reveal Interstate 75 and toll booths. We walk a little farther to where the concrete stops and Lake Huron begins, the great bridge spread out in front of us like a postcard picture, connecting this wild and forgotten part of Michigan to the place we've come from.

"So it's settled then."

"What is?"

"We're going through the UP."

The punch has lost me my right to argue for a while. "I guess we are."

"Are you okay to drive for a while?"

The question makes me shudder. I haven't driven a car since the night of the accident. I don't tell him this. I don't tell him how scared I am. I don't tell him how afraid I am of killing him too.

"We can get off the highway a couple miles up," he says, as if he's read my mind, sensed my fear. "Drive on back roads. It's more scenic," he says. He doesn't have to say they're safer, too.

"Okay," I say.

We walk in silence back to the car. The sun has risen and the air is no longer crisp and cool. It is growing stagnant. Heavy. It is time to start moving.

I get in the driver's seat and take a long time to adjust everything. I double- and triple-check the side mirrors. "Okay," I say, and turn the key. The car purrs to life. I check my seat belt.

"Maybe you can test drive it a few times around the parking lot," Hunter offers.

I nod, shift into drive, but don't take my foot off the brake. My heart beats hard and fast in my chest, threatening to break through. We sit there for what seems like several minutes until Hunter sighs and says, "Why don't I drive a little longer?" I nod again because I can't speak. I'm afraid if I open my mouth, I'll start crying. If I start, I don't know if I will ever stop. Ever since I cried yesterday morning in my mom's arms, it's like the floodgates were opened and now there's only a thin, fragile wall protecting me from drowning.

I put the car in park again and we change sides. Hunter adjusts the seat and mirrors back to match his body. "I'm sorry," I finally say.

"I can't drive the whole way, you know."

"I know."

"You have to get over this."

"I know."

We sit in silence for a few moments. Another car enters the parking lot, another family gathering information for their vacation.

Hunter pulls the stack of tourist brochures out of his back pocket and throws them on my lap.

"Here," he says. "Make yourself useful. Find us something fun to do."

What have I gotten myself into?

Trees. Miles and miles of trees and not much else. The world saturated with deep greens and browns. An occasional boarded-up old house. An abandoned barn. Mossy ghost towns held together with cobwebs. We pick up greasy breakfast burritos at a run-down gas station and eat in the car. All I want is to hurry through this nothing place, get this part of the journey over with so we can arrive at a real destination. I don't understand why Hunter would want to take his time here, would want to wallow in somewhere so empty and sad, why he wouldn't rather drive through as fast as we can and not stop until we reach something nice. But I figure I owe it to him to at least try to be agreeable while he's doing all the driving. Maybe when I get my shit together enough to drive, I can start making some decisions.

We stop for gas and groceries in an Indian reservation. It's not even a town, just a gravelly stretch on the side of the road with a couple of gas pumps, a little store, a mechanics shop that may or may not be in business, and a couple of beat-up old trucks with FOR SALE signs in the windows that look like they've been parked there for years. A girl my age works the register and is very pregnant. Something in her eyes is so much older than me, so worn down. I wonder what she does for fun, if there's anywhere for her to go besides this roadside store. She rings up our groceries like a robot, like she's only barely alive, her heart beating just enough to perform the necessary movements, like the rest of her is sleeping, hibernating, not bothering to wake for this half-life.

"I'll pay," Hunter says, offering the girl his card.

I shove my debit card in front of his, maybe a little too forcefully. "No," I say. "We'll split it."

"It's okay," he says. "I can cover it. I know you don't—"

He stops talking just in time. He can tell by the look on my face that I do not want his charity. The checkout girl sighs and looks out the window at the view of the gas pumps she'll see every day for who knows how long.

"I will pay my own way," I say firmly, and that is that.

It's barely afternoon, but Hunter's already been driving for five hours. "Unless you're ready to take a shift," he says, "we should probably start thinking about where we're going to stay tonight. The map shows a few campgrounds coming up and a waterfall. That'd be cool. We could go swimming maybe, go for a hike."

I don't say anything. I've been watching trees go by since eight this morning. I can't remember why I thought this was a good idea. I can't remember who I was when I made that decision.

"Hello?" Hunter says.

"What are we doing?"

"What do you mean?"

"What are we doing, Hunter?"

"We're driving to San Francisco," he says slowly, unsurely. "Like we talked about."

"But we're going to be, like, *tourists* on the way there? Stopping at every roadside attraction we pass? Going *hiking*?"

"I thought you'd like hiking. You're into all those sports and shit, aren't you?"

"I'm not talking about hiking!"

Hunter doesn't say anything. His face clouds over and for a split second I catch a glimpse of him years younger, a heartbroken boy hiding behind this brooding almost-man. Then it hits me how hard he's been trying to be cheerful for both of us, and I immediately feel sorry.

"So what, you're in a hurry?" he says, the little boy gone, his face a sudden wall of anger. "You want to get there as fast as possible and not have any fun? Because, what, fun is inconvenient? Fun is inefficient? Stopping and pulling that stick out of your ass for one minute is going to make you fall apart, it's going to ruin everything?"

"No," I say. "I—"

"If you're not uptight and in control at all times, then what? You're already miserable, Kinsey. It can't get much worse. What the fuck are you afraid of?"

I don't have an answer.

"Your life sucks. My life sucks. How could your precious speed and efficiency make our shitty lives any better? No one gives a shit where we are or what we're doing. We might as well enjoy it before we have to fucking give up like we know we're going to have to."

"Why do you say that?" I say. "Why do we have to give up?"

"That's what people do. That's what everyone does."

"Even you?"

"Especially me."

I want to ask more. I want to know how the conversation

veered this way so suddenly. I want to know why Hunter of all people, this heavy-drinking, skateboard-riding, indie-music-listening rebel who doesn't seem to follow anyone's rules, is saying all this. But before I have a chance to say anything, he swerves suddenly to the left, into a dirt road I hadn't noticed.

"What are you doing?" I shriek as the side of my head thuds dully on the window.

"The sign said camping."

"What sign? I didn't see a sign."

"It was tiny. This place isn't on the map."

"Camping?"

"Yes, camping," he says definitively. "We are camping. Right here."

My instincts tell me to object, the part of me that wants to be in control, that needs to be the one making decisions. But the tunnel of dense trees opens to a small, almost-empty campground, a handful of quaint, private sites lining the shore of a small, still lake sparkling with sun.

"Fine," I say. "We're camping."

It's hot when we get out of the car. The air is heavy with the scent of pine. My mind immediately goes to setting up camp. Did Hunter bring everything we need? Did we buy enough food? What about sleeping arrangements? But before

I have the chance to say anything, Hunter yells, "Swimming!" tears off his pants but leaves his boxers and long-sleeved shirt on, and runs into the lake just a few steps away.

"Shouldn't we set up the tent or something?" I yell over to him, but he just keeps splashing around, and I'm pretty sure he's pretending not to hear me. The thick summer air is suddenly oppressive, and I notice how my clothes are sticking to my skin. In my haste packing, I didn't bring a swimsuit; I didn't think it was going to be that kind of a trip.

The water is an opaque, coppery brown. Reeds line the shore like long green fingers, waving slightly in the breeze as if beckoning us in. This is the kind of water where things can hide, all kinds of viney monsters reaching up from the mucky bottom for ankles.

"Come on!" Hunter yells, splashing the shore with a wall of water. "It feels amazing."

"I don't like swimming where I can't see the bottom."

"That's the stupidest thing I've ever heard," he says, and dives back in.

It's hot and I'm sticky. Am I really going to let some silly fear of pond monsters keep me from relief? I hide behind the car as I strip down to my bra and undies. I wait until Hunter goes under again to approach the water. I wade in carefully, testing each step with my toe before I move forward. The mud sucks at my feet, but it is benign. There's nothing sharp, nothing grabbing for me.

"Oh wow," I say when I finally make it up to my chest. The heat, the dust, the sweat washes off me. The days of exhaustion and anxiety seem to dissolve into the water. Even my ankle seems suddenly healed. I kick my legs a few times and glide away from shore. There is no pain anywhere in my body. "This lake is magic," I say.

I do a few laps along the shore and Hunter makes fun of me for turning relaxation into a chore. "I'm swimming," I protest. "How is that different from what you're doing?"

"You're doing *laps*, Kinsey."

"So what? I'm swimming in a straight line. Big deal." He laughs and dives under the water, and I realize that I'm kind of enjoying his teasing now. I try to do what he does, just splash around with no real order to my movements, but it feels awkward, unnatural. My body doesn't know how to move that way.

I don't know how long we spend in the lake, but it's long enough to realize I'm starving. And somehow that feeling brings up a whole list of practical concerns. When Hunter surfaces, I ask him about the sleeping situation.

"I brought two sleeping bags," he says. "Though I don't know if we'll even need them, it's so hot. Probably won't cool down too much at night."

"So we're both going to sleep in the tent? Together?"

"Does that bother you?" he says with a playful smile, the afternoon sun making him golden. "Are you afraid you won't be able to control yourself and end up ravaging me in the middle of the night?"

"Shut up. No."

"Seriously, though. If you're uncomfortable with it, we can figure something else out."

"No. I'm fine. It's okay." I'm a big girl. I can handle this. I'm not a prude like Camille always said.

When I climb out of the water, I'm too aware of my underwear sticking to my skin, my white bra now made see-through. I feel the water cascade off my body, the tiny scraps of fabric clinging to me. When I turn around, Hunter is still in the water, watching me. I feel a chill. I don't not like it.

"Aren't you getting out?" I say.

Hunter looks away. Is that embarrassment I see?

"Um, yeah," he mumbles. "In a second." He looks down, into the water.

Oh my god. That's why he's acting weird all of a sudden. He has a boner.

I pretend like it's no big deal, like something incredibly embarrassing didn't just happen. I change my clothes behind the car and start pulling supplies out of the trunk.

Tent. Sleeping bags. Sleeping pads. Cooler. Stove and fuel. Lantern. A couple of flashlights. When all the camping stuff is emptied, the only thing left in the trunk is a cardboard box full of liquor bottles.

"What is this?" I say.

"What is what?" Hunter says, walking over as he buttons his pants. His shirt is soaked but he doesn't take it off.

"This box."

"Refreshments," he says, pulling out a bottle of vodka. "Where's that OJ we bought?"

"Really?"

"Yeah, want a drink? Screwdrivers are the perfect beverage for a sunny afternoon."

"No thank you," I say, and I can hear the primness in my voice.

"Oh, sorry," he says, the playfulness in his voice gone slightly sour. "I forgot. Miss Perfect doesn't break any rules, does she?"

I decide to ignore him. "Does your phone get reception out here?" I say.

"I don't know. I turned it off as soon as we left town."

"What if someone calls?"

"I don't want to talk to anyone who'd call me."

"Can I borrow it?"

"Sure, knock yourself out. It's in the glove compartment."

I get the phone and press the button to turn it on. I have to walk all the way to the main road to get reception. As soon as one bar show up, the phone starts dinging alerts. I try not to be nosy, but I can't help but look at the screen when I dial the number for my house. Nineteen missed calls. Five messages—four from "Mom" and one from "His Majesty."

I'm relieved when the answering machine picks up at my house so I don't actually have to talk to my mother. I can't deal with her sadness right now. "Hi, Mom," I say. "I just wanted to let you know I'm okay and not to worry. I'm with a friend and we're camping. I'm trying to have some fun this summer, you know? Like you said. I'll keep you posted. Love you." Short and sweet and to the point.

When I get back to camp, Hunter's already put up the tent and prepared a meal of turkey sandwiches and potato chips. He hands me a plastic cup. "Orange juice for the lady," he says.

"Thanks."

We sit at the picnic table, eating our dinners in silence, looking out at the early evening sun sparkling on the lake.

"You had some messages," I say.

"Uh-huh," he says.

"Aren't you going to call your parents or something? Let them know you're all right?"

"Why don't you let me worry about that, okay?" He takes a big gulp of the concoction in his cup.

We sit at the table and read for a while, Hunter working on something old and dusty with very small print. With his guard down, he looks almost studious. My eyes start drooping before the sun even sets. I go to bed and leave Hunter at the picnic table with his book and the lantern and his bottle of vodka.

As I crawl into the sleeping bag, it hits me that I haven't felt Camille all day. Will my luck last through the night? Have I gotten rid of her for good? As soon as my head hits the wadded-up sweatshirt I'm using as a pillow, sleep starts taking me and a warm relief spreads through my body. But as I drift away from the day, my heart aches just a little. Maybe part of me doesn't want Camille to really be gone.

SEVEN

I wake up with the sunrise. I don't remember dreaming. Hunter is balled up on the other side of the tent, snoring. I get out and stretch, feel the morning sun warm my body, see it glistening off the still lake. I hop on my left foot and it feels perfect, like my ankle was never even twisted. I can't remember the last time I slept this well. For a few moments, it feels like nothing could possibly be wrong in the world. But then I see the car trunk wide open, muddy paw prints all over our torn shopping bags, our food now only crumbs littered on the ground, at least fifty dollars wasted on a feast for raccoons. Hunter's bottle of vodka is lying on its side on the picnic table, half-empty. I don't know how many drinks that is, but I'm pretty sure it would send me to the hospital.

The cooler in the trunk is scratched with dirty claw prints, but at least the food inside is still safe. I take out an apple and a jar of peanut butter, find a knife on the ground and wash it off, and go sit by the lake, trying not to let my anger ruin this beautiful morning. But it's no use. The sun is suddenly too bright. The ground is too dirty. The lake is too wet. How am I going to make it across the rest of the country with Hunter if this is any indication of how things are going to be?

I hear a rustling behind me and turn to see Hunter stumble out of the tent in his shirt and boxers, barefoot, eyes still closed, and puke behind a tree. When he's done, he emerges as if nothing happened, walks past me, and dives straight into the lake.

"Did you just throw up?" I say as soon as he emerges.

"Uh-huh," he mumbles, then dives in again. Is this normal? Is this the way he usually starts his day?

"Do you want to eat anything?" I ask when he comes back up.

"No," he says.

"Good, because someone left the trunk open and raccoons got into all the food."

"Oops."

"Oops? That's all you have to say? Almost all our food is gone."

"So we'll get more."

"I don't have unlimited money, you know. That food was expensive."

"So I'll pay for it."

"Is that how you solve problems? Just throw money at them?"

"This conversation is boring," he says, then dunks his head under the water.

When he emerges, I say, "Let's go. You need to help me clean up camp."

"Calm the fuck down."

"Don't talk to me like that."

He climbs out of the water and stomps, dripping, to the tent. He starts tearing it down with all our stuff still inside.

"Wait a minute," I say.

"I thought you were in a hurry."

"Are you even okay to drive?"

"Why, are you offering?" he says sharply.

"Um," I say, panic bursting in my chest. "I don't know. I don't think I'm ready." I have lost my right to be mad at him.

"Looks like I'm okay to drive, then."

Hunter is grumpy and silent the entire morning. His

mood is like a poison in the car. Only after stopping at a road-side diner and getting some food in him do his spirits start to lift. He pays for breakfast and some groceries and we silently agree that we're even. He switches the music on the stereo from dark and heavy to something lighter and more melodic. I can feel his hangover dissipate; he comes back to life as the alcohol drains from his blood.

We drive past a ghost town, all the businesses boarded up, faded FOR SALE signs on every window. A bakery, a diner, a gas station, a tavern. Nothing of value left. Even the church is for sale. The stained glass windows have been removed, probably stolen. It's unclear how long the town has been dead, how long it's been since someone sat inside that church and believed God was with them.

With no warning, Hunter pulls off the side of the road and parks.

"What are you doing?" I say.

"Sightseeing." He opens the glove compartment and pulls out an expensive-looking digital camera with a giant, complicated lens.

"Here?" I say, but he doesn't answer.

I follow him around the ghost town as he takes pictures. His hangover seems to have lifted completely, and he's energized, almost frantic, as he climbs the rickety stairs of buildings, as he peers inside the ruined rooms and snaps away with his camera. The more broken something is, the more interested in it he seems. It's like he gains energy from it, but all this place does is make me feel sad.

"I don't know what you see in this place," I say, leaning against a rusty old tractor, sucking down our last bottle of water. "It's so ugly."

"That's why it's beautiful," he says, then disappears behind a dilapidated shed.

I feel like I'm missing something, like this beauty he speaks of is some kind of math equation I'm not understanding. I can't get both sides to add up. There's some variable that's still unknown. I hate this feeling. I hate the thought that maybe Hunter knows something I don't.

After what seems like forever, Hunter approaches with a satisfied smile on his face. He has cobwebs in his hair and his clothes are filthy from crawling around the ruins, but I've never seen him happier. "Want to see some of my pictures?" he says. He stands close and begins flipping through the photos on the camera's tiny screen. I can feel the electricity on his skin.

I walked around the town too, but I didn't see any of the things he saw. His pictures are stunning, art gallery–worthy even, yet sad at the same time. I never even considered that those two things could exist together—beauty and pain. Some things in the photos look vaguely familiar, but also like they're from a different world, a place with different light and different shadows, a place where broken things are indeed beautiful.

"Hunter, you're really talented," I say. He shrugs. "How did you even see that? That doesn't look anything like what I saw."

"You just have to look at things a little differently," he tells me. His smile is sincere. Something about taking the pictures opened him up. Something about exploring the darkness managed to let light in. Something I am far from understanding.

As we drive through the afternoon, the forest gives way to rural ruins of industry. We stop for the night in the shadows of an old abandoned factory on Lake Superior, on the edge of the small boarded-up town that died with it. We camp at what used to be some kind of resort, with rickety little cabins for rent, a playground overrun with weeds, a pool full of green sludge and leaves, and a weathered sign for canoe rentals. A storm-ravaged dock sticks out of the water, a few weather-beaten skeletons of boats just barely floating. A creaking sign points the way to a "campground," but it's not much more than an overgrown field marked by gravel parking strips and decaying picnic tables.

"This place is what Sunset Village would look like if it died," Hunter says when we pull into what appears to be the outline of a camping spot. "It's like a vacation graveyard."

I imagine Gabby's Snack Shack all boarded up, the hot dog warmer, soft-serve machine, and all the other equipment stripped and sold, leaving only the sad shell of the building. What would Bill do if Tourist Hell froze over? Where would he go? Where did all these people go? What happens to a whole town when the one thing keeping people employed there just shuts down?

Hunter runs across what used to be a volleyball court to the lakeshore and sticks his hand in the water. "Holy fuck, that's cold! Why would anyone vacation by a lake you can't even swim in?"

"Apparently they didn't."

According to Hunter, it's my turn to put up the tent. I say okay, not mentioning that I've never put up a tent in my life. I don't want to be that girl who needs a boy to show her how to do things. He'd like that too much.

But I'm hopeless. I have no idea where anything goes. The elastic sticks are unruly and nearly poke my eye out.

"You need some help?"

"No," I mutter.

"It looks like you need some help."

"I'm fine."

"Jesus, Kinsey. There's nothing wrong with needing help. All you have to do is ask."

I won't. I can't. Even if I wanted to, my jaws are clenched tight, like they have a mind of their own, like they've made the decision for me.

"It's a fucking tent. Who cares if you don't know how to do it?" He shakes his head. He feels sorry for me. "Kinsey Cole, you're the most stubborn person I've ever met."

I look at the tent lying deflated and tangled on the ground. I look at Hunter and his eyes are kind, the sourness of his hangover long gone. Just like my mother, he is capable of being two such completely different people.

"Fine," I finally manage to say. "Help me. I need your help. Are you happy?"

He smiles. "See, that wasn't so hard, was it?"

"Actually, it was."

He starts laying out the tent and sticks, explaining how everything fits together as he goes. "How'd you get so good at this?" I ask. It seems so unlike him, this outdoorsy prowess.

"We used to go camping a lot when I was a kid. Before my dad became such an asshole."

"What happened?"

"You mean how'd he become an asshole? He got rich. You

own a couple crappy restaurants in suburban Chicago and you can still be sort of a nice guy. But when you start expanding your empire, you become an emperor, you know? Power corrupts and all that. A corporate mastermind doesn't have time for camping."

"But the Kountry Kitchens seem so friendly," I say, thinking about the cheesy Americana and fake old posters on the walls, the ruffles on everything, the baby-blue color scheme.

That makes Hunter laugh. "Have you tried their chicken-fried steak? That shit is not friendly. It's a nuclear bomb in your digestive system."

Somehow we've managed to get the tent upright. "Now we just have to stake it," Hunter says, throwing me a large rock. "Here, use this."

"You didn't bring a hammer or something?"

"This is more fun."

I bang a stake into the ground with the rock. "I feel like a caveman."

"Exactly," Hunter grins.

When we're done, I stand back and take a good, long look at the tent. It's such a small accomplishment, but I feel ridiculously proud of myself.

"I still go camping a lot, though," Hunter says. "With the guys sometimes. But my favorite is to just go by myself. Get away from my mom. Get away from all the stupid small-town assholes."

"You go by yourself? Don't you get scared?"

"Not at all. Being around people is way scarier than being alone."

I don't know. They're both terrifying. But right now I am thinking of darkness, of things hiding behind trees, in abandoned buildings, of being powerless in the wilderness.

"But there's so much unknown," I say. "You're surrounded by the unknown."

"I'm okay with that," Hunter says. I meet his eyes. Neither of us looks away.

"I wish I was," I finally say. I am the first to blink.

Our eyes lock again and his mouth opens. He's on the verge of saying something; maybe he's about to make this all make sense. But before any words have a chance to come out, we are interrupted.

"Hey!" calls a woman's voice from behind us. It's shocking to hear the voice of a stranger in this secluded place. We haven't seen another human being in hours. For a moment, a spark of fear passes through me. People get murdered in places like this.

"Hey," says Hunter, smiling. I turn around to see a woman, probably in her early twenties, and an older man, probably midthirties, both with long dreadlocks and friendly, dopey grins.

"You found our secret spot, man," the guy says. "This is the best campground in the whole state of Michigan. Totally free, man."

"We didn't even know it was here," Hunter says. "We just kind of fell upon it."

"That's how you find the best stuff," the girl says with a slight Southern drawl. "Happy accidents."

"It was destiny, man," says the guy.

"You can't plan magic," says the girl. They're both nodding mindlessly like bobble heads, like caricatures of dumb stoners, but they are totally serious.

"I'm Chesapeake," says the girl.

"Mountain," says the guy.

"Hunter."

"Such a violent name for such a gentle man," says Chesapeake with a tilt of her head. Was that supposed to be flirting?

After an awkward pause, I realize it is my turn to speak. "Kinsey," I say.

"Cool, cool," says Mountain while Chesapeake keeps nodding and grinning.

I know I'm supposed to be open-minded and not judge without getting to know someone, but I really don't want to keep talking to these people.

"Hey!" Chesapeake says way too enthusiastically. "You

guys should totally hang out with us tonight! We have veggie dogs!"

"Yeah, yeah," says Mountain. "Cool."

"Yeah," says Hunter, looking at me for confirmation. I try to send him a psychic message of NO while smiling, but he does not receive it. "Sounds good," he says. "We can bring some chips or something. I got a bottle of whiskey to share if you're down."

"Oooh!" Chesapeake squeals. "Whiskey goes perfect with veggie dogs."

"And brownies," Mountain adds. "*Magic* brownies." Chesapeake giggles.

"We have to finish setting up camp first," I say a little too sharply. God, I am such a downer.

"Well, come on by when you're done," Mountain says. "We have our own secret spot behind the shed by the dock. Can't see it from the road."

"Will do," Hunter says, eyeing me with a smirk only I can see. He knows how uncomfortable this is making me. And he loves it.

"What did he mean by magic brownies?" I ask Hunter as we navigate through knee-high weeds and what appear to be broken tractor parts to Chesapeake and Mountain's camp. It's twilight and everything is golden orange. It would be peaceful if I weren't so nervous.

"You can't be that naive, can you?" Hunter says. He's carrying a bottle of whiskey and I have a bag of corn chips and a jar of salsa. I feel like the girl in the movie *Dirty Dancing* when she shows up all nerdy at the underground dance party and says, "I carried a watermelon," to sexy Patrick Swayze.

If we didn't already know they were here, we probably wouldn't have even noticed Chesapeake and Mountain's campsite. Their beat-up VW bus is perfectly hidden by a grove of birch trees. Folding chairs and a small table circle the campfire, laundry hangs on a clothesline strung between two trees, a picnic table is covered with a checkered tablecloth and a mason jar full of wildflowers, and they even have a rug laid beneath the bus's sliding side door. It looks like they've been here a long time and don't plan on leaving any time soon.

"Friends!" Chesapeake yells, crouched at the water's edge, completely naked, holding a washcloth and a bar of soap. The water is filmy from her bath. She splashes herself with the freezing water and lets out a yelp, then walks toward us without any shame. "Now where'd I put my towel?" she says. I look away, but there's Mountain climbing out of the bus, also naked. What the hell is going on?

"Hunter," I whisper. I can hear the panic in my voice. I

pull on his sleeve. "Hunter!" He's in a trance, staring at Chesapeake as she bends over to pick her towel off a rock. She seems to be taking her time on purpose, enjoying the attention.

"Oh, hey, guys," Mountain says. "Didn't realize you were here. Let me put some pants on." He gets back in the bus and I can breathe again. Chesapeake grabs some clothes off the clothesline and gets dressed. Hunter watches as she pulls on her jeans, as she raises her arms to put her shirt on. All I can see is the fuzzy blond bush of her armpits.

"Hunter!" I hiss. "Stop staring. It's rude."

"It's only rude if the attention's unwanted," he says, throwing me his signature grin. "Or are you jealous?"

"I hate you," I say.

We sit around the fire and they immediately get to drinking. Hunter pours me a plastic camping cup half full of whiskey. I take a sip but nearly gag. In the time it takes me to consume maybe a tablespoon, the others do a quick progression of more shots than I can count, cheering to things like "freedom" and "chaos" and "sky." Hunter's face is lit in a way I've only seen when he was taking pictures at the ghost town. So now I know there are two things that make him happy.

By the time the veggie dogs are done, everyone is drunk. Even I'm a little tipsy, which, as much as I hate to admit it, is not an entirely unpleasant feeling. It makes these people a little less annoying. But only a little. Chesapeake and Mountain start waxing poetic about life on the road, Hunter in rapt attention, hanging on their every word. They keep talking about freedom, about not having to follow anyone's rules, about being able to follow their bliss wherever it wants to take them. They are so full of shit.

"But you're not *doing* anything," I blurt out. I must be drunker than I thought. Hunter laughs so hard he nearly falls backward, as surprised as I am at what came out of my mouth. But I keep going. I can't stop myself. "How can life be satisfying if all you do is wander around?"

"Not all who wander are lost," Chesapeake says sagely, like she's the first person who ever thought to say that.

"That's just a bumper sticker," I say.

"Excuse my friend here," Hunter says with his mouth full of corn chips. "She's a little uptight. It's my mission on this trip to help her loosen up. As you can see, I have a lot of work to do."

"Cool, cool," says Mountain, smiling at me with wet lips. "We all gotta start somewhere, man." Could he be any more patronizing? Does he really think he's more evolved than me?

"Yeah, like I used to want to be a ballerina," Chesapeake says, her Southern drawl getting thicker the more drunk she gets. "But back then, my name was Edith." That makes her crack up. She laughs uncontrollably while Mountain roots around in the cooler. Hunter just drinks his whiskey like it is completely normal to be getting wasted with strangers in a ghost town.

"This!" Mountain announces as he pulls out a tinfoil package. "My pal Ferret in Denver baked these. Best pot brownies in the country, I'd say, and I've sampled a few in my time."

"Yum," says Chesapeake, clapping her hands like a toddler.

Hunter looks at me and wiggles his eyebrows. "No," I say.

"Your loss," he says as he grabs a smashed glob of brownie out of the tinfoil Mountain offers.

"Bon appétit," Mountain says, and they start chewing.

I don't know why I don't just leave then. I could easily walk back to our camp with my flashlight and leave Hunter there to spend the night with his new ridiculous friends. But for some reason I stay, quietly turning into a spectator rather than participant in the evening. They forget I am even there. I watch them get more and more wasted; I listen to them make less and less sense.

After an hour, they are barely intelligible. Their eyes are slits and their words are jumbled. Is this supposed to be fun? Do they actually enjoy being this fucked-up? I sit silently, like an anthropologist observing some lost tribe whose customs are so unfamiliar it's hard to even recognize them as the same species.

After being invisible for an hour, it is shocking when Mountain suddenly stares me down and says, "Are you loose yet?"

"What?"

"Have you loosened up? Or are you still wound up tight?"

"Tight," Hunter mumbles beside me, only capable of single syllables by now.

"I could give you a back rub," Chesapeake says. "I give really good back rubs."

"No thank you," I say.

"I feel loose," says Mountain.

"Loose," says Hunter.

Something suddenly feels very wrong.

"There's lots of room in the bus," Chesapeake says. "It's really comfy."

"I know Hunter's in," Mountain says.

"In," says Hunter. He can barely hold himself up anymore. His eyes are closed and his head is drooped against his chest. Hunter is not in for anything besides passing out.

It is definitely time to go.

"Hunter," I say, tugging on his shirt. "Hunter, come on. I'm tired. Let's go."

"You can sleep here," Chesapeake purrs. "Both of you." She gets out of her chair and glides over, the reflection of the fire dancing in her eyes. "With us."

"Sleep," Hunter mumbles. "Here."

"No sleep here, Hunter."

Chesapeake puts her hand on Hunter's shoulder and lowers herself onto his lap. He doesn't seem to even notice her weight. She puts her arms around him and attempts to kiss him, but he's too wasted to even try to kiss back. He's like a zombie sitting there, half-dead.

When I stand up, Hunter is startled back to life. "Kinsey," he says. "Don't leave me." He tries to stand, knocking Chesapeake off him.

"Ouch," she says as she lands on her butt, then starts laughing the monotone huh-huh-huh of stoners. Mountain joins her, laughing from his chair on the other side of the fire, eating chip crumbs out of the bag and watching us through half-closed eyes like we're a TV show.

I reach for Hunter's arm as he struggles to get up, but his sudden momentum sends him forward. His leg gets caught in the cheap folding chair. He has no balance. He's blind and falling and I can't catch him. He's going forward, too fast, too hard, into the fire. Into the fire.

"No!" I scream.

Headlights. Metal. Brakes.

Scraping. Smashing. Gone.

Camille.

Going. Going. Gone.

I am blind as I reach for him. I grab onto air.

He is gone.

Burning.

Gone.

He is fire.

I am air.

We are nothing.

No. This is his arm in my hands. This is Hunter falling against me. That is my elbow slamming on the ground, Hunter a lump on top of me. "Huh?" his whiskey mouth says. The dreadlock twins continue their huh-huh-huh.

The fire flickers against the trees, turning the night on and off. And Camille's in the shadows, watching us, laughing.

After several tries, I manage to pull Hunter to his feet. Chesapeake and Mountain have laughed themselves into a passed-out stupor, Chesapeake a lump on the ground, Mountain slumped in his chair covered in chip crumbs. I have to half carry Hunter back to our camp, stopping several times on the way for him to lie down, once to hug a tree he finds particularly beautiful, and once to throw up. "My whiskey," he says, wiping his mouth. "I left my whiskey."

"Fuck your whiskey," I say.

When we finally make it back to our camp, he falls into the tent and immediately starts snoring. I am exhausted, but I am too angry to sleep. I sit outside on the picnic table, listening to the darkness. I lie down and look up at the sky, but where there were once hundreds of stars, there is now just one. Its blinks taunt me, telling me I can never reach it no matter how hard I try.

I hear something splash in the lake. Something big.

The air is cold.

The trees and abandoned buildings seem to thicken, crowding around me, becoming solid, an impenetrable wall, a tunnel.

I look up but all I see is black; even the one cruel, lonely star is gone. There is black everywhere. I could search forever and only find black.

"Camille?" I whisper.

The wind blows and leaves rustle. The rusty swings in the decrepit playground creak. I flip the switch on my flashlight but it doesn't turn on.

A voice sounds in the distance, a cross between a cry and a moan. It sounds pained. Searching.

"Camille, is that you?"

Nothing. I'm being stupid. It's not cold. I try my flashlight again and it sends a beam of light across the campground. The voice was an owl, talking to the night like owls do. Camille is dead and there's no such thing as ghosts. I didn't dream last night. I haven't felt her for two days. She is gone.

When I crawl into bed, Hunter is snoring a sickly, wet snore, the tent full of his drunk breath. I wedge myself as far to the other side as possible, my face against the nylon wall. As soon as I close my eyes, I feel exhaustion pulling me under. Like quicksand. Like drowning.

Is that you, Camille? Are those your hands pulling me under? Are you waiting for me? Do you miss me as much as I miss you?

EIGHT

The golden morning sun sparkles on the lake, but I am not impressed. Is this going to be the ritual every morning? Me getting up early and sitting around waiting while Hunter spends an extra couple hours filling the tent with his rancid breaths? We could be fifty miles from here by now, fifty miles away from crazy Chesapeake and Mountain, fifty miles closer to San Francisco, but I have to wait out his drunken hibernation.

I wonder if he dreams during these sleeps. Or does the alcohol turn everything off? Maybe that's the solution; maybe Hunter is on to something—maybe alcohol is the magic potion for keeping ghosts away.

For three nights in a row, I haven't dreamed; for three nights, I've slept beside Hunter. It's like something about him protects me from my own brain. I hate to give him that credit, but I don't know what else it could be.

I hear rustling. Like a repeat of yesterday, Hunter stumbles out of the tent and immediately pukes. Is this how he starts every day? I don't even want to think about the state of his torn-up stomach, his poisoned liver, his eroded esophagus.

"It's fucking hot," he says, wiping his mouth with the back of his hand. He walks to the lake and splashes himself with water. "This water is fucking cold," he says, then just sits there with his head in his hands, the sand sticking to his bare legs.

"Do you remember anything from last night?" I say. He doesn't respond. "Do you remember almost falling into the fire? Do you remember how those two freaks practically tried to date-rape us?"

"What?" Hunter says, almost soberly. He looks up and is almost able to focus his eyes on mine. But it's too much effort, and his head falls back into his hands again.

"You don't remember that? They wanted us to have some kind of orgy in the back of the van."

"That did not happen."

"Yes it did."

"You are so paranoid. They were probably just being friendly."

"Hunter, you're the one who was so wasted you can't remember."

He mumbles something I can't quite make out, but I think I hear the word "prude."

"What did you say?" My voice is shrill.

"I don't know what's more frigid, you or this water."

"Fuck you, Hunter."

"Yeah, right. It might help, though. Loosen you up a little."

I turn around and stomp back to the tent. I throw out our sleeping bags, the pants Hunter managed to take off in the middle of the night, and everything else I can find. I start pulling out the stakes with way more force than is necessary.

Hunter, dripping and caked with sand, is in his boxers and long-sleeved shirt as he staggers toward me. "Hey, what are you doing?"

"We're leaving," I say. "Right now." I imagine I sound like what normal mothers sound like when talking to an unruly child.

"Don't get my stuff all dirty." He reaches down to pick up his pants, his movements slow and pained like an old man's, his words still noticeably slurred.

"You're still drunk," I say. "I'm driving." My stomach lurches as I say it, fear threatening to change my mind. But there's no way I'm letting him drive in this condition. As scared as I am of getting behind the wheel, I'm more afraid of him.

"Fine with me," he says, pulling down his wet boxer shorts without even turning away. I avert my eyes just in time. "Nap time for Hunter." It takes all my strength not to turn back around and kick him in the balls.

My driving doesn't go very well at first. Luckily, the adrenaline of my anger is strong enough to overpower my panic, but I'm still overly cautious. I drive way too slow at first. I hit the brakes at the smallest surprise. When a squirrel runs across the road, I slam the brakes so hard, Hunter has to open the door to puke. I make him get out of the car and won't let him in until he brushes his teeth and drinks some water.

Hunter is in and out of sleep for the next hour. My knuckles are white on the steering wheel and I can feel every muscle in my body tense, ready to jump out of my skin. Images flash through my head, gruesome snapshots not quite in focus but threatening to solidify the more panic seeps in. The more peacefully Hunter sleeps, the more my chest tightens, the less I can feel my feet, my legs, my hands, until the numbness spreads to my lungs and I can't breathe.

I'm driving. I'm actually driving. I'm driving a car for the first time since I killed my best friend.

I pull over at a gas station just in time. My vision is cloudy as I put the car in park, turn off the engine, and stumble out the door. Only after I slam the door shut can I breathe again. The world comes back into focus. I watch Hunter through the window as he stretches himself awake.

How can he be so calm? How could he sleep while I'm driving? How could he even let me drive? Not after what I did. Not after what I did to Camille.

I must move so I will stop feeling. I must busy myself with a task so I will not think.

I buy him a Gatorade and a muffin and throw it at him. "Eat something," I command. I look at him slouched and haggard in his seat, his greasy hair matted to his face in a dried pool of drool. Anger wipes away the fear and I can drive again.

"I don't eat in the morning."

"It would settle your stomach."

"What do you know about my stomach?"

"It helps my mom when she's hungover."

"Fuck your mom."

I stop the car in the middle of the road. Hunter rubs his forehead where it bumped against the side window. I hope it hurt. I hope it bruises. The anger calms me. The anger makes me strong.

"What the fuck?" he says, as if he's the one with a right to be offended.

"I don't care if you're hungover, Hunter. That is no excuse to be a fucking asshole. You cannot talk to me like that. Ever."

"Okay, whatever."

"And you can't do this every night."

"Do what?"

"Get wasted like this. I don't want to have to babysit a drunk or hungover asshole for the whole trip."

"Well, you should have said that before we left. Because that's what I am. A drunk asshole. Take it or leave it."

He closes his eyes and leans his face against the window, as if pretending to sleep will make me go away.

"No you're not," I say. "You're different when you don't drink. Better."

"But that would require me to not drink."

"So don't drink. It's not that complicated."

"How would you know? Little miss never-been-drunk-in-her-life? Jesus, I can't believe Camille ever thought you were her best friend."

He could have cut me open instead of saying that. He could have stabbed a knife in my chest and carved out my heart.

"What is that supposed to mean?" My voice is only a

whisper. There is no air behind my words. They hang limp between us, barely there.

"Camille was fun. You are so *not* fun."

I want to be strong. I want to find words so cruel they cut him. But I can't. I have no reserves of meanness. I search, but all I find is loss, a sad emptiness where Camille used to be, and all that place stores is yearning, and despite my holding my breath and clenching my jaw so tight it feels like my teeth are grinding themselves flat, the tears come, cascading down my face in a straight, silent line. I've spent my life not crying, but now it seems like I do it every day. I don't want him to see me. I don't want him to know he has the power to hurt me. But after so many moments of silence, he opens his eyes.

"Oh fuck," Hunter says.

I wipe the tears away, blink my eyes and look out the window. But the tears keep coming, a tiny waterfall dripping off my chin and onto my seat belt.

"Oh shit, I'm sorry. I'm an asshole."

I look at him and his face has softened, has lost some of the raggedness of his hangover. Concern warms his eyes just a little.

I sniffle and wipe my eyes again, and this time, no more tears come.

"She wouldn't have loved you," I say.

"What?" he snaps, as if stung. His face hardens again.

"If that's all you were," I say. "If you were just a drunk asshole. Camille never would have loved you for that. She wasn't the kind of girl who goes for guys who treat them like shit. She liked herself too much. So you must be more. You must be someone really amazing."

He's quiet and still, his mouth slightly open, like he's been startled, shocked. Something like pain crosses his face, a ripple of feeling, and just as I notice his eyes getting wet, he looks away. His hands clench and unclench in his lap. Up until now, I've always wondered what Camille saw in Hunter, what it was that made her love him. But now a new thought hits me—did he love her back? Did she take his heart with her when she died?

"Will you keep driving?" he says.

As if driving will save us. As if moving will keep the pain away.

"Camille was a good judge of character," I say. "And she said she loved you."

"Shut up," he says softly. There's no cruelty in his words. Just sadness. Sadness, and maybe a tiny sliver of gratitude.

I keep driving. My anger is replaced by something else, something softer, with a different kind of resistance to fear. I decide to let him sleep for a while.

***

After an hour or so longer on back roads, I feel confident enough to get on what passes as a highway in the UP, which is still pretty much just a two-lane road through the forest. Around one o'clock, Hunter speaks for the first time in what seems like forever: "I'm hungry." Like a child. With no words to communicate anything but the most simple of needs.

We stop at a diner in a little town close to the Wisconsin border. The sign in front advertises the best Cornish pasties in the UP. Hunter pulls the road atlas from the backseat to bring with us. Everything inside the diner is greasy and dusty and at least twenty years old. Faded photos of smiling men holding big fish line the walls. The frumpy waitress doesn't even smile as she leads us to a booth by the window. There are only two tables with customers at prime lunch hour—a booth full of oversize fishermen and a tiny table in the back seating an ancient man slumped over a cup of coffee. The waitress hands us our menus, the cloudy lamination peeling at the corners.

"What the hell is a Cornish pasty?" Hunter says, pronouncing it *paystee*, like the circles strippers wear on their nipples, when it actually rhymes with "nasty." The menu has things like burgers, sandwiches, and fried perch. But the specialty is obviously pasties. They have the traditional chicken and beef options, but also venison, buffalo, pork, and today's special, quail.

"You've lived as close as you have to the UP for the last year, and you've never heard of a pasty?"

He just shrugs.

"It's like a potpie but you can hold it in your hand. The UP was settled by people from Cornwall in England in the mid-1800s. Hence, the proliferation of Cornish pasties in the region."

A little smirk lightens his eyes, which I assume means his hangover is loosening its grip.

"What?" I say.

"You sound like a Wikipedia article," he says. "How do you even know that?"

"I don't know. I just do. I remember things. I like to know stuff."

He laughs, not unkindly, and I feel the morning's anger dissipate. Why is it so easy to keep forgiving him?

The waitress appears to take our order.

"I'll have a chicken pasty," I say. "And a Coke."

She nods and turns to Hunter.

"Cheeseburger and fries," he says. "And coffee. Lots of coffee."

"And water," I add. "For him. He's dehydrated."

The waitress looks at us blankly for a moment, then turns and walks away.

As we wait for our food and Hunter guzzles down two refills of coffee, we look at the map and try to plan our next move.

"What's fun in Wisconsin?" Hunter says, mixing creamer and insane amounts of sugar into his third cup of coffee.

"Cheese?" I offer.

After a big gulp of coffee, Hunter smiles and says, "Boy, you really know how to party." His smiles are coming easier now, as if passing the noon hour somehow turned his Mr. Hyde back into Dr. Jekyll.

"We could go to Madison?" I offer.

"Why?"

"I don't know. It's a big city. There's probably cool stuff happening."

"Madison isn't a big city."

"It's bigger than Wellspring."

"Everywhere is bigger than Wellspring."

"Yeah, so it's big to me."

"Wait a minute," Hunter says, setting his coffee down. "Have you ever been to a city?"

"I've been to Traverse City a few times. I've been to Petoskey."

"Traverse City and Petoskey are not cities. They're largish towns. Really? That's seriously it?"

"I lived in San Francisco when I was a baby, but that doesn't really count since I can't even remember it. I think I went to Grand Rapids when I was four."

"Wow," Hunter says, shaking his head.

"It's kind of hard to travel when your mom doesn't have a car or money."

"This is seriously tragic."

"Which is why I want to go to Madison."

"No way. Madison can't be your first city. Chicago. We're going to a real city. Chicago is a real city."

"Okay," I say, and my stomach jumps a little. Chicago is definitely a real city. A really real city.

"You're being mighty agreeable all of a sudden."

"I'm an expert on a lot of things, but not cities. I trust you on that one."

"Well, I'm honored."

"Don't get used to it."

When the food comes, Hunter asks for another coffee refill. He scarfs down his burger like a maniac.

"How is it?" he says. "Your *paystee?*"

"It's like a really salty, meaty, dry potpie." I poke around in it with my fork. "There's isn't a single vegetable in it."

"Potato's a vegetable."

"Not really."

"What are you talking about? It's totally a vegetable."

"But it metabolizes like a starch."

"Okay, Wikipedia."

"I can't believe I'm saying this, but I really need some vegetables."

"What kind of a teenager are you? Here, have my lettuce." He flings the discarded iceberg from his burger onto my plate.

"This is barely a vegetable. It's just slightly green water."

"You're insane. You are seriously not normal."

"Drink your water."

We study the map as we wait for the check. "I say we head in the general direction of Chicago," Hunter says.

"You mean south?"

"Don't be a smart-ass," he says. "Yes, we head south. And when we get tired, we'll head toward one of these green spots on the map with the little tent symbol. Then wake up early tomorrow and go to Chicago. I should call my buddy to see if we can crash with him."

"Will I like this buddy?"

"You'll love him."

"Is he going to try to have an orgy with us in the back of a bus?"

"Only if you feed him enough Ecstasy."

"Oh, Lord," I say, but I am smiling.

I stop in the restroom before going out to the car. The tiny room is rank with the smell of cheap potpourri and bad plumbing. It looks like someone vomited up pink everywhere; even the toilet seat is pink.

As I wash my hands, I feel the strange sensation of a smile on my lips. How is it possible that I'm happy enough to smile right now when just this morning I wanted to kill Hunter?

But when I look up, what I see in the mirror makes me stop smiling.

My heart stops. All the pink drains out of the room.

"It took me a while to find you," Camille says.

It is her face in the mirror, not mine.

It is her long brown hair exactly the way she used to wear it.

It is a shirt I recognize.

But everything is backward.

Something is off.

Something in her eyes.

Something flat and dark and dead.

"Aren't you going to say something?" she says. It is her voice. It is unmistakably her voice.

"What am I supposed to say?" I whisper, afraid of someone hearing me talking to myself in the bathroom. "You're not real."

"That hurts my feelings, Kins. I'm not real? Then why are you talking to me?"

I close my eyes and shake my head, as if that will reset some kind of misfiring connection in my brain. But when I open my eyes, Camille is still there.

"You like him, don't you?" she teases.

"What? No. Are you crazy?"

Did I really just ask her if *she's* crazy? I'm the one talking to a ghost in a bathroom mirror.

"'Oh, Hunter, you are so amazing,'" she says in a singsong voice. "'Why don't you know how amazing you are? Let me show you how amazing you are.'"

"Shut up, Camille. You know I wouldn't do that."

"Wouldn't do what?"

"Wouldn't hook up with your boyfriend."

"Oh, honey," Camille says, her voice patronizing and cruel, so unlike her. "That's so sad. Pathetic, really." She wrinkles her forehead and looks down on me in mock sympathy. "Dead girls can't have boyfriends."

"Dead girls can't talk, either," I say. "Dead girls don't hang around diner bathrooms in the UP."

"That's very closed-minded of you, Kinsey. Very small-town thinking. I thought you were better than that."

My lack of sleep must have caused some kind of brain damage. Maybe those crazy hippies put something in my drink. Maybe I did eat a pot brownie and don't remember it. Maybe I'm turning crazy just like my mom. Worse than my mom. Hallucinations are much worse than mood swings.

"Hello?" Camille taunts from the mirror. "Anyone there?"

I try the doorknob but it doesn't turn. I try the lock but nothing happens. I am trapped. She has trapped me.

"But I just got here," Camille says. "You can't leave already. Don't you miss me?"

"Of course I miss you."

Why am I still talking to her?

"You know, it's kind of fun being a ghost. I can do all kinds of fun stuff. Watch this."

All of a sudden, the room goes black. All light is gone; even the tiny window that looked out onto the street seems to have disappeared.

I can't see my hands in front of me. I can't see Camille. I can't see anything.

"Stop it, Camille!"

"Stop what?"

"Turn the lights back on."

"Or what?"

"Just do it."

I feel something whoosh around me.

"Are you scared, Kinsey? Are you scared of the dark? I thought you weren't scared of anything."

Wind blows at me from every direction. Camille's voice comes from above, below, behind me, everywhere.

"You always had everything figured out," she says. "A perfect plan for everything so there'd be no surprises. So there'd be nothing to be scared of."

"Turn on the lights!" I scream. I don't care anymore about anyone hearing me.

"But you're scared now, aren't you?"

"Do it!"

"What's your plan now, Kinsey? What happens if you can't see where you're going?"

"Camille, stop it!"

The room is spinning. I am spinning. Everything is spinning.

"Just admit you're scared."

"Turn on the lights."

"Say it. Say you're scared."

"I'm scared!"

Then, as fast as it started, everything is still. Warm light shines through the window. Birds chirp brightly outside, mocking my fear. Camille is nowhere. I am looking at myself in the mirror, shaking and pale.

That wasn't Camille. She would never say things like that. There's no such thing as ghosts. All those nights of not sleeping must have flipped some switch inside me, some latent insanity just waiting for me to crack. And now I've cracked. I'm crazy.

No. I can fix this. I can handle it. That's what I do. I handle things. I keep going. No matter what. If I work hard enough, the pain goes away.

I am fine. I am normal. I just went to the bathroom. My hands are not shaking. Those fat men in that booth in the corner are not looking at me weird. The sun is shining and I'm smiling. Hunter's leaning on the car waiting for me and we're going to San Francisco and we're having fun and everything's going to be okay.

"I thought you fell in," Hunter says.

"Let's go," I say. I get in the car and put my sunglasses on. Maybe then Hunter won't be able to see the crazy in my eyes.

He gets in the driver's seat. "So I called my buddy in Chicago. He said he'd love for us to stay with him."

"That's great."

"He has an apartment with his girlfriend downtown."

"Great."

I can tell Hunter's staring at me but I don't look at him.

"Are you okay?"

"I'm fine."

"You seem weird all of a sudden."

"My stomach is kind of upset," I say. "I think the pasty didn't agree with me."

"Oh." Nothing like alluding to digestive disturbances to shut a boy up.

Over the next few hours, rural northern Michigan gives way to suburban Wisconsin. We drive past strip mall after identical strip mall, which the map claims are separate towns.

"Would you call this a city?" Hunter asks me when we pass an area with a handful of buildings over two stories tall.

"Probably," I say.

"That is so sad."

I take control of the stereo and flip through news stations and talk shows, anything with people talking. "Why can't we just listen to music?" Hunter whines. I don't tell him it's because music allows my mind to wander; it makes space for me to think about things I don't want to think about.

We decide to sleep at a campground a few miles off the freeway. But first, dinner. A sign for the next exit lists a bunch of fast food chains, a pizza place, and a Kountry Kitchens.

"Ooh, let's go to Kountry Kitchens," I joke.

"I'd rather kill myself than set foot in one of those places willingly," Hunter says a little too sharply.

"Jesus, I was kidding."

"It wasn't funny."

"What's your problem?"

"I just didn't think it was very funny."

"Fine."

"Fine."

We decide on the pizza place. I load up at the salad bar and Hunter calls me a hippie. I think of crazy Mountain and Chesapeake. I think of my mom's weird friends. I think of my mom and how she uses being a "free spirit" as an excuse to not deal with her problems.

"My mom's the hippie," I say. "I am not."

"But the apple doesn't fall far from the tree." He has no idea how much that burns right now, how scared I am of taking after her. Eating vegetables is one thing; mental illness and being a failure at life are other things entirely. It's not Hunter's fault, but I still want to hurt him back.

"Then that would also apply to you and your dad, wouldn't it?" I regret the words as soon as they leave my mouth.

Hunter doesn't say anything, just looks down at his pizza sadly.

"I'm sorry," I say.

"I guess we're even as far as bad jokes go."

We finish eating and drive in silence the rest of the way to the campground. Hunter's phone rings a few times but he doesn't answer. After the fourth call, he turns it off and throws it in the glove compartment.

"Forgot to turn it back off," he says.

"Who was that?" I ask, but I already know.

"Nobody," he says. His parents. The world he's running away from.

The campground isn't much more than a crowded RV park with a couple of dusty patches of grass for tents. It's already dark as we set up the tent, but the night is lit by the glow of RV windows and the blinking of the televisions inside. As ugly as it is, it makes me feel safe. This is not the kind of place ghosts hang out.

"Should we make a fire?" Hunter says.

"No, I'm tired. Let's just go to bed so we can wake up early and get out of here."

"I'm going to stay up a little longer to read."

As I zip myself up in my sleeping bag, I hear Hunter opening the car trunk and rooting around inside. I hear the clink of a bottle being removed.

NINE

Hunter manages to wake up without a notice-able hangover and we get on the road early. He's surprisingly easy to motivate when he has something to look forward to.

It suddenly strikes me that we've never once discussed San Francisco since we left. I've told him nothing about my plan and he's told me nothing of his, if he even has one. What if his expectations are different from mine? What if they get in my way? We have to talk about it soon. Before we get any more wrapped up in each other's lives and it's too late.

But I can tell now is not the right time to bring up San Francisco. Hunter's in the passenger seat, finally listening to his voice mails, and he is not happy. His eyes are squinted in anger and his jaw is gnashing. His left hand is a pulsing fist.

He turns the phone off and slams it into the glove compartment. He looks out the window like he wants to smash everything he sees. I could pretend I don't see how upset he is, I could try to keep us safe from that discomfort. Or I could just ask him what's wrong. Maybe we're capable of being that honest with each other.

"Fuck," he says.

"What?"

"Fuck," he says again.

"Hunter, what happened?"

"What happened is my dad's a fucking asshole."

"Do you want to talk about it?"

"No."

Silence. He looks out the window at the miles and miles of pasture. "Fucking cows," he says.

"What'd the cows ever do to you?"

"Did you know they're one of the top contributors of greenhouse gasses?"

"Yes, I did know that."

"Of course you did."

"Is that what you want to talk about?"

He takes a deep breath, closes his eyes, and leans his head back. "So my mom leaves these messages, crying," he says, his eyes still closed. "Begging me to come home, to at least call her and tell her I'm okay."

"That seems reasonable," I say, wondering what it feels like to have a mom who wants you around that much.

"Yeah, except my dad's in the background screaming the whole time about how he's going to kick my ass, and my mom's like whispering now, 'Your father's really mad,' like that's going to make me want to come home. And then *he* starts leaving these messages saying how he's going to call the cops and report the car as stolen, how he's going to cut me off for good, he can't believe a piece of shit like me is even his son, he can't understand why my mom keeps forgiving me and making excuses, and he calls her an idiot, a dumb-ass piece of shit just like her son, and I can hear her in the background crying, and who knows what that asshole did to her, and—"

Hunter's voice cracks. His throat is full of tears. But his eyes are steel. Dry. Hard. "Fuck!" he says, and pounds the dashboard with his fist.

"I'm sorry," is all I can think to say. I reach over and put my hand on his. My fingers wrap around the rock of his fist. I hold it there until the fist loosens, until the rock becomes flesh again.

"Can we stop here?" he says.

"Stop where?" I put both hands back on the steering

wheel, suddenly aware of the warmth of our touching, the thin strength of his fingers.

"Right up there." He points at a tiny white roadside chapel next to a hand-painted sign that says, STOP. REST. PRAY.

"I need to stop, rest, and pray," he says, trying to sound sarcastic, but I have a strange feeling he's not really kidding.

I pull over and we get out, Hunter grabbing his camera from the glove compartment. "I'm going to check that place out," he says, motioning to the building, just barely big enough to fit four people, like a fancy dollhouse with its tiny stained glass windows and little cross on top. Someone spent a lot of money building this thing.

"Want to come in?" Hunter says.

"No thanks, I'll stay out here." Any kind of religious building, especially miniature ones on the side of the highway in the middle of a cow pasture, creep me out. "Can I use your phone to call my mom?"

While Hunter's inside the chapel taking pictures or praying or whatever it is he's doing, I dial my number. I half expect to get the answering machine; Mom sometimes goes weeks without answering the phone. But after the sixth ring, just as it's about to click over to let me be a coward and leave a message, my mom picks up. "Hello?" she says, her voice weak and sad and far away.

My first instinct is to hang up. I hold the phone against my ear, not breathing.

"Hello?" she says again. I still can't speak. "Kinsey, is that you?"

"Mom?"

"Are you okay?"

"Yeah, I'm fine. I'm good. I just wanted to call and tell you that."

"Thank you."

She's being too polite. Something is wrong when she's too sad to be mean.

"Mom, are you okay?"

"Yes, of course." She makes a feeble attempt to sound cheerful. "I'm fine. Guess what?"

"What?"

"I got a cat."

"A cat?"

"Yeah, isn't that wild? I named him Frida, after Frida Kahlo of course."

"Why'd you get a cat?"

"Oh, my friend Marnie—you know her, she's the Reiki healer—she said it'd be good for me to have a companion, someone to love and be responsible for, to keep me accountable, you know? It's really helping."

A cat. A cat is helping my mom be responsible. A cat is giving her something to love.

"Are you taking your medication?" I say.

She sighs. She hates it when I talk to her like she's a child. This is when she usually blows up. This is what makes her slam doors and not talk to me for a week. But all she does is say, "Yes," softly.

"I'm sorry," I say.

"Oh, Kinsey," she chokes. I hear the tears. I can hear the echoes of her all alone in that empty house. "You have nothing to be sorry about."

"But I left you there by yourself. I shouldn't have left."

"Kinsey, I'm proud of you."

In all my eighteen years of life, I can't remember her ever saying that to me, not for the perfect report cards, not for the soccer trophies, not for the races won, not for the countless spelling bees and science fairs and various academic awards I've been collecting for as long as I can remember. None of that has impressed her, none of my hard work and training and sleepless nights studying. And now she finally says it, now that I've done possibly the stupidest thing I've ever done, now that I've run away from home with a troubled boy she's never even met in a car that may be reported stolen.

"Why the hell are you proud of me?" I can't help the acid in my voice.

"You're brave, Kinsey." Her voice is tired, almost pleading. "Braver than I ever was. You're not going to get trapped like me."

"Mom," I say, and nothing else.

"I love you." She says it for me.

Hunter emerges from the chapel. The highway rumbles with passing trucks and the air is thick with the smell of exhaust, hay, and cow manure.

"Mom," I say again. It must be so quiet there, so dark with the shades drawn, so still.

"I'm going to let you go now," she says.

"No, Mom. Wait."

"Good-bye."

Silence. Wind. Cars. My mother proud of me for finally being lost.

"Did you get ahold of your mom?" Hunter says, suddenly and miraculously cheerful.

"Yeah," I say, handing him the phone, offering nothing more. I don't want to talk about it. I don't want to think about it. "Did you get ahold of God?"

"As a matter of fact, I did." Hunter grins, and I'm pretty sure he's serious.

* * *

"Is this Chicago?" I say.

"This crap? No way."

"Is this Chicago?" I say fifteen minutes later.

"Jesus, Kinsey. We're still in the suburbs. We're in the suburbs of the suburbs."

The buildings keep getting taller and taller and the houses closer together.

"This is called stop-and-go traffic," Hunter says, my cynical tour guide. "It means we're almost there."

I feel silly being so excited. I'm practically breathless. My face is glued to the window. I know I look ridiculous, but for now, I don't care. How sad is it that driving through suburbs feels like the most exciting thing I've ever done?

"That apartment building is huge," I say. "How can people live like that?" A series of massive window-dotted concrete blocks at least twenty stories tall block the horizon.

"Those are the housing projects," Hunter says. "Now we're in Chicago."

The freeway takes us through a poor part of town. We are elevated, cut off from the city by fence and barbed wire, but I can still see the weed-cracked sidewalks, the broken playgrounds, the rows and rows of dilapidated, boarded-up houses. The few people on the sidewalks seem to be moving in slow motion. There's no point in hurrying if you've got nowhere to go.

"This is Chicago?" I say, unable to hide the disappointment in my voice. My giddiness has been replaced by something like embarrassment. Why did I expect the city to be all sparkling chrome and art museums? Of course people suffer here like they suffer everywhere.

"This is part of Chicago," Hunter says. "I'm trying to get through it as fast as I can."

"We don't have to rush," I say. "I'm not in a hurry to get anywhere." He turns to me and gives me a funny smile, and I realize how out of character that was of me to say.

"Good girl," he says.

"Don't patronize me." That just makes him smile bigger.

We crawl along the freeway half an hour longer. The residential area gives way to office buildings that get taller and fancier until the sky opens up for a brief moment, revealing in the distance the tallest of them all.

"Is that the Sears Tower?"

"Yep," Hunter says with, I think, a tinge of pride. "Second tallest building in North America, after the new World Trade Center in New York. Except it's technically called the Willis Tower now. But no one calls it that."

"Are we going there?"

"Nope," he says, then suddenly changes lanes and gets off at the next exit.

We weave through city streets, a mix of retail, offices, apartments, and condos. I can't imagine living on top of people like this, knowing that just under you are floors of people eating, sleeping, bathing, having sex, literally feet away doing all these intimate things, separated by just inches of drywall or brick or concrete. Everything is so tidy—the trees are young and trimmed, poking out of the sidewalk through perfectly round holes of dirt. The only flowers grow out of boxes or heavy pots. Hedges frame apartment building doorways with perfectly chiseled ninety-degree angles. Everything, as far as the eye can see, was planned by someone.

"And here we are on the Magnificent Mile," Hunter announces, turning onto a busy street. "The only magnificent thing about it is there's lots of expensive shit to waste your money on. But the Museum of Contemporary Art is a few blocks over there, and it actually is pretty magnificent."

"Are we going there?"

"Maybe tomorrow. Tonight we have plans."

"What plans?"

"You'll see." He taps on the steering wheel in time to the music on the stereo.

Women in high heels totter down the sidewalk carrying shopping bags marked with labels I recognize from the fashion magazines Camille loved. These are not the kind of stores they have at the mall an hour away from Wellspring.

Hunter opens his window and yells, "Consume! Consume!" at the top of his lungs.

"Hunter!" I scold, though I'm not sure why. It's my instinct to not want to make too much noise, to not draw attention to myself. But right now, we're on the move, anonymous, in a big city. Right now, none of my usual fears seem to matter.

"Woo hoo!" he shouts. "Hello, Chicago! Kinsey, say hello to Chicago."

"Hello, Chicago," I say.

"That's all? You're in the big city for the first time in your life and all you have is that wimpy 'Hello, Chicago'?"

"Hello, Chicago," I say louder. I can feel my face getting hot with embarrassment. Why should I be embarrassed? Who am I afraid is going to see me?

Hunter opens my window with his controls. "Now out the window," he commands. "Really tell Chicago how happy you are to meet her."

"Hello, Chicago!" I yell out my window.

"Hello, Chicago!" Hunter yells out of his.

"It's nice to meet you, Chicago!" I yell, then start laughing. A woman with giant boobs and a bad fake tan squints at us from the sidewalk, and her equally badly tanned boyfriend yells, "Shut up!" but I don't even care. I'm in Chicago. For the first time in my life, I'm *somewhere*.

After blocks and blocks of shiny retail, we cross over a small bridge, take a left, and are suddenly at the foot of Lake Michigan. "Oh, wow," I say. The tall buildings of downtown are to our right, the endless expanse of blue at our left, and we are tiny, driving straight through the middle.

"Pretty awesome, huh?" Hunter says.

"The lake looks so different from this side. It's so much more . . ." I search for the right word.

"Magnificent." Hunter finishes my thought.

He starts pointing in various directions, listing all the places within a few blocks of where we are—the Navy Pier, Millennium Park, the Art Institute, Buckingham Fountain, Shedd Aquarium, the Adler Planetarium, the Field Museum. "If you want to go to an art museum, it should definitely be the Art Institute. It'll blow your mind. There's a traveling exhibit there right now I really want to see."

"Is that a jogging trail?" I say, pointing to the left.

"Yeah," Hunter says. "That thing goes on forever. The best part is where it goes through this like bird sanctuary where there are some cool sculptures and a pretty nice beach. My buddies and I used to love getting high out there and walking around."

My body suddenly aches for movement. I need to get out of this car. It's been so long since I've run, so long since I've felt my lungs and muscles burn. I don't care if my ankle isn't completely healed yet. "I need to go for a run," I say.

"Not today," Hunter says, pulling off Lake Shore Drive and onto a side street. "It's dinnertime."

We drive a few blocks as Hunter consults a scrap of paper in his lap. "Aha!" he says, and does the quickest parallel park I've ever seen. "We're here," he announces, practically glowing. There's something childlike about his excitement, something pure.

We carry our bags to the front door and Hunter presses an apartment button. "We don't want any!" calls a scratchy voice over the intercom.

"Well, you're gonna get some anyway," says Hunter with a grin. The buzzer sounds and we climb the stairs to the third floor.

A tall and very handsome black guy in an apron greets us with a huge smile. He and Hunter embrace for what seems like a long time for a dude hug, and I can't help smiling a little at yet another one of Hunter's surprising quirks— the photography, the reading highbrow books, the possibly praying in a roadside chapel, and now this open affection for a male friend.

"I'm Eli," the guy says, then hugs me, too. He smells comforting, like herbs and fresh laundry.

"Come in, come in," he says as he ushers us into his apartment. A beautiful platinum-blond girl sits at the kitchen counter chopping vegetables. Her arms are covered with tattoos and her nose is pierced in the middle like a bull, but her eyes are bright and kind, confusing what I instantly recognize as my prejudices about people who look like her.

"This is my girlfriend, Shelby," Eli says, and she comes over and hugs us too.

"I've heard so much about you," she says to Hunter, holding his hand in hers.

"Uh-oh," he says, and we all laugh.

We sit at the kitchen counter while Eli finishes cooking. Hunter seems suddenly calmer in Eli's presence, less troubled. "This is a nice place," he says, looking around the apartment. It's clean and bright, with art on the walls, plants, and a mix of IKEA and secondhand furniture. "It almost looks like grown-ups live here."

"Yeah." Eli laughs. "It's a far cry from my parents' basement, huh?"

"I liked your parents' basement."

"We got in a lot of trouble down there."

"Exactly," Hunter says.

"I've heard all about that basement," Shelby says. "It's kind of famous."

I want to say, "Tell me about the basement." I want them to tell me everything about Hunter and his life before he moved to Wellspring. But I don't want him to know how curious I am. I don't want him to know how much I care.

Eli sautés vegetables in a pan, expertly flipping it one-handed. "Wow, you look like a real chef," I say instead.

"He is a real chef," Shelby says proudly.

"Just finished my first year of culinary school," Eli says.

"Tell them the other thing," Shelby nudges.

"Oh yeah," he says humbly. "I found out I got a summer internship at Chez Jardín."

"It's like the best restaurant in Chicago," Shelby says. "People apply from all over the world. He was picked from literally *thousands* of applicants. Right, honey?"

Eli just grins and shrugs, turning his focus back to his cooking.

"Wow, man, that's awesome," Hunter says with so much sincerity I have a sudden urge to hug him. "That's like the best news I've heard in a long time. Seriously."

They share the kind of look reserved for best friends, and I am hit with a sudden ache for Camille. I remember when I had someone to look at like that, when a few seconds of eye contact could communicate things we could never say with words.

"I had a pretty gourmet childhood thanks to this guy," Hunter says. "His parents' basement was like a little apartment with its own kitchen and stuff. We'd get really high and Eli would turn into this like food magician and whip something up out of whatever ingredients he could find. It was like watching *Top Chef*. What was that one you made, that epic meal we couldn't stop talking about for months?"

Eli laughs. "Oh shit, I forgot about that." He takes on a fake high-class accent and points his chin in the air. "Cheetos-and-cashew-encrusted tilapia with fruit-punch-infused rice and water chestnuts."

Shelby and I both groan in disgust.

"It was so good," Hunter says with no hint of irony.

"This will be much better," Eli says. "I promise."

Shelby lights candles and we all sit at the dinner table. Eli lays the food out in front of us, each plate perfectly constructed like a work of art.

"Tonight," he says in the hoity-toity voice, "we are featuring fresh Alaskan salmon with a balsamic fennel glaze, a ratatouille of eggplant and summer squash, and mashed new potatoes with green garlic and sun-dried apricot."

"It smells incredible," I say.

Eli sits down, takes Shelby's hand, and reaches across the table for mine. "Just humor me," he says. "I have this thing about saying grace before meals."

I don't think I've ever said grace before a meal in my life. I look at Hunter and he just smiles like this is perfectly normal behavior.

"Thank you for this food," Eli begins. "And all the energy and love that went into growing it. Thank you for old friends and new friends and the warmth around this table. Thank you for love. Thank you for the ability to always grow. Amen."

"Amen," we say, and start eating.

I take a few bites. "Oh my god," is the only thing I can think to say. This may be the best meal I have ever had in my life. My mother is an incredible cook and I know I've been luckier than most Midwesterners in my exposure to good food, but somehow this seems different. Maybe it's because we've been eating on the road for the last few days. Maybe it's the warmth and love in the room. Maybe I can taste that. Or maybe it's because Eli is simply a genius.

"You know what would go great with this?" says Hunter. "Some wine. We've been here an hour already and you haven't offered us a drink? Where's the hospitality, Eli?"

I can tell Hunter is trying to make it sound like he's kidding, but I know he's not. And I'm pretty sure Eli knows too. I kick Hunter under the table.

"What?" Hunter says to me. "It's a perfectly reasonable question. Right, Eli? That's what we do."

Eli and Shelby share a look that sends another ache through me. I don't know what that look feels like. That one's reserved for people in love.

"Yeah," Eli says. "That's something I've been meaning to talk to you about, but I wanted to do it in person. We don't have any booze here. I don't do that anymore."

"What, like you're taking a break?"

"No, like I quit. I'm sober. Got one year clean a couple weeks ago."

Hunter looks confused for a second, then it hits him what Eli is saying and he looks almost sad, like he's lost something precious. But then his face warms into a smile and he gets up out of his chair and walks around the table and throws his arms around him. Eli looks surprised but relieved as he hugs him back.

"That's cool, man," Hunter says. "That's really cool." He looks a little embarrassed as he returns to his seat, and before I even know what I'm doing I find my hand wrapped around his under the table. I squeeze once and let go. I look up and catch Shelby's eye across the table. We share a smile and I feel a smooth warmth growing in my chest, and I wish I could stay here with these people forever.

When everyone's done eating, I excuse myself to the bathroom. I look in the mirror and all I see is my own reflection. Camille, where are you? Are you gone for good now? Are the nightmares over? Was that visit in the diner bathroom a one-time thing? Did you get what you wanted?

Did I?

My eyes fill with tears. I wipe them away before they have a chance to fall. I miss Camille so much I can't stand it—the real Camille, not the skewed version of my nightmares. But I think I would take her, too, just to see the face and hear the voice that are almost hers, even if it scares me.

When I return, the table has been cleared and everyone's sitting in the adjoining living room in the middle of a conversation. Eli and Shelby are draped across the love seat and Hunter sits on one side of the couch. It could be my imagination, but the mood seems somewhat somber as I curl up on the other side.

"Were you any good?" Shelby says.

"We sucked." Eli chuckles.

"Were they good at what?" I ask.

"Our band," Eli says. "Though I use the term 'band' very loosely."

"We weren't that bad," Hunter says. "We could have been good if we actually practiced."

"But we'd only ever play for half an hour," Eli says. "Then we'd be too drunk to do anything but keep drinking."

"Those were the days," Hunter says. A weird silence fills the room. Shelby and Eli seem so comfortable and relaxed, so free, so at home in their bodies. But Hunter sits upright in the corner of the couch, his body tight and anxious, like he's ready to break out of his own skin. "It was so much fun back then," Hunter says. I can't tell for sure, but I think his hands are shaking.

"Yeah," Eli sighs. "Until it wasn't."

"It was just that one night," Hunter protests weakly.

"No it wasn't, Hunter. It was tons of nights. Nights and mornings and afternoons, too many to count. Just because we only got caught once doesn't mean shit wasn't fucked-up the rest of the time."

A tinge of hostility sharpens the airs, the warm post-dinner coma suddenly gone.

"What happened?" Shelby says, and I want to tell her to shut up. Doesn't she know talking about these things will just make them worse? It's better to ignore them, better to deny them until they go away.

"What happened was Eli killed a dog," Hunter says flatly.

"Oh, I've heard this story," Shelby says like it's no big deal.

"Wait a minute, what?" I say. "You killed a dog."

"It wasn't on purpose," Eli says. "We were really drunk and high on Ecstasy. Me and Hunter and our old friend Caleb."

"Whatever happened to Caleb?" Hunter says.

"I have no idea. When I got back from rehab and said I actually wanted to try staying sober, he just sort of disappeared, like there was no reason to try to stay friends anymore." Eli is quiet for a moment, thoughtful. "Anyway, I was driving Caleb's car because—get this—we decided I was the most sober."

"Yeah, I remember," Hunter says. "And what was your blood alcohol level?"

"Point one six. Two times the legal limit. Plus I was seeing triple from the X."

"So you ran over a dog?" I say.

"Yep, then crashed into a tree and totaled the car. And when the cops came, smart guy Hunter over there decided it'd be a good idea to punch one in the face."

"You punched a cop?"

"That's what they tell me."

"You don't remember."

Hunter shakes his head and I can't tell what he's feeling. His face is blank, closed.

"We'd probably both be in jail if it weren't for your dad pulling whatever strings he pulled."

"Yeah, and he never lets me forget it."

"Got me sent to rehab," Eli says. "Best thing that ever happened to me." He runs his fingers through Shelby's hair. "That's where I met this fine lady."

"Got me sent to Bumfuck, Michigan," Hunter says cruelly.

"Maybe everything happens for a reason," Shelby says.

"Maybe there's something you needed to learn there. Or someone you needed to meet."

Hunter looks at me for a second, then his eyes dart quickly away. Was it Camille he was meant to meet? Was it me?

"Can we stop talking about this now?" he says.

Shelby sits up and says matter-of-factly, "Gelato."

"Yes," Eli agrees.

"Gelato and a stupid movie will solve all our problems."

Hunter nods, but I can tell by the look of discomfort on his face that he doubts their logic. Is he thinking about drinking? Is he thinking about how even though it's created so many problems in his life, it is still his only solution? Is he thinking about how it was a drunk driver who crashed into us and killed his girlfriend?

We eat the fancy ice cream as the movie starts—something about mistaken identity and the ensuing hijinks. Our laughs gradually dwindle over the next hour until my eyes shutter closed, and I am vaguely aware of someone turning the TV off and laying a blanket across me. I think for a second that I should get up, brush my teeth, wash my face. But sleep seems like such a better idea, and it wins.

TEN

The first thing I notice when I wake up is I'm not alone. My legs are touching skin that is not mine. This warmth has not all been generated by me. The second thing I notice is my back is killing me.

As the world comes into focus, I realize the source of both of these things—I slept on the couch all night. With Hunter. His head is at the other end, our legs entwined under a blanket. My first thought is I should get up. My second thought is I like the feeling of his skin against mine; I like not knowing which part of his body my foot, my knee, my calf, is touching; I like the mystery of our bodies under the blanket. It is this second thought that convinces me I definitely need to get up.

I try to untangle myself from Hunter and the blanket as stealthily as I can, but Hunter's eyes pop open just as I'm attempting to unwedge my right foot from under his upper thigh.

"Oh." He blinks. "Good morning."

"Good morning," I say, stumbling away from the couch. I run to the bathroom before he has a chance to say anything else. I stall as long as I can, washing my face, brushing my teeth, retying my ponytail over and over again.

When I get out, I am grateful to see Eli and Shelby in the kitchen. The blanket we slept under has been folded and set somewhere out of sight. Hunter is sitting at the counter drinking coffee.

"Hey, Kinsey," Shelby says cheerfully. "How'd you sleep last night?"

"Fine," I say.

"We made the executive decision to not wake you. You both looked so peaceful."

I tell myself not to look at Hunter, but my eyes move on their own. My face burns as our eyes meet briefly. I swear he is smirking.

"I have class in a couple hours and Shelby has to go to work," Eli says. "So after this gourmet breakfast I'm about to make you, I'm afraid you're on your own until about five."

"That's cool," Hunter says. "We have sightseeing to do. Right, Kinsey?"

"Right."

After the huge breakfast of frittata, potatoes, and homemade blueberry muffins, I'm grateful to be walking. We pass the convention center, surrounded by hordes of people in business suits and name tags.

"If I ever end up one of those people, please kill me," Hunter says.

The sky opens up to blue infinity on the right; the lake is flat and calm. Sailboats drift by, leaving slow-motion shivers in their wake. We walk along the waterfront trail for a while, joggers passing us. I want to join them. I want to go fast. But part of me also wants to take my time, to do this as slow as possible to make it last.

"I've always dreamed of running the Chicago marathon," I say.

"So do it," Hunter says, like it's no big deal, like it's so obvious. For some reason that makes me laugh. I think I've laughed more in the last two days than I've laughed in the previous two months.

"What's so funny?"

"You're right," I say. "I should just do it."

"Duh," Hunter says, which makes me laugh even more. "Laughing looks good on you," he says. "You should do it more often."

That shuts me up.

"You should also learn how to take a compliment."

I pretend I didn't hear him and we keep walking.

Our first stop is the Art Institute. I pick up a map but Hunter says he doesn't need one.

"Now you're just showing off," I say.

"Hey, man," he says. "I have so little going for me, just humor me, okay?"

I roll my eyes, but I can tell he takes pride in this, and I am in fact impressed. I wonder if his parents even know this about him, that he cares so much about art. I wonder if it would make them proud.

Hunter takes me through the permanent exhibits. We start on the third floor, with European Modern Art, then move to the second floor, then end up on the first floor for the special exhibit. I'm pretty much shocked into silence for much of the tour; I've never even been to a real art museum, let alone one of the best in the country, and with an amazing tour guide. Hunter explains how different artistic movements evolved into others, how each period's defining characteristics reflected what was going on socially and politically at the time. He waxes poetic about how artists are our modern-day shamans, in tune with a higher plane, charged with the heavy responsibility of turning reality into symbol and then back again, of finding truth in the shadows, of being blessed and cursed with the power of seeing too much. He's passionate as he says this, serious, without a trace of his usual sarcasm, his voice strong and confident, his eyes clear and full of fire. I feel the sudden urge to catch his flying hands, to tame them in mine, to kiss his lips and make him quiet, as if that could somehow contain his energy, as if I could save it, as if I could keep it to draw on for strength, as if I'm afraid he'll use it all up now and there won't be any left for later.

"Why are you looking at me like that?" he says.

"What? Oh, nothing. I'm just . . . impressed."

He smiles. "I'm not as dumb as I look."

"How do you know all this stuff?"

"Before I moved to Wellspring, I went to this pretty awesome private school in Chicago. I know, I know—private school. I'm a privileged white bastard. But they had this incredible art teacher, Mrs. Laughton, and as long as I took all the college-prep-type classes, my parents didn't care what I did for my electives. So I took at least one art class every semester."

According to Hunter, he has saved the best for last—a

traveling exhibit of one of his favorite contemporary artists, a Spanish painter named Arturo Reyo.

"These paintings were last in Stockholm, Sweden," he tells me. I'm guessing this is supposed to be an impressive fact. "Reyo is compared to Francis Bacon a lot because they painted around the same time and are both pretty dark. But where Bacon can be kind of grotesque at times, I think Reyo captures more of the sublime. There's hope in his darkness. See there." Hunter points at the first painting in the series—a large abstract of black and blues and reds, with hints of discernible figures swirling in and out of focus, body parts, pained faces, displaced eyes full of terror. I see hope nowhere.

"That light," Hunter says. I follow his finger to a space in the corner of the painting, where the darkness opens up into bright whiteness. "See how they're all pointing toward it? See how it reflects off of everything, just barely?"

"Yes," I say. "I see it."

We walk slowly through the exhibit, Hunter taking his time with each painting. I look at them with him, but I obviously feel done way before he does. I'm not sure what else there is to look at; I don't know what else he sees. His eyes are open in a way mine aren't.

We come to a painting that is especially gruesome. It seems vaguely familiar; I guess it must be famous enough for even me to recognize it. It is obviously the prized piece of the exhibit, huge and central, with a wall all to itself. Hunter and I join the crowd around it.

I don't know anything about art. I don't know what style or movement this guy is. I couldn't tell you anything about his technique or symbolism or influences. All I know is when I look at this painting—so huge it is the only thing I see—it feels like I am falling into it, getting sucked into its darkness, until all there is is darkness, until I am lost in it and can't get out. I realize I am not breathing. My heart is racing. Did art do this to me? Is it really that powerful?

I turn to Hunter, excited to tell him that maybe I'm starting to understand this thing he loves so much. But when I look at his face I see tears in his eyes. His lips are trembling.

"Hunter," I whisper. "What's wrong?"

He shakes his head. "Nothing." He smiles, but it's a small, private smile, as if he's sharing an inside joke with himself. "That's the thing, isn't it? Feelings are *good*, even when they're uncomfortable. They're not things to run away from."

"What are you talking about?"

He doesn't answer and he doesn't look at me. He just says, "What did you feel while looking at this painting?"

I try to think back to a few moments ago. "Fear," I say. "I felt afraid."

"Perfect," he says.

"What's perfect about being scared?"

"It proves you're human. It proves you're alive. All this darkness—in a lot of ways it's ugly, right? But it's beautiful at the same time. It's beautiful because it shows what we're capable of surviving. It shows how deep we can feel. It's so easy to forget that. We live in this world that's so full of artificial crap, with so many tricks to make things easier, so we don't have to go to those deep places anymore, we don't have to experience this darkness. And people think that's a good thing. But that's what makes us whole, you know? The darkness with the light."

"Are you scared?" I say as softly as I can.

"Of course I am." He laughs sadly, as if the effort deflates him. He turns to me just barely, the corner of his eye all that's capable of making contact. "Why do you think I drink so much?"

"Do you think I'm scared?"

He turns to me, looks me fully in the face, and smiles kindly. "You're one of the most scared people I've ever met."

A tiny voice says to fight, to defend myself, to argue his statement away. But a louder voice says he is right; it says I don't care if he sees it. I *am* scared. I'm terrified. But maybe that's okay. Maybe I am brave enough to feel it, brave enough to go to that dark place, to just be with my fear. Maybe that's the secret to surviving. Maybe facing it is all I really have to do to tame it.

I break off our eye contact. I am full of a different kind of fear now, one that has to do with Hunter, a fear that is unfamiliar, that energizes, that is also a little blissful. Maybe I'm a coward to want to run from it, but I need a break from all this feeling. Just for a second.

"I have to pee," I say, and Hunter laughs, breaking the spell. Suddenly there's a crowd around us. We're not the only people in the world. We're surrounded by stark white walls covered by these giant squares of sadness, but I'm the happiest I can remember feeling in a long time.

As I'm finishing up in the bathroom, I realize I'm humming. I am not the kind of person who hums. I don't think I've ever hummed in my life. But something about being here, being with Hunter, is making me feel unlike my normal self.

I think about San Francisco. What if I adjusted my plans a little? Maybe I don't need to start school right away. Maybe I can take some time off and see what it feels like to not be a student for a while. Maybe Hunter and I can even be friends. Maybe there's a group of weirdos in San Francisco that has room for both of us.

"You better watch out."

A high-pitched scream escapes my mouth. I open the stall

door and look around. No one. I look in the mirror and there is just me. I run down the row of stalls punching the doors open. Nobody. Nothing. I am alone.

"I'll admit it—he's pretty good at making a girl feel special," says the voice.

"Camille?" I can't tell where the voice is coming from. It could be in the air vents. The faucets. The hand driers. It could be coming from inside my own head.

"Those eyes of his. The way they look at you and seem to see your soul. The way they convince you that you see his. It's a neat trick, isn't it? But they're just eyes, Kinsey. Just body parts."

"Where are you?"

"It's not real, you know. I hate to say this, because you seem so happy for once, but really you could be anyone right now and he'd be acting the same. He just wants to get laid and you just happen to be here."

How can something said by someone who doesn't even exist hurt so bad? What the hell is going on?

"Why are you telling me this?" I say. "Why are you following me?"

Why am I talking to her as if she's real?

"Because I care about you," she says. "Because I'm trying to help."

"You think insulting me is going to help me?"

"I'm trying to protect you."

"Or maybe you're jealous."

I'm fighting with my imagination. I'm trying to hurt a ghost's feelings.

She laughs, and the sound tears through me. I know it's not her—that mean, spiteful sound could never have come from the real Camille—but it hurts as if it is, as if I'm being mocked by the person I've loved more than anyone.

"Jealous?" she says. "Oh, Kinsey, don't flatter yourself."

Camille would never say something like that.

"I'm trying to help you."

"How is freaking me out in nightmares and sneaking up on me in bathrooms supposed to help me?"

"I have to get your attention somehow, don't I? I have to make you listen. Why aren't you listening to me?"

I'm talking to air. I'm talking to my own reflection in the mirror. There's nowhere to look but into my own wide eyes.

"I'm listening, Camille. What do you want to tell me?"

But the door to the restroom opens and a loud group of women enters, their grating voices taking over the space. I wash my hands, trying to look as normal as possible, doing everything I can to avoid looking up and catching a glimpse of myself in the mirror.

When I step back into the exhibit, the previous magic of the space is gone. The paintings are just paintings, giant canvasses covered with haphazard blobs of paint that mean nothing. They are being stared at by pretentious people who are just pretending to understand what they're looking at, but really they're all terrified that someone will see through their act and discover what a fraud they are. That's all any of us really do—try to convince everyone we have our shit together, when really we're stupid or weak or insecure or, in my case, lonely and crazy and haunted by ghosts.

I can't find Hunter. I walk around the exhibit but he's gone. Panic seizes me from the inside; all my muscles and organs wrench tight. Maybe he's left me here. Maybe he's finally gotten sick of me. Maybe he's gone the way of so many other people in my life—my father, Camille, my mom in her various ways—and just disappeared forever.

No. He would not do that. I'm letting the crazy voice win. I cannot listen. I cannot believe her.

I enter the bright bustle of the museum lobby. Sunlight streams through the wall of windows. People stand in line for tickets. People stand in line for bag check. And there, in the corner away from the crowds, is Hunter, still here.

I'm relieved as I approach him. I want the magic of our last conversation back. I want him to replace my fear with happiness. But as I get closer, I realize that's not what's in store. He's on the phone, his face red and contorted in anger.

"Mom, what did he do?" I hear him say. I stand a few feet away, far enough to give the false impression of privacy. I know I shouldn't be listening, but I can't help myself.

"Did he hurt you?" Hunter says. My heart drops. I take a few steps away, but not far enough.

"Mom, please," he pleads, his voice low and strong and steady. "Tell me the truth. You don't have to protect him."

Silence as he listens.

"I'll come back, Mom. I'll come back if you need me to."

Silence.

"Do you promise? You're not just trying to make me not worry?"

He turns around and looks at me. I try to send him all the kindness I can through my eyes. I try to replace all the feelings I have from my run-in with Camille with concern for him, for his mother, for this woman I never met and this boy I barely know. If I think about them, I don't have to think about Camille. If I care about them enough, I don't have to think about myself.

"Okay," Hunter says to the phone. "I love you, Mom." My heart breaks a little. "I love you," he says again, then turns the phone off and puts it in his pocket. He takes a deep breath and closes his eyes, like he's trying to create stillness, silence, just for a second, like he's trying to regain his bearings. When his eyes pop back open, he says decisively, "Let's walk."

It seems somehow inappropriate that it's such a beautiful day. The sky is blue and the temperature is perfect, flowers are blooming everywhere, and everyone we pass seems to be smiling more than they should. I stay quiet as we wander south through Grant Park; I figure Hunter should be the one who decides when we're ready to talk again.

After several minutes of walking, Hunter finally breaks the silence. "You know what's crazy? My dad's here somewhere, like right around here. My mom says he left Wellspring yesterday. His office is close to here, in one of these high-rises. And his new condo is somewhere downtown. I've never even seen it."

I don't say anything. I just keep walking, matching my footsteps with his.

"It's weird to think he could be blocks away right now. We could run right into him by accident."

He stops walking. "Oh, this is Buckingham Fountain," he says. We're standing in front of a giant ornate fountain, surrounded by tourists taking identical photos in front of it. "It's one of the largest fountains in the world."

"You don't have to be tour guide right now," I say.

He smiles, turns around, and starts walking in the opposite direction. "Let's go this way."

After a few moments, I say, "What would you do? If we ran into him?"

Without a beat, Hunter says, "I'd kick his ass." But then he sighs a sad laugh and says, "Or I'd probably run away as fast as I could."

We walk the entire length of Grant Park north into Millennium Park. It's a place I've heard about my whole life, this great oasis in the big city, this triumph of green space in urban planning. Despite the expanses of grass and flowers and growing things, something about it strikes me as sad, the way everything is perfectly planned and manicured, the trees so evenly spaced, the bushes carved, the flowers bunched in measured arrangements. Something has been lost by taking out the wildness, something true. In taking out the variables, in making all this life a little more convenient, it's lost some of its soul.

This seems profound. It is something I'd like to talk about with Hunter, something I know he'd understand. But right now, I'm enjoying our silence. Maybe talking isn't always the best form of communication. During our walk, we've managed so many light touches of the hand or bumping of shoulders, which neither of us acknowledges. I don't know if these nearnesses are accidental. All I know is I like them. All I know is the closer I am to Hunter, the farther away I get from Camille, the farther away I am from the part of myself that needs her.

We approach a giant globular silver structure that I immediately recognize as the famous *Bean* sculpture. We walk around it like all the other tourists, watching our reflections morph in and out of the curved mirrored surface. We walk under it, into the cavelike tunnel that opens up underneath. We stand in the middle, looking up at the bulbous ceiling. It's hard to find ourselves among all the other distorted faces, but there we are, flipped upside down, our mouths stretched into grotesque grimaces, our eyes swirled like scrambled eggs, our noses and ears ripped apart and glued where they don't belong, everything unrecognizable, everything deranged, everything made ugly and inhuman.

"That's the real me," Hunter says softly, looking up at his distorted reflection. I lean into him, my shoulder pressed against his. I circle my fingers around his wrist, for a brief moment, then let go.

We keep walking.

After another gourmet meal by Eli, we stay up late talking, drinking tea, and playing board games. I want to get used to this new version of Hunter, this one content with spending the evening sober, this one who laughs and tells funny stories. We're leaving tomorrow morning, and I want to take this Hunter with me.

After a particularly exhausting laughing fit, Hunter says breathlessly, "I can't remember ever having this much fun sober."

"Well, you haven't given it much of a chance," Eli says.

"True," says Hunter. There's silence for a few moments in the wake of these statements, but it's not entirely uncomfortable. I remember friendship like this, when you trust someone so much you can say or hear anything. The ache of missing Camille thuds dully in my chest.

Discussion of tonight's sleeping arrangements ends up a little awkward. This whole time, Shelby had assumed Hunter and I were a couple, so she's excited to tell us about the full-size futon in the spare bedroom that she made up for us. I don't know why sleeping next to each other on the bed seems so different from in the tent, but it does.

"Oh, um," I say.

"Crap," Eli says. "Shel, I guess I forgot to explain their relationship. Or lack thereof."

Hunter pretends to look out the window.

"We're not together," I say. "We're just, um, friends."

"Oh," Shelby says, her face turning a bright shade of red. "I'm so sorry. I just assumed— You guys seemed so—"

"It's okay," I say.

"I'll sleep on the couch," Hunter says.

"No, it's okay. You can have the bed. I'll sleep on the couch." I don't say anything about enjoying how we slept last night. I don't say anything about being afraid to sleep alone.

"No, you should have the bed," Hunter says. "I want you to have the bed."

"No, really, it's fine. I'm fine sleeping on the couch."

"Oh shit," Shelby says. "Look what I started."

"You get the bed and that's final," says Hunter, and I sense an edge to his voice. "I'm being chivalrous." He grins. "You being the weaker sex and all."

"Oh thanks," I say. "You're so kind."

Not the ground. Not a tent. Not a couch. Not even a bed.

Sand, but more like dust.

Sky, but more like wasted breath.

Your head on a cloud, a makeshift pillow. Your face, an eyelash away from mine. Your smile, a sickle that cuts through time and mourning.

"I miss you," you say.

"I miss you, too."

"I don't believe you."

I feel the movement of your words on my skin, but there is no heat to your breath, no smell. Just the displacement of air.

"I'm sorry about what I said earlier," you say.

"It's okay."

There are two of me, one who wants to be with you and one who wants to stay here, solid, where light does not shine through me, where I make shadows instead of getting lost in them. The world of you has a hole inside where wind passes through. A hollow place. A wound that does not heal.

We are in the place that does not heal. From white to black to red. The night cut open like a scar.

"I knew I was dead," you say. "I knew my body was on its own. I was somewhere else, above it all, watching the whole thing. I saw Hunter leave me there and save you."

My eyes are your memory. We watch the scene as you narrate: a dead girl and one almost, a brave boy who no one sees.

"I saw him run through fire," *you say.* "You were out. He thought no one saw him, but I did."

"I see him," *I say.*

White. This nothing world. This place of waiting.

"You think you do. He looks up at you with those eyes of his and you think he's showing you everything."

Black.

"Aren't you tired, Kinsey?"

I am a cloud but I feel like mud, like tar, like quicksand, like something that wants to be solid.

"Just surrender, Kinsey. Just stop fighting. Aren't you tired of fighting?"

"Yes."

"Come with me."

"How?"

"You know."

"No. I don't. I don't know."

"Leave him."

"I can't."

"He doesn't love you, Kinsey. Don't be stupid."

Wind. Tiny pieces of glass. Too many cuts to measure.

"I never said he did."

"You can't trust him. He'll let you down like everyone else. He's just using you. There's only me. There was only ever me."

You are the wind, the hand caressing my hair, your voice like morphine. It is almost you. I am almost taken.

But still. *"Maybe you're wrong," I say.*

"Oh, Kinsey. You're so naive."

"Maybe you're lying."

The warm breeze turns sharp. The caressing turns to pulling. The soft white turns cold, harsh and buzzing like fluorescent lights. The air pinches my skin. Your sweetness turns sour. Rancid.

Black.

"You're pathetic, Kinsey."

Black. Red. Red. Red. We are in the fire, burning. We are in the car, trapped. You are holding me hostage. I look forward into flames and cracked glass. I will not look at you.

"You can't do anything by yourself. That's your big, pathetic secret. Your big lie. I'm the only one who knows the truth. You've fooled everyone else, haven't you? They all think you're so strong, so independent, so smart. 'That Kinsey, she's going to do something with her life. That Kinsey's going to get out of this stupid little town.'"

Your blood pools around my feet. I will not look at you.

"Just because you were quiet and got good grades, because you acted like you were so much better than everyone else, you tricked everyone into thinking that meant you were so focused, so serious, so mature. But I knew what it really meant. I knew how scared you were, how terrified of failing. I knew why you didn't talk. I knew it was because you were so afraid no one would like you if they really knew you. And guess what, you were right."

Red.

"Shut up," I say.

"What are you going to do without me? How can you go to college with some stranger as a roommate, reminding you it was supposed to be me? It was only ever supposed to be me. I took care of you. I was the only one who ever did. Who's going to take care of you now? Not your mom. She's too crazy. Not Hunter. He's too drunk to even take care of himself."

"He hasn't gotten drunk in two days."

Your laugh shakes the windshield, the maze of cracks spreading like rivers.

"Two days? Wow, what an accomplishment. Do you realize how pathetic you sound?"

The cracks are veins in the window, throbbing with red. Your blood is up to my calves now.

"Shut up," I say again.

"I don't blame you. He's hot. Whatever. Have some fun. But I feel so sorry for you, Kinsey. Two days sober and you think he deserves a medal? Two days sober and you're ready to fuck him?"

"Fuck you," I say.

Your blood is up to my knees. I will drown before I burn. You laugh and the windshield shatters; shards of glass circle me like a blizzard.

"You think he likes you? You think you're something special?"

Glass in my mouth, crunching in my teeth, cutting me from the inside.

"You're not special."

"You're not Camille."

Glass in my throat, my lungs. Your blood up to my waist now, warm and thick and poison.

"Stupid girl," you say.

"Shut up!"

Finally, I turn to you. Your face is gone. It is only a hole filled with meat. You are nothing but cruel, desperate flesh. I reach for you but you grab my wrist, grab my throat. So many hands, strong and hard and freezing. All your warmth, drained out. I am bathing in it, stuck in your blood like tar. You squeeze my throat and the glass cuts. I too will be headless soon.

"Look at me," you say. I stare at meat. I stare at nothing. I close my eyes, feel your hand around my throat, feel my breath sucked away, and I become your pain.

"There's only me," you say. "There will only ever be me."

ELEVEN

No light. No breath.

Invisible hands around my neck.

Cold hands. Yours.

Pain where your thumbs press tight.

I am absorbing your death.

Oh god, not this again.

I jump out of bed. I gulp down air, filling my lungs back up with life. But it hurts, this living. Every breath bruises; every molecule of air stings and cuts.

Would it hurt less to not breathe? To just quit this world where no matter what I do, I can't outrun pain? Is that it? My only option? To join Camille where she is so she will stop chasing me here?

No. I am in Chicago and it is almost morning and just hours ago I was happy. That was real. That was not a dream or a hallucination. My throat aches too, but that is not all there is. Pain is real. But there is more than pain.

I open the bedroom door. I stumble down the hall into the living room. I watch Hunter sleep in the last of the moonlight and I am instantly calmed.

I sit on the arm of the couch, trying to match my breath with his, trying to find the rhythm of this rare peace. What is it that makes me feel so much safer when I'm near him? Why can't Camille find me when we're together? Why can't she hurt me when he's around? It can't be what she said, that the connection I've felt with him the last few days is just an act. If it is an act, wouldn't she be able to break through it? Wouldn't she be able to find me even when I'm with him?

Hunter's face is so still, so calm. It makes me happy he can find relief in sleep, that he can take a break from his usual brooding turmoil. I wonder if it will last for a while after he wakes up. Which Hunter will it be today? The surly asshole, the one with the scowl and the sharp tongue? Or will it be the boy who hides behind him, the one who tucks his hair behind his ear so I can see his eyes, the one who talks in a soft voice and admits how lost he is?

It would take only a few steps for me to reach his lips. I could wake him up with a kiss.

What am I thinking? It's before sunrise and I'm in the dark staring at a sleeping guy like some kind of creepy stalker. I have to get moving. I have to get out of here before I do something crazy.

So I throw on my running clothes and make a quick trip to the bathroom. I do everything as fast as I can; I do my best to avoid looking in the mirror. But just as I'm leaving, I catch a glimpse of myself that makes me stop. Are those bruises? Did Camille really strangle me? There are faint red-purple marks on my neck. They could be anything. A rash. I could have scratched myself in my sleep. They could be anything.

This is crazy. I'm going crazy.

If I run hard enough, maybe I will forget all of this.

I scribble a note that I'm going for a run and leave it on the kitchen counter. As soon as I get out the door, I start running. I know I should warm up first. I know my muscles and joints need to take it easy after so many days on the road. I know my ankle is still not 100 percent. But I don't care. I need this. I need to feel my breath sting from something other than fear.

Maybe I should be scared running through the streets of downtown Chicago when it's still dark, but there's so much else to be scared of. I run by dark huddles in corners. Mysterious cars slow down as they pass me. But I keep running until I find the lake, where the sky is starting to lighten purple in the east, somewhere close to what used to be home.

The water laps the shore as I fall into my rhythm. I pass a few other crazy early-morning runners, but they're all decked out in hundred-dollar tech shirts, blinking safety lights, and ergonomic water-bottle carriers, when all I've got is a ratty sports bra, stained T-shirt, and pair of secondhand basketball shorts.

"Pick up the pace, Cole."

Really, Camille? Out here? While I'm running? While I'm doing one of the only things I have left that makes me feel safe?

"Aren't you going to say hi?"

Out of the corner of my eye, I see the figure of Camille running beside me, and it feels so normal, like we are just two girls going for a run together. Am I getting used to this? Are these appearances of hers just part of my life now?

But I know it can't really be her. Camille would never run. The real Camille had an aversion to exercise. Unless you count riding a horse exercise.

"You're not talking to me now?"

"You're not real," I say.

"Those bruises on your neck would disagree, don't you think?"

I run faster. If it's really Camille, she won't be able to keep up with me for much longer.

"Sorry about that, by the way."

"Whatever."

"*'Whatever.'* God, Kinsey. You sound like such a teenager."

I pass a runner who seems to be making an extra effort not to make eye contact. I guess it's probably wise to avoid people who appear to be talking to themselves in downtown Chicago before sunrise.

"Speaking of wounds," Camille says. "You know what I've been wondering? I'm curious—do you remember anything about being in the hospital after the crash?"

Another runner passes. The sky turns a lighter shade of purple.

"No? I guess you were pretty doped up. Not that you needed it. I mean, you barely had a scratch. But I guess they wanted to give you a chance to take a little nap before finding out you just killed your best friend."

"I had more than a scratch, Camille. I had two bruised ribs and a concussion."

"Yeah, but I was dead."

I trip on a crack in the pavement and barely catch myself from falling on my face. The sun peeks out of the lake. The figure of Camille seems to fade just a little.

"No one came to visit you, you know. I mean, your mom showed up because she had to sign some papers and stuff, but she was complaining the whole time. Even your grandma didn't come. She just gave your mom a check to pay for the hospital bill and the cab ride there. If it was me in there, the whole school would have shown up. The whole town probably."

"Death isn't good for you, Camille. It's turned you into a conceited bitch."

"I'm just telling the truth. Did you know my parents didn't even visit you? Kind of surprising, huh? After all those years of treating you like family. They'd never admit it, of course, but they were pissed, Kinsey. Oh sure, later they hugged you and cried and told you it was an accident and not your fault and they love you, blah blah, but they hated you those first couple of weeks. They wished it was you who died instead of me. Everyone did. They still do."

I run as fast as I can. I run faster than I should. I run until I hurt, until I find a new pain to push this pain away. I run until I can no longer hear the echo of Camille's cruel laughter. But still, the tears come. The sun rises and I leave the ghost behind, but my eyes won't stop. My breaths turn into sobs. My legs turn into noodles. All of my strength, all of my speed, is suddenly gone, and I collapse, just barely making it to the grass. I hug my knees to my chest, the morning dew soaking through my shorts. I try to catch my breath, but it is impossible through the tears. I am hyperventilating. I am gulping sadness.

It should have been me. It should have been me who died.

The sky is too beautiful. I do not deserve it. I do not deserve this sunrise or this grass or this breath. I do not deserve the beautiful boy and our meandering road trip and treating my days like they're endless, as if happiness and freedom and time are some bottomless pool that never runs out. How could I be so stupid? Of course it runs out. It ran out for Camille. It's running out for Hunter. It will run out for me.

We have to get to San Francisco. No more of this wandering around, acting like we have all the time in the world. All we have is a destination and we must get there. We must focus. It is the only way to stay in control. Above all, I must stay in control.

I stand up, a little wobbly. I check my ankles and knees and hamstrings and am relieved to find no major pain. I dust myself off and break into a steady jog—a reasonable speed for a reasonable person. I will pretend to be a reasonable person, someone with the security of a destination, and we will make it to San Francisco as planned and everything will be under control.

When I get back, I do my best to act like nothing's wrong. I take the fastest shower of my life, then join the others for breakfast. This is our last morning with Eli and Shelby. In a couple hours, it will be just Hunter and me again.

We look at the map over smoothies and scrambled eggs. Hunter traces some crazy route through South Dakota and Wyoming. "Don't you want to see Mount Rushmore?" he says. "Yellowstone?"

"I want to get to San Francisco," I say, a little too harshly. "The most direct route is through Iowa and Nebraska. We can take the eighty all the way through."

"Iowa and Nebraska?" Hunter says. "Where's the fun in that?"

"I think it's time for us to start thinking about efficiency instead of fun."

I try to pretend like I don't notice Hunter's face drop or Eli and Shelby exchanging surprised looks. "But—" Hunter starts to protest, but I stop him.

"It's my turn," I say. "You've been choosing the way long enough. I want to get to San Francisco."

"That's bullshit."

"How sweet," Shelby says. "They're learning to compromise like a real couple." I want to smack her. Eli attempts an awkward laugh. How can they act like there is nothing wrong with what we're doing? What about Camille? Why doesn't anyone think about Camille? How can Hunter act like we're on some stupid vacation together—as if we're friends, as if we mean something to each other? Has he moved on that fast? Has he moved on to *me*?

I've single-handedly destroyed the blissful vibe of our little group, but that's not surprising. I was never easygoing and likable like Camille. I'm the one who ends conversations. I'm the one who makes things awkward. But I don't care. I don't need to be liked. All I need is a destination. All I need is to get there.

Hunter and I pack up our stuff. Shelby hugs us good-bye and runs off to work. While Hunter carries our bags to the car, I thank Eli for the food and letting us stay at his place, but before I have a chance to finish, he wraps me in a bear hug and whispers, "Thank you."

"For what?"

"For taking this trip with Hunter," he says. "For believing in him. He really respects you, you know? You bring out the best in him."

I can feel myself blushing as I pull away. I don't want to think about that right now. I don't want my mission to be complicated by emotions.

Hunter returns and Eli embraces him. I hate long good-byes. I hate all this sincerity and earnestness. Why can't we just leave? Why can't we skip this part?

I hover by the door while Eli and Hunter say their good-byes. I try to pretend like I'm not listening. Hunter says how great it is to see Eli so happy, so stable and successful. "Honestly, I never would have imagined," Hunter says. "I mean, you were the most fucked-up of all of us. No offense."

"I got lucky," Eli says. "It could have gone all kinds of ways. I could have ended up like Caleb and just disappeared. I could have ended up dead."

"Or you could have ended up like me. Going nowhere. With no future."

"Fuck that, Hunter. Don't start with that self-pity shit. You could do anything."

Hunter chuckles sadly. "I've got so much potential, right?"

"You're the smartest person I know," Eli says. "And that's your fucking problem. You're so smart you won't listen to anyone else. You won't admit when you need help."

"Shit, Eli. I think I liked it better when you were a loser like me."

"You're not a loser. *She* doesn't think you're a loser."

I pretend to be looking at my nails and oblivious to the fact that Eli is talking about me.

"Yes, she does," I can barely hear Hunter whisper.

"Hey," Eli says. "Stop feeling sorry for yourself. I love you, man."

"I love you, too."

"Now get out of here. You've got a pretty lady waiting for you." Eli catches my eye and winks, and I know he knows I heard everything. "Call me anytime," he says to Hunter. "I mean it. About anything."

"All right."

"Promise?"

"Yeah."

"Don't lie to me. You know I can kick your ass."

"I promise."

As we walk to the car, Hunter says out of nowhere, "Let's go to the aquarium."

"What?"

"Shedd Aquarium. Have you ever been? Have you ever seen a fish besides a trout or perch?"

"Isn't it expensive?"

"My treat."

"But we need to get on the road."

Hunter stops walking and looks me sternly in the eye. "Listen, Kinsey. I'll give you Iowa and Nebraska. The least you can do is give me a couple hours at the fucking aquarium."

Hunter drives us there in silence and pays way too much for parking.

"We could have walked here from Eli's house," I say.

"Shhh," he says. "Can you stop complaining for one second?"

As tense as things are between us, it's impossible not to be impressed by the exhibits. The whole aquarium is like a real-life Animal Planet show. I even get to touch a stingray. The fact that Hunter is sulking and distracted and texting on his phone the whole time hardly even bothers me.

"There's a café a couple blocks away where we can get lunch," Hunter says as we step back out into the bright, sunny day.

"It's already almost two," I say. "We really need to get on the road."

"No," Hunter snaps. I have no idea why he's so on edge. Was it the conversation with Eli? Can he really be that mad at me about skipping South Dakota? "We're having lunch at this café," Hunter says, and that makes it final.

The café is nothing special, just a nondescript downtown lunch place with standard sandwich, soup, and salad choices. I know it couldn't have any sentimental value for Hunter. It isn't the kind of special hometown place that would hold any kind of nostalgia. I have the weird feeling that Hunter is stalling, that there's something he's not telling me, something he's trying to hide.

We order our lunches and take a seat in the corner in the back of the restaurant. The customers are a generic mix of downtown office workers and tourists. Hunter keeps fidgeting and checking his phone.

"Are you expecting a call?" I say, just trying to make conversation, but he fires back with "Why would you say that?" His voice is sour and suspicious.

His phone buzzes at the same moment our food arrives.

Hunter looks at the text message, then at me, and I think I see a brief flash of regret in his eyes, like an apology. "I'll be right back," he says. "Go ahead and eat." Then he gets up and hurries around the corner to the front of the restaurant where I can't see him. Maybe he's just going to the counter to buy a Coke. Maybe he's calling his mother and wants privacy. Or maybe he's walked out the front door and left me stranded in Chicago without saying good-bye.

I take a bite of my turkey sandwich. It's dry and flavorless. Hunter's lunch sits untouched on his plate. I look around at the stone-faced workers in suits, the sunburned tourists in khakis and tacky T-shirts, and I wonder if I'll end up like these people, these two versions of the same soul, one in uniform to make money, the other in uniform to spend it.

I force a few more bites of my sandwich and Hunter finally returns, looking slightly relieved.

"Just had to use the bathroom," he says, though I can see the sign for the restroom right behind him, which is not the direction he went. But I don't have the energy to confront him right now. I don't care where he was for the last five minutes. I just want to get out of here.

"Are you going to eat your sandwich?" I say.

"I'll take it to go," he says. "Let's get on the road."

* * *

The car is silent for the rest of Illinois. Suburbs thin until we're in the rolling hills of Iowa farmland. We keep passing semi trucks pulling the long white pieces of wind turbines, a hundred feet of smooth white blade, like the polished bones of dinosaurs. The car goes up a hill and we can almost see over the top, like there's some promise of a horizon, but then all there is is more of the same, hill after hill after identical hill, as far as the eye can see. Then we go back down to repeat it all again. The terrain doesn't change, but I'm nagged by the impatient feeling like it should have by now, but I missed it, just barely, and I'm being tricked somehow, stuck in some kind of twilight zone where we're cursed to do the same thing over and over again, going up and down these hills forever but never really getting anywhere.

Hunter's sandwich is untouched and sweating on the dashboard. It has been there for hours. "The mayonnaise is going to go bad," I say.

He picks up the sandwich, rolls down the window, and throws it onto the Iowa freeway.

"That was dramatic."

He just shrugs his old apathetic shrug.

"What the hell is going on with you, Hunter?"

He shrugs again.

"Oh, come on. Don't try that shit with me. I'm not going to beg."

Hunter sighs.

"Is this about Eli?"

He looks at me—tired, defeated. He looks back at the road.

"He's changed," Hunter says. "A lot."

"For the better, sounds like."

Hunter nods.

"So?"

"So I haven't."

"You've been doing it for the last three days," I say. "You haven't had anything to drink."

"Three days." He laughs sadly. "You know what's the saddest part? It's been really hard. Three fucking days."

"You seemed happy."

He says nothing.

"You fooled me." I don't know why, but I feel hurt. I know this problem has nothing to do with me, but some part of me thinks he should have been happy enough to forget about it. *I* should have made him happy enough. "I thought you were happy," I say, and I don't try to hide the hurt in my voice.

"I was. I am. Shit, Kinsey. I'm sorry. It doesn't mean I wasn't having any fun. It doesn't mean I wasn't having any fun with you. All it means is I'm a fucking idiot. Okay? It means I'm a pathetic piece of shit who has to sabotage everything good that ever happens to me."

"So stop," I say. "If you're so miserable, why don't you just stop doing the shit that makes you miserable?"

"It's not that easy. You don't get it. I'm not like you. I'm not perfect like you."

"Perfect? Are you insane?"

"You're beautiful and smart and talented and people respect you," he says. "You respect yourself." I stare at him hard, trying to find a hint of teasing or insincerity. But all I see is sadness. He really believes what he is saying. Even the beautiful part.

"I'm a mess, Hunter. You have no idea. I'm just really good at hiding it." The words come out so easy, despite the fact that this is the first time I've ever said them, not even to Camille. "Sometimes it feels like hiding is the only thing I'm good at. At least you're honest. At least you know who you are."

"I hate who I am." His voice breaks. I look away, wishing I could give him some privacy. What can I say to that? What can I do to let him know he is so much better than he thinks he is?

A single tear drops down his cheek, making a line through the unshaven stubble. Before I have time to even think about what I'm doing, I lean over and trace the wet trail with my lips, placing a final salty kiss on the side of his mouth. He turns and looks at me, surprised out of his sadness. I smile and he smiles back, as close to shy as I've ever seen him.

We don't talk for the next several miles. The car is so charged with electricity, there's no room for words. Somehow, I manage to doze off for a while. When I wake up, we are pulling into a rest stop and I can tell by the color of the sky that it is close to sunset.

"Can you drive for a while?" Hunter says gently as I stretch myself awake. "The map says there's a campground in about two hours. We should be able to get there before it's too dark."

"Sure," I say. Neither of us mentions the earlier conversation or half kiss.

The sky holds on to the last of its light and lightning bugs blink on and off as we pull into the "campground." There are only a few actual campsites, which are not much more than a line of concrete slabs so close to each other that your tent is practically on top of your neighbor's. If there were neighbors. The place is empty except for a couple of lonely cars parked on separate sides of the property. A vacancy sign still blinks optimistically, but even it seems to know it's only a few steps away from becoming another abandoned roadside business like the overgrown place where we camped on Lake Superior. The majority of the campground is made up of varying sizes of cabins for rent. We're exhausted and neither of us feels like setting up camp, so we decide to splurge on their cheapest one-room cabin. I never knew I could be so excited to sleep on a real bed between real walls.

"There's no bathroom." The tiny woman at the front desk coughs between wheezing breaths. She's puffing on a long, thin cigarette with an oxygen machine attached to her nose with plastic tubes. She's ancient, her face as wrinkled and dry as tree bark. One of her eyes is completely clouded over with cataracts. Her thin white hair is clumped haphazardly with pink plastic little-girl barrettes.

Hunter and I look at each other. "Um," I say. "Then where are we supposed to—"

"Shared bathroom," she croaks as she stubs out her cigarette in an overflowing ashtray. "Between cabin seven and cabin nine. Next to the vending machines. They're out of order by the way."

"The bathroom?"

"The vending machines!" she shouts, looking at us with hatred in her one good eye. She lights another cigarette with a lighter decorated with surfboards that says *Hang ten, dude!*

"Okay, thanks," I say, wanting to get out of here as quickly as possible. Hunter hands her his credit card and I look in my wallet for cash to pay him for my half.

Her one eye squints at us. "You two are married, ain't you?"

"Married?" says Hunter.

The woman points an arthritic finger at a faded and smoke-stained poster of Jesus on the cross, gory with his blood and suffering. "He's watching, you know. He sees *everything*."

"Yes, ma'am," I say. Then it hits me: We're staying in one cabin. With one bed.

She has the keys to our cabin in her hand, but she's holding on to them tight like she's thinking twice about giving them to us. The credit card machine beeps its acceptance and spits out a receipt, making the decision for her. She hands Hunter the keys, her eye still squinted, and says, "Cabin four. To the right of the Dumpster."

"Thanks," he says, and signs the receipt, and we can't walk out of there fast enough.

"Young lady!" the woman shouts just as I'm about to walk out the door. "You obey your man," she says. "You bow to him."

"Yes, ma'am," I say, and manage to get out the door before Hunter and I burst into laughter.

"I saw a pool on the other side of the office," I say as we carry our bags into the cabin. It's not much more than four walls and a lumpy queen-size bed, but it feels extravagant. "Want to go for a swim?"

"Hey," Hunter says. "I'm supposed to have the ideas around here, woman. You're supposed to bow to me."

"Sorry, Master. Please forgive me."

"Just this once. A night swim, huh? Isn't that kind of

dangerous? Aren't you worried about the lack of lifeguard or something?"

"Very funny."

"You're living on the edge."

Just carrying my bag the few feet from the car has me already drenched with sweat. Even with all the windows open, it's stuffy inside the tiny cabin. I thought Michigan summers were hot and humid, but this Iowa night takes it to a whole new level.

"Hey, where are you going?" Hunter says.

I pull my shirt over my head and throw it on the bed. I'm in a sports bra and shorts, the closest thing I have to a swimsuit. I can feel Hunter's eyes burning into my back as I walk out the door. If only the gruesome Jesus poster could see me now.

The pool is tiny and shallow, but the water feels like heaven. As I slide through it, the weight and dirt of the day washes off me. Everything I've been carrying—all the pain, all the regret, all the fear—all dissolves and floats away, gets sucked into the pool filter, where who knows what happens to it.

I lift my head out of the water and see Hunter coming my way. He looks uncharacteristically shy as he unbuttons his long-sleeved shirt and sets it on a cheap plastic chair, and I realize this is the first time I've seen him with his shirt off. The moon paints his skin silver, makes shadow slivers where ribs turn into tight abs, lights the small forest of chest hair that turns into a trail under his shorts. But on the surface of his thin, toned body is something else, something he has been hiding, a layer of pain and memory he will never be able to wash away.

The skin of one of his arms and half of his chest is grotesque—melted, cratered and pocked, deep burns barely healed, still raw and shiny with newness. This is what the crash did to him.

I say nothing as he steps into the water, as he swims a few circles around me. When he emerges, he is just inches in front of me. I trace my fingers across the lava flow of his arm. I feel where he was melted.

"Does it hurt?" I say.

"Sometimes."

"Does it hurt right now?"

"No. Nothing hurts right now."

His wet hair is slicked back and his eyes are big and bare in the moonlight. Exposed. Vulnerable. Brave.

I place my hand on his chest, on the place above his heart, the place where the burn stops, where the bubbled pink turns to smooth tan skin.

"You saved me," I say. "You pulled me out of the car."

"I didn't think you knew," he says softly. "You were out. Unconscious."

"You didn't tell anybody?"

He shakes his head.

"Why not? You were a hero."

"What, like I'm going to go around saying, 'Hey, guys, guess what, I'm a hero'?"

His breath is warm on my face, my lips.

"You should have told me."

"But I didn't have to. You remembered."

"I remembered."

My mouth is inches from his. Just as I realize I'm holding my breath, he looks down.

"Pretty gross, huh? My skin. I didn't want you to see it."

"It's not gross."

He meets my eyes again.

"Thank you," I say.

"No problem." He grins. "I'd pull you out of a burning car any day."

"Thank you for everything. For this trip, for reaching out. For being persistent even though I was a bitch."

Hunter shrugs and I can tell he's embarrassed. He doesn't have a witty comeback for so much sincerity.

"You're a good friend, Hunter."

His face hardens. The lightning bugs blink off. The magic fizzles away into the darkness. That was the exact wrong thing to say.

He smiles sadly. "Yeah." He pulls his body slowly through the water back to edge of the pool. "I'm tired," he says, his voice trailing behind him. "Time for bed."

Way to ruin a moment, Kinsey.

I follow him out of the water and back to our cabin. I know I should say something, do something to fix what I broke, but nothing seems right. We stand on opposite sides of the bed with our backs to each other, silently root in our bags for towels and a change of clothes. I change into a dry tank top and pajama shorts inside while Hunter changes out on the semiprivate porch. By the time he comes in, he's already sweating.

"There's no way I'm getting under those blankets," he says, doing his best to sound cheerful. Now that I've finally seen his scars, I guess he doesn't feel the need to wear a shirt to bed. He lies on one side of the bed in just his boxer shorts. I lie on the other side, being careful not to touch him. We are all skin. We are sweat and heat.

"Good night," he says. He lies on his back with his eyes closed. He is not sleeping. I will not be able to sleep. Not with his skin so close. Not with this heat and humidity. The air is too heavy to keep pretending we're just friends.

A voice inside tells me what to do. It is not Camille's voice. It comes from somewhere deep down, somewhere Camille can't touch.

I roll onto my side and face him. "Hunter," I whisper.

"Yeah?" he says, his eyes still closed.

I lean over and place my lips softly on his. He does not startle or seem surprised. He opens his mouth as if he was expecting me, as if he'd been waiting all this time, all these days and nights, for me to kiss him. I can feel him smiling.

He reaches out his arm and pulls me close, his hand on the small of my back, strong and confident, guiding me toward him. Our skin touches, all the heat and sweat of it, our arms, our legs, our hands, our faces, but it is not enough. Hunter's hands are under my tank top, circling my ribs, his thumbs under my breasts, inching their way up. I pull my top over my head. I want every part of me to touch him. His chest slides against mine. The muscles in his back flex under my hands. His mouth is on my ear, my neck, my breast, my nipple. We are panting, feral. I have never felt so wild.

But there is another voice, a familiar voice, not the one that told me to kiss him. It's the voice that tells me no, all the time, no—don't do this, don't do that, don't be stupid, Kinsey. This pleasure is not yours. You do not deserve it. There has been a mistake. Give it back, you foolish girl.

His hands slip beneath the waist of my shorts. My body wants to bend to him, open, let him in. But the want is my curse; it is the mark of what's forbidden. My mind senses it and says no, clenches tight, punishes my body for daring to be so free.

"No," I say, but so quietly I hope he will not hear.

He freezes where he is, his hand motionless on my hip.

"No?" he whispers, as out of breath as I am.

I want to take it back. I can't take it back.

"I can't do this," I say.

"Okay," he says, pulling away. "Okay," he says again, as if in pain.

"I'm sorry."

"Were we going too fast? We can take it slower."

"No. I mean, yes. I mean, I don't know."

"What is it?"

I can't speak. I see Camille in my memories, blissful, telling me she's in love.

"Kinsey, *you* kissed *me*."

"I know. I'm sorry."

"You're sorry you kissed me?"

"No." A million words swarm around in my head and none of them are right. I have no idea how I feel. I have no idea what I want to say. Why does this seem so easy for him, this forgetting of Camille? Did he love her as much as she loved him? Did he love her at all? Or was he just using her? Was she just some girl he fucked who happened to die?

"I want to understand," Hunter says, a tinge of anger entering his voice. "I think I deserve that."

The heat in the cabin is oppressive. The humidity is suffocating. I search my mind for an explanation. I grasp for an excuse.

"You're my best friend's boyfriend," is what comes out of my mouth.

The room is filled with deadly silence. I can't see Hunter's face in the darkness, but I can feel his disappointment and anger pushing out all the air. He sits up. The wood floor creaks with his steps. He opens the door and is outlined with the blue of moonlight.

"Where are you going?"

"I need to get out of here," he growls. "I need to be alone."

"Don't go," I plead. "I'm sorry."

He doesn't respond, just walks out and shuts the door hard behind him.

"I'm sorry, Hunter," I cry as his footsteps pound down the steps.

"She's dead, Kinsey," he hisses, and even filtered by the cabin walls, the words are strong enough to take my breath away. "You need to fucking move on already." A wave of hurt and sadness rushes through me; a pit of loneliness opens up and sucks everything away. Tears mix with the sweat on my cheeks.

But then something else. Fire in my throat. Claws tearing

through the sadness, drawing blood. "Fuck you," I say quietly. "Fuck you!" I say louder.

He says nothing but I know he can hear me. I hear the muted but familiar sound of the car trunk opening, Hunter rooting around, a glass bottle knocking against something hard. Then a new sound, something small and slightly musical, like a rattle, like pills shaking in a bottle.

"You're right," I holler. "She's dead. Your girlfriend is dead. And you're trying to fuck her best friend. That's been your plan this whole trip."

The words slice through me. I want to hurt him, but I just tear myself open even more. I cannot breathe through my sobbing. I choke on my shame. We're both to blame. We've both betrayed her. I'm sorry, Camille. I'm sorry.

And so old Hunter has returned, gone off into the night to destroy himself. And old Kinsey is here as well, too scared to let go. The only difference is the tears, the shame, the raw emotion rushing through me in waves. There was a time I didn't feel things like this, a time when I didn't feel anything, when I could turn off my heart and go cold. But now that is not so easy. Now there's a crack in my armor where feelings pulse through, an irreparable hole where I let somebody in, then pushed him back out again.

Again, white. The pale, dusty infinity of no-man's-land. This place where you live now. This place where you want me to join you.

I can't see you but I can feel your hand on my wrist. Cold. Sharp. Your skin made of wind.

"You should leave," the wind says.

I keep walking even though I know there's nowhere to go.

"Just take the car and run. Just leave him. Just go."

"I can't do that to him."

"Why not? He'd do it to you. How do you know he's not already planning it? Now that he knows you're not going to put out. Now that he knows there's no point in keeping you."

So cold. The wind and the emptiness. This ice in my veins.

"I'm not the cold one," you say.

The sky swirls around us, outlining your empty space. You are a window. You are a door. The blizzard makes a halo around your body. A storm of snow, a storm of ash—the white-gray flakes don't know the difference between freezing and burning.

I never knew thunder could laugh. "Frigid!" the clouds burst. "Prude!" the sky roars.

"Stop it!" I try to scream, but it comes out all wrong—warm and thick and slow.

"Cock tease!" The sky shakes, and the ground shakes with it. So above and so below, heaven and hell laughing, and I am the joke.

"God, you're worthless." It is your voice now—closer, sharper. "Not even good for a lay."

"Shut up!" I try to shout, but my words turn to ash, to snow.

"It should have been you," your voice booms. The sky is falling. Heaven cracks into tiny splinters.

You're right, Camille. It should have been me who died. Hunter's scars are worth nothing.

TWELVE

I am tied down.

My arms can't move.

I am in a tunnel, a cave, and it is burning.

I am in a bag.

The fire gets closer.

I am sweating rivers, but it is not enough to stop the heat.

I fight my way out of the blankets that are tangled around me. The air in the cabin is thick even though the windows are opened to their screens. Hunter is not beside me. I open the door but it offers little relief. The air outside is almost as hot, made even worse by a buzzing swarm of mosquitoes.

I stand on the porch, swatting the air. My skin is sticky

with sweat, chlorine from the pool, traces of Hunter, and the residue of uncertainty of whether or not I did the right thing. I don't know if the regret I feel is for starting what we did last night or stopping it.

What I need is a shower. Immediately.

There's an empty vodka bottle tipped over on the ground between the cabin and where the car is parked in the gravel spot next to it. Half a dozen crows scatter as I approach, leaving the remains of a torn-open bag of chips. I look for other signs of Hunter's trail of destruction—the trunk left open, our belongings a haphazard mess spilling out, his wadded-up shirt on the ground next to the driver's side door in what I'm guessing is a puddle of vomit.

"Jesus, Hunter." My stomach turns as I catch a whiff of his puke on the hot breeze.

The side of his face is pressed against the window. What is he doing in there? The windows aren't even cracked. It must be at least a hundred degrees inside the car.

But I don't care. Let him roast in the juices of all he drank last night. Let him breath in his own toxic air.

I grab my toiletries bag out of the chaos of the trunk and head toward the bathroom. What am I so angry about? Why am I even surprised to find him like this? How could I be so stupid to expect anything different? Camille is right. Hunter hasn't changed. Maybe he's not even capable of it. Maybe no one is, including me. I am frigid like she said. I am a prude. What was I thinking last night, throwing myself at him? Like I could ever be that kind of girl, someone sexy and confident. That was Camille, not me.

I know I shouldn't go in the bathroom. I know it is empty, that Camille is in there waiting for me. But I don't care. I need a shower more than I need to hide from a ghost.

I take my clothes off and step into the musty concrete shower. The cold water stings, makes my mind sharp. I can't even count how many days I've been on the road, but it feels like we've gotten nowhere.

No more tourist stops, no more scenic detours, no more sightseeing. I can't remember why I wanted to go to San Francisco in the first place, but I can't think of any good reason to go back, either. I'm just lost somewhere in the middle of the country, between a beginning that never felt like home and an end that never really felt like a destination. What happened to me? I've always had a plan, always had such a sure vision of where I was going, every detail in high-definition. But now, every possibility seems so unsure, so precarious. Every path has a million detours that wind around in tangled webs. I can't tell which ones intersect, which ones dead end, which ones lead me off a cliff plummeting to my death. Which path is the right path? I always thought I'd be able to tell. But now I don't even know if there is one.

The fluorescent lights flicker. The stall doors bang violently open and closed. The shower water turns so hot I have to jump out.

I am getting so sick of this.

"Fuck you, Camille," I say, toweling off. "This shit doesn't scare me anymore."

"Oh really?" says her voice, echoing off the concrete walls.

The room darkens and turns cold. A force pushes me against the stall door and onto the wet, filthy tile of the floor. The room seems to suddenly lose pressure, like an airplane descending, and my ears ache. The sound of a faucet dripping is magnified and echoing inside my head. I try to pull myself off the floor, but Camille pushes me down again.

She doesn't have to say anything. I know why she is angry.

"I'm sorry I kissed him," I say.

The mirror above the sinks shakes so hard it breaks, sending glass shards flying. I cover my eyes and feel the glass fall around me. A sound like an animal screaming throbs inside my head; claws tear at my skull.

"Camille, stop!"

"You think he loves you?" she cries. "You want him to?"

"No!"

"You just want to win. You've always wanted to win. You've always thought you were better than me."

"That's not true."

"Don't fucking lie to me! I hate being lied to." She slams me in the chest and my head pounds against the wall. Pain shoots through me and the room goes even blacker.

"Hunter!" I scream, but I know he can't hear me. No one can hear me.

"Oh, poor Kinsey, crying for her little boyfriend to save her. Can't be alone for three minutes without getting scared."

She pounds my head against the wall again and I actually see stars. All sound is sucked away.

My body is frozen, immobile, except for my right hand crawling across the floor. I try to stop it. I try to make a fist, but it moves without me, finds a shard of glass on the floor. My fingers curl around it, feel it cold and hard against my skin, the sharp edge cutting into my palm.

A force moves the blade against my wrist, pushes slightly, teasing. Blood beads just barely on my skin.

"Camille, stop!"

"Say it, slut," Camille says. "Say I win."

The blade presses harder against the bulging vein in my wrist.

I could just give up. I could just let her take me with her.

"You win," I say.

I close my eyes, ready for whatever she wants to do to me.

"You win, Camille."

The light turns back on and the bathroom returns to normal; even the mirror is still intact. I look at my wrist and there is only a benign little scratch. It could have been made by anything.

But she is not really gone. She's playing with me, tossing me around like a cat with a mouse, having some fun before she sinks her teeth in. She'll come back. And next time, it will be worse.

I gather my stuff and run out of the bathroom as fast as I can. I am shaking. My head hurts. The scratch on my wrist stings. I have to wake up Hunter. We have to get out of here.

A knot of anxiety burns in my gut as I walk toward the cabin. I rehearse in my head what I'm going to say to him, something about how I don't care if he's emotionally wounded, or an alcoholic, or whatever the hell is wrong with him; I'm not looking to hook up; I just want to get to San Francisco like we planned.

I won't say anything about being sorry. I won't say anything about being afraid of his dead girlfriend's revenge.

I open the car door, ready for my speech, but Hunter falls out, lifeless, into his own vomit. He doesn't wake up, doesn't even seem to notice he's on the ground.

"Hunter," I say. "Wake up."

Nothing.

"Hunter, this isn't funny." I nudge him with my foot. His shoulder slides a few inches in the slimy old contents of his stomach. My brain tells me to stay calm, but my heart is already pounding too hard in my chest. This is not a hangover. This is something else.

"Hunter." I can hear the desperation in my voice. I nudge him with my foot harder, more like a kick, and he still doesn't stir.

The forest morphs into a too-familiar place; Hunter becomes someone else, another broken person I love without wanting to. The pine needles are carpet. The trees are walls. Hunter's muscular arm is now my mom's thin one. She is splayed on the floor like a shattered ballerina. They share the same pale skin, the same smell of poisoned insides. I am a seven-year-old girl trying to shake my mother awake, trying to convince her to come back to me, begging her to believe I'm worth it.

"Don't leave me," I cry, to Hunter, to my mother. I put my face close to his, listening for anything. I feel nothing, hear nothing. His lips are blue. He smells like death. I shake him. Nothing. The day is already too hot but his skin is so cold.

"No!" I scream. "No no no no no no." But there is no one here to hear me.

Mom, on the floor of her bedroom, bathed in morning shadows. Mom, so sad she couldn't wake up. Despite my fear, I was a good girl. I called 911. I called Grandma. I remember the silence of waiting. I remember curling tight around her still, limp body. I remember promising to go with her wherever she went.

No one told me anything. No one ever said the word "suicide." I had to stay with my grandmother while Mom recovered in the hospital, and she never once hugged me, never bothered to tell me everything would be all right. She might as well have been a ghost, floating through her big old house, just out of reach. I searched the place, snuck from room to off-limits room against her orders, looking for something that might comfort or entertain a scared kid, some artifact of my mother, but the whole place was musty with loneliness.

The mosquitoes buzz a good-bye song.

"No!" I punch Hunter in the chest as hard as I can. "You can't leave me." I punch him again. I keep punching over and over. I will beat life back into him. My cries will give him breath.

And then, just barely, his mouth opens. I hold my breath. I am immediately still, my senses sharp, focused. The world is a tiny pinprick. I hear the faint whisper of the intake of breath. It is not mine. There is life in him, somewhere deep and stubborn, still holding on.

"Hunter, what did you take?" The only response I get are his faint, shallow breaths.

I remember the prescription bottle next to my mother, the little white pills I thought were candy.

I remember Hunter storming out of the cabin last night. I remember the sound of rattling. I remember his mysterious disappearance from the café in Chicago, the secretive texting while we were at the aquarium.

I look on the ground around him, but all I see are pine needles and gravel.

"Hunter, what did you take?" I say again, but I know he can't hear me. I look in the car—the glove compartment, the cup holders, the floor. I feel a bump under the floor mat. I lift it up, find a half-empty pill bottle.

Diazepam. Valium. WARNING: Do not take with alcohol.

Even as he was starting to die, he went through the trouble to hide his drugs.

To my grandmother's and my relief, Camille's family offered to take me in until my mom "felt better." I remember dinner that first night at her house—everyone was being so nice to me; Camille's mom made sloppy joes and didn't even make me eat any vegetables. I remember the table going silent when I asked what pumping someone's stomach meant. Camille's dad carefully explained how it's what doctors did to make someone throw up when they ate poison. No one had to fill in the rest, that that's what the doctors did to save my mother.

So now, eleven years later, at a campground in the middle of Nowhere, Iowa, I stick my fingers down my friend's throat to make him throw up. There's no 911 this far away from everything.

"Come on, Hunter." I roll him onto his side. I feel his teeth on the back of my hand, his soft tongue on my palm, the squishy length of his throat. It's still warm inside him at least, still alive. I push my fingers deeper, feel the strange fleshiness of his tonsils. I push and poke frantically, my finger searching for the magic spot that will trigger him to live.

And then I feel the spasms starting in his throat, the constriction and release. I feel his whole body shudder where my arms hold him, hear him gagging. I remove my hand and tip his face toward the ground just in time as he starts emptying his insides.

The sound and smell are horrible. I try to do as I'd done before with Camille the couple of times she drank too much— rub his back, hold his hair away from his face, say "let it out" over and over. Except I can't hide the terror in my voice. I can't stop my hands from trembling.

Once he starts, he can't stop. He empties himself in waves,

his whole body contorting in spasms, then resting briefly before the next round. Even after there's nothing left, not even bile, when all he has are dry, empty heaves and streaks of blood from his ravaged throat, his body acts as if it still wants to purge itself of something that goes much deeper than his stomach, something at the core of himself.

After what seems like forever, the vomiting finally stops. Hunter is slippery with sweat and limp in my arms. His breathing is still shallow but closer to normal and some pink has returned to his skin. His lips are no longer blue. The area around his eyes and throat are bruised red and purple with broken blood vessels. He smells and looks like shit, but he is alive and I think he's going to stay that way, at least for a while.

His eyelids flutter but don't open. "Hunter," I say. "Are you okay?" Such a stupid question.

His mouth moves and some sounds come out, but nothing coherent.

"Can you eat?" I say. "Can you drink some water?"

Air escapes his lips in the shape of the word "Camille."

"What?" I say.

"Camille," he mumbles.

"No, Hunter. This is Kinsey."

"Camille, I'm sorry."

"Hunter, do you see her? Is she here?" Of all the things to

feel right now, I am suddenly excited. Maybe he sees her too now. Maybe I'm not crazy. Or maybe we both are.

But he does not hear me. He's in a different world, somewhere between here and the place of my nightmares. "Camille," he says. His eyelids flutter. "I'm dead now too."

My chest clenches tight and my throat turns to concrete. I cannot hold him close enough. "You're not dead, Hunter."

His eyes open to slits for a split second, hinting at a sliver of reluctant life inside.

"Yes," he says. "I am."

It takes me a long time to drag him up the stairs and back inside the cabin. There are a few brief moments when he regains just enough consciousness to move his legs in a semi-crawl, but I do most of the heavy lifting. I leave the windows open for a breeze, but it will be unbearably hot in a couple of hours.

I fill a jug with water from the bathroom and use it to wash him off. I wipe off the sweat, the remnants of vomit, the dirt and leaves and pine needles from the ground. I am as gentle as possible across the terrain of his scars, the bubbly pink new flesh he earned from saving my life. What scars have I earned from saving his? I try to make him clean, but I know there's no way I will ever be able to wash away his pain and sadness and desperation.

Then I feel a hard whack against my calves.

"What the hell?" I turn around and see the woman from the front desk, humpbacked and tugging on her oxygen machine, with a broom in her hand pointed at me.

"You two! You get out!" she yells, swatting at me with the broom. "You bring the devil here with your liquor and your fornicating!"

"My friend," I plead. "He's sick. We just need to stay one more night."

"No!" She hits me in the knee. "You leave now! He's sick with the devil." Then she whacks Hunter in the shins, but he doesn't even move. I pull the broom out of her hand and it takes all my strength not to hit her with it. I throw it out the door and she looks at me in horror, lets out a bloodcurdling scream, and scoots away in her ragged pink slippers, tugging her oxygen machine along behind her.

"My gun!" she cries as she shuffles away. "My gun!"

"Shit!" I throw our stuff in the trunk and somehow manage to drag Hunter into the backseat. I will deal with making him comfortable later. My hands shake on the steering wheel, but this is no time to be scared of driving. Survival trumps fear. I speed away from the campground as fast as I can.

Once my breath gets back to normal, I pull over to cushion Hunter's head with a pile of clothes and set an empty pot on the floor in case he has to throw up. He doesn't open his eyes, doesn't acknowledge me as I bend and twist his body. But he is breathing. His skin is warm. I convince myself that is enough. It has to be.

I spend the next few hours flipping through radio stations. I can't focus on the words, can't decipher their meaning. It is just noise to fill my head, to crowd out the fear. When it threatens to take over, when panic fills my head with static and I feel the car drifting out of my hands, I count my breaths. I count signs. I count trees. I count everything.

I check on Hunter constantly—barking his name, reaching back and shaking him to semiconsciousness. I leave him alone only when he grunts acknowledgment. I look in the rearview mirror for signs of life—a tiny twitch of the eyelids, his chest moving in and out. He does not speak and his eyes are always closed, but his absence is a relief for now. I am not ready for him to be awake. I am not ready to talk about this.

But talking is inevitable. He cannot stay asleep forever. And I cannot keep driving for the rest of my life. I have to stop sometime.

"Kinsey." It is several hours later when I finally hear his weak, strained voice from the backseat. The late-afternoon sky is dark purple with clouds. The radio says a storm is coming.

What am I supposed to say to him? "Hi, how's it going? How was almost dying?"

"Kinsey," he says again. I look in the rearview mirror and see him halfway propped up on one elbow, his hair disheveled, his eyes bloodshot, the skin around his eyes and throat bruised from the force of his vomiting.

"You need to drink water," I say as sternly as I can. If I act angry enough, he won't see my fear.

"What happened?" he says, looking around the car as if for clues.

"You're asking me what happened? You're asking *me*? You overdose and almost die and you're asking me what happened?"

"Almost died? What are you talking about? I didn't almost die." But I can tell he doesn't fully believe what he's saying. I can tell he's scared too.

"You weren't breathing, Hunter. Your lips were blue. For all I know, you have fucking brain damage."

"Oh god," he says, sinking back down onto the seat.

"Oh god is right." I pull the pill bottle out of my pocket and throw it at him. "This is what you were sneaking around Chicago for?"

I watch his reflection as he picks up the bottle and looks at it sadly. "They're for anxiety." I can't imagine his voice sounding any more pathetic.

"Is that a doctor's diagnosis? Was it a doctor you bought it from?"

He tosses the bottle back weakly. It hits the dashboard and rolls onto the car floor. "Take them. Throw them away somewhere I can't find them."

"How many did you take, Hunter?"

"I don't know."

"How many? Five? Ten? A hundred?"

"I don't know. The bottle was full."

The bottle is half-empty. There are at least twenty pills missing. "Jesus, Hunter."

He meets my eye in the mirror for a second, then looks away in shame. "I don't remember taking all those."

"I don't care. I'm done caring about you."

"Don't say that," he says. I can't bring myself to look at his sad puppy dog eyes. As mad as I am, I know I'm no match for those.

"This is the deal," I say. "You will be sober for the rest of the trip. You will not touch me. We will drive as much as possible. We will stop only when necessary. We will not fuck around. We will get to San Francisco and we will part ways. Then you can drink and do drugs as much as you want. You can overdose and die for all I care because I am never going to see you again anyway." Thunder cracks in the distance and a white vein of electricity pulses in the clouds.

A sound like choking escapes his throat and for a second I think he's getting sick again. But when I look back at him, I see his face in his hands and his shoulders shaking and hear a guttural sound and I realize he is weeping. My chest caves in and all I want to do is go to him, wrap my arms around him, and make him stop hurting. But I cannot do that. I am done trying to fix Hunter. I keep my eyes on the road and I drive.

"I'm sorry," he cries. "I'm so sorry, Kinsey. I don't know why I'm like this."

I don't respond. I just keep driving into the storm.

I want this day to be over. I want to close my eyes and have it magically disappear, and when I open them again it'll be tomorrow or, better yet, days from now, when we reach San Francisco and I can finally rid myself of Hunter, rid myself of his drama and all the feelings I have wrapped up in him. With him gone, maybe I can stop caring. Out of sight, out of mind. Maybe.

But it is only afternoon, still hours until sundown, though the sky is already as dark as night. The clouds rumble over us and a light rain starts to fall. I look at Hunter in the rearview mirror and he is already out, cried himself to sleep like a baby. I feel like a guard, and Hunter is my prisoner. How did this become our relationship?

I reach down and pick the pill bottle up off the floor. The

prescription is for someone named Hong Kim. Is Hong Kim the one who sold them to Hunter? How much did they cost? Or were they stolen? Did someone get hurt for these? Someone besides Hunter?

I roll down the window and throw the bottle onto the freeway.

The clouds roar above us, shaking the car. Lightning flashes a split second later, way too close. The sky has cracked open and now it's dumping water, not even raindrops but gallons, bucketfuls. I turn on the wipers full speed but they do nothing. I am driving through an ocean. I can see nothing but gray waves pounding against the windows. I can't see the road. I can't see the lights of other cars.

It is not black. There is no forest, no drunken headlights. It is too wet for fire. But still, I am driving. Hunter is in the backseat. A too-familiar configuration. My hands shake. I do not feel them. I can't hold on if I cannot feel them. I can't keep driving if I cannot breathe, if my head fills with static, if I close my eyes and drift away to wherever Hunter's dreaming.

I can barely make out the sign for an exit. I turn the wheel and we are flying off the freeway.

And then, silence.

Then black.

Red.

Screaming metal.

We are thrown through space in slow motion.

Camille is screaming.

My head hits the window.

A force like God's fist pounds us back into the ground. I don't know which way is up, don't know if we are on the ground or in it, don't know if this is rain or fire, home or road, Camille or Hunter, life or death.

"Kinsey!" Hunter shouts from the backseat. Now I know where I am. Camille is not next to me. I am not drenched with her blood. I am in a world where Hunter says my name.

I spin the wheel and press the gas and the car shudders as it finds its way back onto the road. My body is shaking so hard I can barely keep my hands on the steering wheel. A burst of lightning illuminates the road for a split second, and now I know which way is forward. If I just go slow, we'll be okay.

"There's a sign," Hunter says. His hand is on my shoulder. "Take a left here."

I am gulping air. I am drowning.

"Stop the car."

Stillness. Muted rain pounding on metal. The car intact. There is no fire.

"Are you okay?"

There is no room for words in my mouth.

"Just breathe. We're okay."

My hand reaches forward and turns off the car. It is not connected to me.

And then the door opens. The rain suddenly amplified. Hunter vomiting into the storm. The sound wakes me up, focuses my eyes. I see a rickety old building in front of us. A broken fence. A sign that says DANGER.

"I can't be in the car anymore," Hunter groans. His head is hanging off the side of the seat, out the open door, getting pounded with rain.

A sign says QUARRY. This shack must be the office. The windows are boarded up. A broken lock hangs from a crooked door. A NO TRESPASSING sign is covered with graffiti.

"We can't stay here," my voice croaks.

"Yes we can," Hunter says, and stumbles out of the car into the rain.

"Hunter, wait!"

But he's lurching toward the shack, stepping over the fallen fence, kicking garbage and broken things out of his way. He trips and lands in the mud and the rain pounds him into a puddle.

"Fuck!" I hear him yell through the thunder.

I get out of the car and am immediately drenched. Hunter pushes me off when I try to help him up. "Get back in the car,"

I say. "We shouldn't be here." But he ignores me as he stumbles toward the shack, as he climbs the rickety steps to the small porch, as he kicks open the door and enters the darkness.

As soon as he gets in, he slumps on the floor and curls up on his side. "Tired," he says. "Need sleep." I try to pull him up but he's too heavy, dead weight. We aren't going anywhere until he decides we are. I slide down the wall onto the floor because I don't know what else to do. I sit on the dirty floor next to Hunter's already sleeping body, a puddle forming beneath us from our drenched clothes. The rain pounds on the tin roof of the porch, a sharp percussion replacing the low roar of the storm. It is dark in here, with only a few patches of pale light where boards do not completely cover the windows. The floor is covered by a thick layer of dirt, and cobwebs line the ceiling. A few pieces of broken office furniture have been pushed into one corner. In another, someone had made a bed out of piled cardboard. The melted remains of candles make a waxy mound on the floor beside it. Rusty tin cans are piled in another corner.

But it is dry. The air is still. The storm is muted. And Hunter has crawled over to the pile of cardboard and made himself a nest.

"Hunter, that's dirty! You don't know what kind of bugs are in there." But he's asleep. He will be for a while. I'm stuck here until he wakes up.

I must keep myself busy. I must keep my hands and mind full. If I don't, I don't know what will happen. I don't know what kind of madness will sneak its way through, will find me cowering and trapped in this hovel, trading thunder and lightning for darkness and filth.

I run a few things over from the car. I make the trip as fast as I can but still they get wet. Somehow I manage to help Hunter into drier clothes and his sleeping bag, though his eyes remain closed the whole time. I tidy up the space a little, find a table and chair to push against the wall, hang up our electric lantern on a nail in the corner, pull a loose board off a window to let in a stream of pale, sickly light. I can see how this might be a decent home for a pioneer or a hobo. So I guess it makes a decent enough detox for a rich, troubled boy and his hapless attendant.

I have no idea what time it is. I have no idea where we are. I lay out my sleeping bag on the hard wood floor and try to sleep, but every time I close my eyes I see flashes of red, feel myself flying through space and jerking awake. There is just barely enough light to read by, so I try to focus on the book I brought. But the words all look like little scratches, like bite marks, like hostile, angry scars. I can't remember what the book is about. It feels weird and heavy in my hand, like it's no longer made of paper.

And then something cold around my wrist. Something wet and fleshy.

I freeze. My body goes numb.

I can't feel anything but the tight grip, the long dead fingers, my own pulse fighting its capture.

I jump up, my arms flailing. I throw the book into the dark, cobwebby corner. I hop around and brush myself off spastically. I look around and of course there's nothing. Hunter's still sound asleep on his cardboard bed. If he's here, why am I scared? If he's here, how can the darkness touch me?

I crawl closer to him. There is just enough room on the cardboard for me. I am too tired to care what kind of vermin have made their nests inside. I curl next to him in my sleeping bag and notice I am shaking. I can feel how close to the edge I am, can feel myself teetering on the fine line between staying in control and losing it.

Even though his back is to me, I can still smell Hunter's sick, rancid breaths. I fall asleep breathing in his poison mixed with the wet, musty air of this ruin we have found ourselves in.

Why is it so dark?

Where am I?

Where's Hunter?

I am trapped here.

She has finally caught me.

I am finally hers.

My throat pulses where her fingertips branded me. I try to scream but nothing comes out, like someone reached in and stole my voice. I am not dreaming. It didn't even take a nightmare to get me here. It is dark and this is real and I am taken.

No, I am in a different kind of hell. This shack, in the middle of nowhere, next to a toxic boy. It is still the same day. The rain has let up, but random drops still bang on the tin roof, sending bullets through my brain. I feel antsy. I need to move.

I stand up, stretch my legs, and walk to the car. The ground is a giant mud puddle. The air is still thick with moisture. Water falls in fat drops from trees. I find Hunter's phone in the glove compartment, on top of a stack of brochures and maps we've picked up at rest stops along the way. I know there's no reception here, but maybe I can listen to some music or play a mindless game on his phone. I press the power button, but nothing happens. The phone is dead. Of course.

So I take the pile of brochures instead. At least they'll kill time. At least they're something to look at with pictures, with empty words that don't require much more than a short attention span. I sit on a bucket on the porch of the shack and start going through them slowly, one by one, trying to imagine all these places I will probably never see. Parks and lakes, outlet malls, a town where it is always Christmas, a petting zoo where all the animals are pygmies, a reptile farm, the world's largest coffeepot, and countless other tourist traps. But I am not a tourist. Not anymore. I am simply in transit. This is just a stop in the middle of nowhere, on my way to somewhere.

After a brochure about a combination cherry farm/go-cart track/paintball course, I flip to one with a picture that looks eerily familiar. I stare at it for a long time, trying to figure out where I've seen this particular scene before—the fence, the small building with the tin-roofed porch, the mottled sunlight painting the canopy of old oak trees. It could be any old building in any old ghost town, but I shudder when I recognize it as the one I'm sitting in right now. The weather in the picture is more cheerful, making it look more like a setting for a historical building and artifacts rather than the broken-down shed and garbage I assumed it was. Without thinking, I turn around, as if to check to make sure there's no photographer standing there right now. It's as if someone took a photo of this place, Photoshopped out the rain and mud and darkness, then erased me. It is a picture of the world without me.

The heading on the brochure reads "Old Quarry Historical Site." My heart races as I skim through the information about the surrounding flora, fauna, and geology; trail maps; safety information; and history of the abandoned quarry. My heart rate starts to slow back to normal as I come to a picture of its towering chiseled walls, the nine-hundred-foot sheer limestone cliff. What am I getting so worked up about? It's just a brochure. They included a photo of this building because it's part of the history.

But just as I am about to throw the brochure on the ground with the other ones, I see something strange in the photo of the quarry. On the rim of the cliff, at the very top, is a tiny figure. The cliff is lined with a fence, but the figure is standing in front of it. How could the brochure makers have missed that? Surely they'd want to avoid picturing someone so obviously breaking the rules.

I look closer and my heart stops.

New details suddenly seem more visible than before—long, straight dark hair, skinny jeans, a tank top with a logo just barely out of focus that looks shockingly similar to my high school's. And the face—it's so tiny I can't be sure, but the proportions are exact. The figure in the photo is Camille.

"What the fuck?" I say out loud.

I look at the picture again. The figure is still there. I don't know if I am imagining the smirk on the gray, smudged face, but it seems to be taunting me, laughing at my fear. Camille never smirked in real life, but there she is, in two dimensions and less than a centimeter tall, daring me to come find her.

I turn to the page with the map of the park. Just a short hike from here to the top of the quarry. I am aware of a small voice inside shouting for attention, wanting to talk some sense into me, but that voice is distant and out of focus. The only voice I hear clearly is the one that says I have no choice—I must see what's at the top of that ridge. I must find Camille.

I shove the brochure in my pocket and get up. As I trudge through the mud to find the trailhead, the leaves shiver above and around me, filling my ears with a glassy hum. I just keep walking, barely seeing anything except what's right in front of me, as if everything else is out of focus, as if the only thing that's real is the path that will take me to the top of the quarry.

The trail gets steep and I feel my legs burn from disuse. A couple of weeks ago, I could have probably run up this hill without breaking a sweat, but now my body feels suddenly old and weighed down. My legs are heavy and slow. The sky rips open and the rain starts again, even heavier than before. I am wading through a lake, an ocean. Lightning flashes and the whole sky is on fire for a split second. My ears pop with the electricity.

I am drenched and panting when I reach the top. I didn't bother to look anywhere but in front of me on the way up, so I only now notice the dramatic view. I lean against the wooden fence and look down. My knees wobble with vertigo as I scan the sharp shelves cut into the cliff, the lonely stranded trees that took root in the eroded piles of rubble, the pool of collected rainwater at the bottom, all made eerily more sinister by the gray blanket of rain dancing in twisted formations, pushed this way and that by the wind. I step back and close my eyes, put my hand on the fence to steady myself, take a few deep breaths to regain my bearings. The voice I ignored earlier is suddenly crystal clear:

What are you doing here? What do you hope to find?

I hear movement.

I hear spongy footsteps in wet leaves.

I feel the breath of air as something passes by me.

I open my eyes and there is nothing.

"Camille?" I call out. The wind blows as if in response, and every bone in my body shudders with the certainty that she is here. The rain dances in the open sky in front of me; a gust of wind sends it swirling into a circle, a semblance of a face, and then it is gone. The sky rumbles and darkens and gets closer to night.

I hear the leaves again and feel the air shift around me. I look down at the ground and am paralyzed by what I see.

Indentations. Foot shaped. Coming toward me.

I can't move. I can't scream. I close my eyes again, squeeze them tight. If I shut the world out hard enough, maybe it will go away. Maybe it won't scare me.

A breeze inside my ear whispers, "Kinsey, Kinsey." A gust of wind blows the leaves against my bare legs and arms, and they feel like wet fingers scratching their way across my skin.

When I open my eyes, the footsteps are gone.

The leaves flutter in slow motion down into the quarry like sad confetti, like the afterthought of a party no one came to but me.

A few last leaves follow the others, but these ones take their time, swirling in dizzy circles around my ankles before taking the leap, like they're pulling on my leg, begging me to come play with them. I look out across the quarry, this giant man-made scar, and am impressed by how completely it's been reclaimed by the trees and grasses and pooled water, how it looks almost natural now, as if it is meant to be here. There must be some meaning in this, and I feel so close to figuring it out, something about how something wrong can turn into a right, something bad can be really good.

I am so close to the truth now, just on the edge. I have been brought here to find it.

There is a reason the leaves were blowing around me. There is a reason this fence is so easy to climb over. There is a reason I am standing here now, on this thin lip of solid ground, looking hundreds of feet down, no barrier between me and nothingness.

Maybe this is what I've been looking for all along. Maybe home is at the bottom. Maybe that is where I'll find Camille, the real Camille of my memories, not this cruel one who's been following me. Maybe home is where I can be with her again, forever.

"Yes," Camille says. "You are supposed to be with me."

"You're the lucky one," I say. "You were always the lucky one."

"Come with me," she says. "Let go. You've been working so hard your whole life. Aren't you tired?"

"I'm so tired." I feel my eyelids droop. My legs are weak. The wind blows raindrops against my calves, pushing me gently forward.

"Take a break. You deserve a break."

"I deserve a break." The rocks under my toes crumble and fall slowly away.

"You can stop now. You can rest."

I could fall asleep right here, standing up. I can barely keep my eyes open. The wind is so strong now. I sway with it.

"Come with me," Camille says, her voice so clear up here, away from the noise of the world. "There's nothing left for you here. We can be together forever, like we always planned."

I close my eyes, feel the wind nudge me toward the edge.

"I miss you," I say.

"Come with me."

The wind gusts.

Thunder shakes the sky and earth.

Rocks crumble and I am airborne.

I am whisked away by strong arms. The ground is gone.

I have been rescued from this pain by somebody who loves me.

But I am not falling.

"Dammit, Kinsey! What the fuck are you doing?"

The world comes screeching back into focus, all sharp lines and hard edges, a sharp pain on my shin from knocking into the fence, arms tight around me, the smell of poison sweat.

"Kinsey, say something." Hunter's sour breath, frantic.

"Oh" is all I can manage.

"I was screaming at you. You acted like you didn't even hear me."

His arms are still around me, rescuing me again. We are still so close to the edge.

I blink my eyes as I look around. None of this looks familiar. I am groggy, disoriented, like I was just woken up in the middle of a dream. What is this place? How did I get here?

"What were you doing? Why were you on the other side of the fence?"

I say nothing. I am shaking now, uncontrollably, but I am

not cold. It comes from somewhere deep down.

"Kinsey," he says, this time more gently. Our eyes lock and I am steady. "Were you trying to get yourself killed?"

I look away. I can't look him in the eye. I don't know the answer to his question. I don't want to know the answer.

"Oh fuck." He grabs my arm. He squeezes too tight. He pulls me to start walking. "No. No way."

"Ouch," I say. My voice tastes strange in my mouth. "You're hurting me."

He stops and looks me in the eye. "Fuck you, Kinsey. You cannot kill yourself on my watch." He turns and keeps walking down the hill.

"I wasn't," I cry after him. "It wasn't me."

"I can't believe this shit."

"I have nightmares," I blurt out. I don't know what I am trying to say. I don't know how much I want to tell him.

"Nightmares? Like, what, you were sleepwalking?"

"No. Nightmares. About Camille."

"What do nightmares about Camille have to do with throwing yourself off a cliff?"

"I wasn't. That's not why I came up here. I was . . . looking for something."

"What could you possibly have been looking for at the edge of a cliff?"

"I don't know." I know that's not the answer he wants to hear, but it's the only honest one I can think of.

"Why did you go over the fence?"

"I don't know."

We're both quiet for a few moments, the only sound our footsteps muted on decaying leaves, the low roar of the rain. Somewhere beyond the rain, the sun is setting. The sky is almost black. Hunter turns on his flashlight.

"What a fucking pair we are," he says with a hiss of disgust.

"I'm sorry" is the only thing I can think to say.

Hunter turns around so quickly I bump into him. "At least I don't try to blame my shit on Camille," he shouts. "At least I'm honest about how fucked-up I am. I don't pretend I'm perfect. I don't try to act like I always know everything."

"But I can't stop thinking about her," I say. It's an explanation for nothing. He looks at me like he doesn't even know me, like I'm some crazy stranger he found in the woods. But I keep talking. I need him to understand. "No matter how hard I try, how hard I try to block her out, she keeps coming back."

"Maybe that's your problem," he says. "Maybe you're not supposed to block her out. Maybe you're not supposed to stop thinking about her. You can't control your feelings like that."

We stand in the drenched, black forest, two crazy people with a death wish staring each other down. I know there is some truth here, something important that's been revealed, but we are both too blind to see it.

"Let's get out of here," Hunter says as he turns away. "Let's get out of this fucking state."

"But you're sick," I say.

"Look who's talking."

The rain lets up to a drizzle as we pack up the car in silence, everything wet and musty, staying as far away from each other as possible. I try not to think about how just a few days ago we were in Chicago with Eli, Hunter was sober, I was happy, even relaxed, and everything seemed so full of promise. Now we're both miserable and crazy and on our way to a city I don't even know I want to go to anymore.

I get in the driver's side, where just last night Hunter sat with poison racing through his veins and slowly killing him. He gets in next to me, slams the door, pulls his phone out of the glove compartment, plugs it into the charger, and puts his earbuds in. He has made it clear that he doesn't want to talk to me.

As I pull onto the freeway, Hunter's phone buzzes back to life. Just before he presses play, he says, "We're even now."

THIRTEEN

Nebraska is the worst place in the world. It is silent and flat and desolate. It is heartless and lonely. It is miles of identical nothing. Hunter and I do not speak unless absolutely necessary. The car is cold with air-conditioning and anger.

I drive into the night while Hunter sleeps. I don't wake him, even when I'm nodding off from exhaustion, even when it's clear I should no longer be driving. It's not safe. I'm a hazard. But it's better than the alternative. It's better than not moving.

Even though I'm inches away from Hunter, Camille keeps trying to break through. But it is not the Camille of the nightmares, not the Camille of the hauntings. It is the real

Camille, the one I remember loving for practically my whole life. Hunter cannot protect me from her.

Her face keeps flashing in front of me, lit softly, turned up to the sun, smiling her ecstatic smile. I try to fight the memories, but my mind is weak and exhausted. I've worked so hard fighting the ghost of Camille, now I'm no longer strong enough to block her memory.

She comes to me in short, painful bursts. She pulls at my ribs, worms her way through my throat, up into my brain, where she flashes pictures of our innocence—sleepovers on her bedroom floor where we'd tell each other our benign secrets in the dark, her few laughable attempts at teaching me to ride a horse, walking the country roads for hours just for something to do, sitting at her favorite table at the coffee shop while she made hilarious commentary about everyone who passed by, Camille and her parents cheering at my soccer matches when neither my mom nor grandma ever showed up.

But then other memories come, blank spaces where she should have been, holes in the months leading up to the crash, when she started leaving even before she left. These memories are the worst, the ones where I can't see Camille at all, where there is darkness where her face should be, where there is just me, alone, missing her.

I squeeze my eyes closed to stop the tears, to stop the

barrage of images like machine gun fire in my gut. The steering wheel is in my hand but it is connected to nothing.

I am driving air. I am not in control. Sleep seeps in like warm water, filling me up as I float away.

"Fuck, Kinsey!"

Hands on mine, squeezing.

Wheels screaming. The world tilting.

Red and white lights blur by as I try to focus.

The night is too dark.

"Pull over!" Hunter shouts, his body heavy on mine as he leans over from the passenger side, his hands on the steering wheel. "Fucking pull over right now!"

My eyes and brain are able to focus enough to bring us to the side of the freeway. We are so still now. And I am suddenly so awake.

"Get out," he says. "I'm driving us to the next rest stop."

"I'm sorry," I say. "I think I fell asleep."

"Why didn't you wake me up if you were getting tired?"

"I'm sorry," I say again.

"Luckily there aren't that many cars on the road. Jesus, Kinsey, you could have killed us. You may have a death wish, but you're not taking me down with you."

I nod because I can no longer speak. I am shaking too hard to acknowledge the irony of his statement. The car is still now but I feel it on replay, the car drifting out of its lane and into the next one over, the jarring tug of Hunter steering it back.

"Get out," he says again. My hands shake as I unbuckle my seat belt. My feet are unsteady as I walk around the car. A semi truck barrels by and I am nearly grounded by the force. I put my hand on the side of the car to steady myself. Hunter is in front of me, the night loud with insects and the rumble of freeway. The ground does not feel solid. I do not feel solid. I slide against the car and fall to the ground.

My head is in my hands, my shoulders shaking, the sound of my cries absorbed by the deafening night. "I'm sorry," I say.

He doesn't say anything. He remains standing. Solid. Stone.

"For everything," I continue. "I'm sorry. I'm having a hard time."

"That's the understatement of the year," he says, and I can't tell if his words are tinged with cruelty or kindness.

"Are we okay?" I say, barely audible.

He's quiet for too long. I can't remember why we're fighting. I can't remember which of us screwed up more. All I know is there's a hole in me now the shape of him.

"Get in the car," he finally says. He turns to walk to the driver's side, but stops and stands there for a moment. He looks up, deep into the night, then turns back around and offers me his hand. I take it, stand up, and brush the dirt and gravel off my legs.

It is only a few more miles to the next rest stop. Hunter pulls in and parks and we head to the restrooms without speaking. I stand outside the ladies room and wait for someone to walk in before I enter to make sure I won't be in there alone. I can't deal with Camille anymore today.

When I get back to the car, Hunter is laid out in the backseat, eyes closed. I get in front and recline the seat as far as it will go without crushing him. Despite the sadness threatening to consume me, at least I feel safe, and I fall quickly into a dreamless sleep.

I wake up suffocating in the trapped heat of rolled-up windows. I can't get out of the car fast enough. The backseat is empty. Maybe Hunter left, maybe he walked off into the night, maybe he finally figured out I'm more trouble than I'm worth.

I fish through the trunk for my toothbrush and a change of clothes. All of his stuff is still there, his cardboard box half full of liquor bottles. I know he wouldn't leave without those.

The bathroom is full of chattering women. As I awkwardly change my clothes in a stall, I find the crumpled brochure for Old Quarry Historical Site in my pocket. I'm just about to throw it on the floor when I have the sudden urge to open it, to look at the photo of the quarry one last time. There, nestled among text about geology and mineral deposits, is the image of the massive cliff face. And there, where there used to be a tiny figure in the shape of a teenage girl, is nothing.

I squint my eyes and look closer. Still nothing. No girl. No Camille. Nobody.

Did I imagine it? Did the figure magically get erased? Is this the same brochure? Can ghosts be so tiny and fleeting and made out of ink?

I squeeze my eyes tight, shake my head hard, and say, "No," loud.

"Excuse me?" someone in the bathroom says.

I tear up the brochure before I open my eyes. I tear it into little pieces. I make the pieces so small there's no quarry left, no photo, no fence, no place where Camille should be. I throw the paper in the toilet and flush.

I exit the stall. I brush my teeth and wash my face. It is so strange to think I must resemble a sane person to all these strangers in the bathroom. They must think I'm some young woman on a road trip just freshening up in a rest stop. I'm not someone unraveling, unraveled. I'm not someone who has lost her mind.

When I get back to the car, Hunter is standing there with a guy not much older than us—tall, pale, skinny, and kind of twitchy; with thick glasses, stringy black shoulder-length hair, thrift store jeans, a colorful top that may be a woman's, and a thick knitted scarf wrapped around his neck even though it's already pushing eighty degrees. He's leaning against the car next to a giant backpack. I have a very bad feeling about this.

Hunter's cleaned up and looks close enough to healthy. He sucks on a Styrofoam cup of coffee as I approach, eyeing me through his sunglasses. I stand before them, waiting for an introduction. The guy looks at me with a dopey grin, then at Hunter, shifting from foot to foot as if it's impossible for him to stand still. Hunter says nothing. He's enjoying watching me squirm. He enjoys knowing something I don't.

The guy finally thrusts out his hand and says with a high, squeaky voice, "Hi, I'm Terry. Pleased to meet you."

I reach my hand out tentatively to meet his; he grabs it and shakes way too enthusiastically.

"There's nothing more important than a firm handshake," he says. "Especially if you're a man. Especially if you're kind of a sissy like me." He blows a thin wisp of black hair from his eyes and cocks his head to the side. "It's essential if you want to be taken seriously. Do you take me seriously?" His thick glasses magnify his eyes so they look like they're bulging out of his face, giving him an owl-like appearance. The scarf around his neck is hideous, old, and poorly made with a hodgepodge of unmatching yarn fragments. His clothes are dirty with the road.

I look at Hunter for an explanation. With a blank face, he says, "This is Terry. He's coming with us."

I am speechless.

"I found your pal Hunter by the vending machines," Terry says cheerfully. "He appeared to be having a rather hostile and spirited discussion with a small black electronic device. Something told me I should talk to him. Do you believe in fate? I do. I think we're meant to be great friends, you and me."

"Let's go," Hunter says, moving to get into the driver's seat, as if the matter's already settled, as if this is not one of the stupidest and craziest things he's ever done.

"Shotgun!" Terry squeals, clapping his hands.

"Wait a minute!" I finally manage to say. Terry is already in the front seat, fastening his seat belt, pushing buttons, opening and closing the glove compartment like a hyperactive kid. "Hunter, what is this?" I say. "What the hell are you doing?"

He lifts his sunglasses from his eyes and stares me down defiantly. "My friend Terry here needs a ride. We're giving him a ride."

"Are you crazy? This guy? A fucking hitchhiker you met at a rest stop?"

Hunter shrugs.

"Don't I get a say in the matter? Were you going to consult me?"

"He's going to chip in some cash."

"I'm rich!" Terry exclaims from inside the car.

"Since when do you need Terry to chip in some cash?"

"Yeah, about that," Hunter says, scratching his nose. "I just got off the phone with His Majesty. He canceled my credit card."

For a few moments, I can only stare at him. "What does this mean?" I finally say. "Don't you have any cash? A debit card?"

"I have a little money in a checking account he can't touch," Hunter says. "But that has to last me until I get settled in San Francisco. It's an expensive city, you know. More expensive than New York, some say."

Why is he being so calm about this? "But we don't even know this guy. He could be an ax murderer." We simultaneously turn our heads to watch Terry tying his mop of black hair into a bun, trying out several pursed-lip poses in the rearview mirror as if for a photo shoot.

"I really doubt that," Hunter says. "I think he'd have a hard time even lifting an ax, never mind swinging it hard enough to hurt us."

"No," I say. "Hunter, this is ridiculous. You can't do this."

He opens the driver's side door and sits down. "Well, guess what? This is my car. And I want to do it. And quite frankly, I'm looking forward to having some company besides you."

I'm too mad for that to even hurt.

"You can stay here if you want," he says. "Catch a ride with a nice trucker."

"I would not recommend that," Terry yells from the front seat. "I'm a recent escapee from a truck driver. He was not a polite man. All hands. And I'm not nearly as pretty as you are."

Hunter turns the car on. Terry keeps babbling, "Which way are we going? Staying on the eighty? Going to Wyoming? Are we going to meet cowboys? I love cowboys!" I can't believe Hunter would rather spend hours in a car with this person instead of me.

Hunter pulls his door shut and the car starts moving. I run after it and pound on the side until he stops. I get in the back and slam the door, and Hunter starts driving again.

"Road trip!" Terry squeals.

"One more thing," Hunter says, merging onto the freeway. "We're taking a detour to South Dakota."

"What? No. That's going backward. That's not the plan."

"Change of plans." Hunter drifts into the left lane and starts driving fast, too fast.

"We didn't talk about this. You can't just decide that."

"My car. My decision. What do you think, Terry?"

"South Dakota! I bet there's cowboys in South Dakota. There were some in Nebraska where I'm from, but they didn't like me very much."

"See, Terry's on board."

"Just tell me why."

Hunter guns the engine and passes a car on the right. "If His Majesty canceled my credit card, it probably means he thought to look at how I've been using it, which means he can trace our whole trip along the eighty."

"So?"

"So he can pretty easily figure out where we are if we stay on it."

"Why does that matter?"

"Oh, did I forget to tell you that part? He reported the car as stolen. Got his friends in the police department to send out an APB or something. Or so he claims. He could totally be bluffing. But better not to take any chances."

"Ooh, we're on the run!" Terry exclaims. "Like Bonnie and Clyde! And their sidekick Terry!"

"Jesus, Hunter! Now we're fugitives?"

"Not you, just me."

"But I'm like an accessory or something."

Terry claps appreciatively. "You guys should have your

own reality show." He tears open a bag of Skittles and pops one in his mouth. "I would totally watch it like every week, even the commercials."

"I can't believe this." I lean back in the seat and close my eyes. I feel the beginning of a headache.

"You're free to leave any time," Hunter reminds me. But what does that even mean? Where would I go? Back to Wellspring? How would I even get there? What choice do I have but to stay with these crazy people?

"This is going to be such a fun trip, you guys," Terry says, then reaches back and shoves his bag of candy in my face. "Skittle?"

"No, thank you."

"Tell me about yourself, Kinsey. What are your hopes and dreams? What are your biggest fears and regrets?"

"Those are big questions, Terry," Hunter says.

"Small talk is for small people, Hunter. That's what my granny used to say."

"She sounds like a wise woman."

"She was. Until her brain got all chewed up." Terry buries his face in the bulky scarf, closes his eyes and mutters something, then comes back up for air. His big blue eyes bore into me. "Kinsey, why are you so sad?"

"Who said I was sad?"

"I got the sense that—"

"You don't know anything about me," I snap. "And I don't want to talk about my hopes and dreams with you. I don't want to talk to you at all. I don't even know why you're in this car."

Terry just blinks. Did I break through his crazy cheerfulness? Did that really shut him up?

"I think you need some candy," he finally says, presenting me with a bag of M&M's. In that short time, he already inhaled the Skittles. "They're kind of melty, but you can stick your finger in and get a good scoop and lick it off. Here."

I swat his hand away harder than I mean to.

"Ouch," he says. Is his bottom lip trembling? Will I get that satisfaction?

"Jesus, Kinsey," Hunter says. "Stop being such a bitch. He's just trying to be friendly."

"I don't want to be his friend. I don't need any friends."

"Everyone needs friends," Terry says, bubbly once again. What is his problem? Why can't he stay hurt like a normal person? "Friends are the most important—"

"Terry, shut up!" Hunter and I say in unison.

"Sorry," he says, then makes a motion like zipping up his lips. Why is he so resilient? Can't he feel pain? Why do I want to hurt him so much?

"Kinsey, what is wrong with you?" Hunter says. "I think I like the sad you better than whoever this is."

"What's wrong with *me*? What's wrong with *you*? You're the one who picked up some crazy hitchhiker at a rest stop." I don't care that Terry's here. I don't care about hurting his feelings. "What's that about? What, I turned you down, so you like boys now?"

"Whoa, Kinsey, you are fucking out of line."

"Can you please stop fighting?" Terry pleads, wrapping the hideous scarf tighter around his neck.

"You're upsetting the kid, dear," Hunter snarls.

"Fuck you."

"Fuck you, too."

"You must really mean a lot to each other if you have to fight so much," Terry says, sticking his finger in his bag of melted chocolate. "Otherwise, why would you bother? Right?" He inspects his chocolate-covered finger. "You have a very passionate relationship." He sticks the slimy thing in his mouth. "So that's a positive way to look at things." I can hear the fragments of candy coating crunching between his teeth. "You guys are great," Terry says, grinning a rainbow-speckled, brown-toothed grin. "I'm having so much fun already, and we've only gone, like, six miles."

Hunter drives in silence and I continue to sulk in the backseat. Luckily, Terry fell asleep after finishing his fourth bag of candy, which is good for him because I think I might have really hurt him if he kept talking for much longer. With his silence, I feel a little less on edge. But I am slightly nauseous with Hunter's fast driving, the vending machine breakfast, and the alternating waves of anger and sadness rushing through me.

The monotony of Nebraska gives way to the grassy, flat nothingness of South Dakota and I realize I haven't talked to my mother in several days. Never in my life did I think I would *want* to talk to her. But now, I'd settle for anything familiar. "Can I use your phone?" I ask Hunter when we stop at a gas station, breaking nearly three hours of silence.

"Be quick," he says. "We're just stopping for gas."

I disconnect his phone from the stereo and switch it off airplane mode. It pings with new voice mails and text messages.

I don't know who I was expecting to find on the other end. Maybe the tired, sad Mom who told me she was proud of me. But that woman didn't last long. She has already been replaced by her more familiar evil twin.

"I hope you're using protection," is the first thing she says when I tell her it's me.

"No, Mom. It's not like that."

"Don't lie to me. Don't try to pull your little prissy Puritan act. Watch, you're going to end up getting knocked up too young just like me and ruin your life. Stupidest thing I ever did."

I try to ignore the blades tearing into my heart.

"We're in Wyoming," I lie. "It's pretty."

"Don't bother coming back," she says. "I won't be here. I'm going to Italy."

"With who?"

"Steve."

"Who's Steve?"

"None of your business."

"Is he your boyfriend?"

"I'll leave your stuff in the house if you want it."

"When are you going to Italy?"

"As soon as possible."

"Do you already have tickets?"

"The mosquitoes are homicidal this summer. Fucking bastards."

"Mom, when are you leaving?"

"God, I can't wait to get out of here."

"When?"

"I'm never looking back."

"Mom, *when*?"

"Jesus, you're annoying. Like a mosquito going 'buzz buzz buzz' in my ear when I'm trying to sleep."

"I just want to know when you're leaving."

"I swat and swat at you but you never go away."

Something small and round hits me in the shoulder. Terry is standing by the car with a new bag of candy. "I got snacks!" he says. He throws another piece and it hits me in the heart. Such a stupid little gesture, but he has no idea how much it hurts.

"Mom?" I say, but the line is dead. She is not there. She hung up.

I swallow the lump in my throat and walk to the car. My only choice right now is to be numb, to push this feeling down so deep I won't feel it. I don't know if I can survive anything else. My only choice is to just let go of any foolish hope I'm still hanging on to, any expectation that she could be someone different. This is the mother I have. This is the mother I will always have.

"I'll keep driving, but we're switching at the next stop," Hunter says as I walk toward the car. He does not know my heart is broken. He does not know I have finally accepted that I am an orphan, that I am truly on my own. When we get to San Francisco, I won't even have him. We will part ways and I will be a lost country girl in a big city and no one will even know when it eats me alive.

As we drive through the endless grasslands of South Dakota,

I feel more and more disgusted with myself. Every thought that goes through my head is some version of "Poor me," and I'm so sick of it, but I can't stop the litany of self-pity. Hunter's sitting next to me, yet he's so far away, locked into his own prison of self-loathing. Terry's in the backseat, looking out the window and dreaming his strange dreams. What a bunch of miserable, lonely creatures we are.

"Fuck!"

I wake to the sound of Hunter cursing and kicking the car. We are on the side of the freeway. I have never been hotter in my entire life. I slip in my own sweat on the leather seats as I crawl to the door. I can't get out of the car fast enough. But it's even worse outside with the sun beating down on my skin.

"I can see why these are called the Badlands," Terry says. He has his scarf wrapped loosely around his head now, like some desert nomad.

"Fuck, fuck, FUCK!" Hunter screams.

"What? What happened?"

"The air conditioner died," he says. "It's a hundred and seven degrees outside and the air conditioner just fucking died."

"Can you fix it?" I say, already feeling faint from the heat.

"No, I can't fix it. I'm not a mechanic. Are you? Terry, are you a mechanic?"

"No, but I worked on a farm last summer. I know how to pick tomatoes really fast. "

"We have to get out of here," I say. There's nothing but brown-red rock as far as the eye can see. Nothing living except us. Not even a cactus. Not even dead grass. This could be hell. This is hell.

"Hunter, we have to move. I'll drive. We'll roll the windows down. That's all we can do. The sun will set soon and it'll cool off. We can stop at the first town we get to."

"Wall!" Terry exclaims. How he manages to stay so enthusiastic in this heat is beyond me. "That's the first town after the Badlands. That's where Wall Drug is. America's Favorite Roadside Attraction! Seventy-six thousand square feet of retail wonderland. They give you a free bumper sticker even if you don't buy anything. I looked it up."

I get in the driver's seat and drive as fast as I can, but we keep getting stuck behind tourists going slow, taking pictures of the desolate scenery out of their rolled-up windows, comfortable inside with their AC blaring. Terry's panting out the window like a dog and Hunter's groaning in the backseat. We're in purgatory. Our sins are getting sweated from us. Hell is driving through the Badlands in the middle of summer with a broken air conditioner, stuck behind slow vehicles, too weak to speak, too sick to protest Terry's ongoing commentary. His voice adds to the surreal landscape, the unearthly heat, the smell of dust and creosote caking my nostrils.

"Do you think there's cowboys out here?" Terry says.

"Do you see any cows, Terry?" Hunter says. "There's no grass or water or cows or cowboys. There's nothing. This whole place is dead."

"But I bet cowboys could survive out here. They'd know how. Cowboys can survive just about anywhere. They're really quite versatile."

"Will you both please stop talking?" I say. "I have a really bad headache."

"You two sure are negative," Terry says. "The negative vibes in the car are suffocating. I know a lot about vibes, which may surprise you since I'm from Hazeldon, Nebraska, population eight hundred and seventy-three, which is not really a hotbed of alternative thinking. But there was this girl at my school, Sadie, and she was from Seattle, like the *city* Seattle in Washington State, where grunge music and coffee were invented, and she lived on this farm outside of town—in Hazeldon, not Seattle—with all these people with long hair who taught me all about chakras and auras and stuff, and also how to pick tomatoes really fast, and that's where I'm going, Seattle. Have you ever been there? Sadie says there's a market where they throw fish at you."

Neither Hunter nor I answer. I am light-headed from the heat. I am too weak to even say something mean.

"Hey, cheer up!" Terry says. "Your best friend may have just died but at least you still have each other."

I almost swerve off the road. "What did you say?"

"Huh?" Terry says.

"Hunter, did you just hear what Terry said?"

"I stopped listening to Terry several miles ago."

"Terry, what did you just say?"

He looks at me, perplexed. "I don't remember. If you haven't noticed, I just sort of talk all the time. I don't really pay attention to what I'm saying."

Sweat pours down my face, and my legs stick to the black leather seat. My brain is probably boiling inside my skull, becoming a mushy stew. It is so hot I'm hallucinating.

"Terry," Hunter says from the backseat. "Why the hell are you wearing that scarf?"

"My granny made it."

"It's over a hundred degrees. Don't you think your granny would want you to take it off? Just looking at you is making me ill."

"She's dead."

"Oh shit," Hunter says. "I'm sorry."

"Don't be sorry. You didn't kill her. Or at least I don't think you did. You don't seem like the killing type to me. She had old-timers' disease. The one where you forget stuff and then you die. I took care of her for a long time. Then the hospital did because I'm no doctor, in case you didn't notice. Then she died. But she never forgot how to knit, even after she forgot who I was. So even when she couldn't talk anymore and was peeing her pants all the time, she still kept knitting. It's not the prettiest thing, I'll admit. I didn't say she could knit well. I mean, how well can a person possibly knit when they're busy peeing their pants? It still smells like her. Not like pee, like her skin. Without pee on it."

"What about your parents?" I say. Maybe it's the heat and I don't have the energy for blind hatred, or maybe it's his sad story, but I feel a sudden warmth toward Terry, like maybe I don't want to leave him on the side of the road anymore.

"Oh, they were already dead. Meth lab explosion when I was five. I'm not even kidding. Cross my heart and pinkie swear. There should be a reality show about me!"

"I'd watch it," Hunter says.

"The worst part was cutting her toenails. Old people feet are gross. No offense, Granny, may you rest in peace. The nails just keep growing and growing, all thick and yellow-like. Did you know that nails keep growing after you die? So my granny's in the ground with some long fingernails and toes. But not my mom and dad or your friend because they burned up."

"You did it again!" I say. "You said something about Camille!"

"Kinsey, you're tripping," Hunter says.

"I don't know anyone named Camille. Pretty name though. If I was a girl, I'd like my name to be Camille. Sometimes I wish I was a girl. After Granny forgot who I was, she kept thinking I was a girl. The nurses thought it was funny. I liked it when she called me 'she.' Do you think you get manicures in heaven? I hope so. Like there's angels there that go around with their little lunch boxes full of colors, and you're sitting on a vibrating cloud chair? That would be great. I never got one before. I tried but Cathy, the lady in town who cuts hair out of her trailer, she wouldn't do it since I'm a boy and all. Oh well. Hey, did you know that I have a lot of money now? Because of my granny's life insurance policy?"

"Terry, you shouldn't tell people that," I say. "They might take advantage of you."

Terry sighs loud, melodramatically. "What I wouldn't give to be taken advantage of."

After a moment of silence, Hunter laughs. Then Terry laughs. Then the two of them are chuckling together like old friends, and I know something was just funny but I can't bring myself to feel it. So I just keep driving while they laugh without me, my sweat pooling beneath me on the leather seat.

"Terry, my friend," Hunter says. "You're like pathologically cheerful. It's not natural."

"What choice do I have?" he says, then sticks his head out the window, closes his eyes, and grins.

"Oh no!" Terry cries. "It's closed!"

His face is smashed against the front-door window of Wall Drug. The sign says it closes at 9:00 p.m. It is currently 9:13. We're just barely out of the Badlands and the cooler temperatures of the Black Hills are still so far away.

"Maybe we can go in the morning," Hunter says, patting Terry on the back.

"Promise?"

"Sure. Yeah."

It's Monday night, and the only things open in town are a cheap motel, a gas station, and an all-night diner.

"Guess we're splurging on a room tonight," Hunter says.

"Good thing I'm rich," Terry says.

A bell rings off-key when we enter the motel office, which smells like burned coffee and sweaty socks. The windows are steamy and an old TV in the corner is turned to the Home

Shopping Network. Bulletproof glass separates us from the front desk.

Hunter dings the bell on our side of the bulletproof glass. A small, hunched creature comes lurching out of a dark back room.

"How can I help you?" the person says with a croaking, indefinable accent. His (or her) face is droopy and unmoving on the left side, that eye bulging out like a frog's.

"Do you have any rooms?"

"One left. Two queen beds."

"Ooh, cozy," says Terry.

"Forty-nine ninety-nine. Complimentary bar of soap."

"Do you have a cot or something we can use?"

"A what?"

"A cot."

He/she just looks at me like I'm speaking a different language.

"Nonsmoking?" I say.

"All rooms are smoking."

"We'll take it," Terry says, slapping his ripped and bulging pink wallet on the counter.

To say the room is disgusting would be an understatement. Everything is old and dingy and unmatching, with cheap aluminum ashtrays on every surface and sad faded decorations from the 1970s. It smells like a mix of decades-old cigarette smoke and heavy-duty, probably toxic, cleansers. I try to open a window but they're all painted shut.

"I'm not sleeping in those sheets," Hunter says.

I press on the bed and it is nothing but squeaky, loose springs. My hand feels immediately dirty. I go to the bathroom to wash my hands and there, as promised, is the complimentary bar of soap wrapped in plastic. I look at myself in the cracked mirror and what I see scares me. It could be the fluorescent lights, it could be a combination of poor sleep and so many days on the road, but I look disturbingly like someone who belongs in a place like this. Disheveled. Broken. Lost.

"I can't tell if I'm hungry or if this place has made me lose my appetite," Hunter says.

"I'm starving," Terry says.

"Let's go to the diner," I say from the bathroom, attempting to pull my hair into a tidier ponytail. "It can't be much worse than this."

The night is black and violent. The hot wind howls apocalyptically and seems to grab at us from all directions, more like hands than air. A small child could be lost in this kind of weather; if you let go, he'd be swept away to disappear into the night with all the other garbage.

The diner is empty. A faded sign on the wall reads DOT'S DINER. It has been decorated to look like something nostalgic out of the 1950s, with red-and-white-checkered tabletops and red vinyl booths, except all the booths are ripped, exposing yellow cigarette-smoke-stained stuffing; the linoleum floor is peeling; and the ancient jukebox in the corner is empty of records and isn't even plugged in.

"Let's leave," I say, suddenly feeling so depressed I can barely stand. But Terry is already spinning in circles on a stool at the counter.

An ancient, wiry woman pops out from the back. "Hi there!" she says way too cheerfully. Her hair is blue in the way only old ladies' hair can be blue, done up in a rat's-nest bouffant that appears to be held together by about a pound of bobby pins and a gallon of hair spray. Her face is caked with makeup, as if it's been spackled on over the years, layers and layers of it, applied with the expertise of a toddler. She's wearing a short skirt that might have been cute on someone fifty years younger, but all it does for her is show off her wrinkled knees and spider veins and orange-tinged support hose.

"You're in for a treat," she says. "You got me all to yourselves tonight."

I want to flee.

"Great! Are you Dot? My name's Terry. Pleased to meet you."

"I'm Cindy," she says. "But you can call me anything you want." She winks at Hunter. "Sit wherever. But if you sit at the counter you get to talk to me." She smiles big and reveals a huge pink smear of lipstick on her cracked yellow teeth.

"I'm staying here then," Terry says, but Hunter slides into a booth and I join him. "Don't worry, Dot," Terry whispers. "It's not that they don't want to talk to you. They have some things to work out. You know, lovers' quarrel."

I open my mouth to protest, but realize it's not worth it. Hunter and I sit at the booth, facing each other but not looking up. I pretend to be looking at my menu, but mostly I'm wishing I had gone straight to bed instead of coming here.

"Where's the cook?" Terry says.

"You're looking at her," says the waitress.

"Where's the dishwasher?"

"That's me."

"You're here all alone?"

"Yep."

"Aren't you lonely? What if you get busy and you need help? Are you scared? Is it safe? Should I be worried about you, Dot?"

"I'm a tough cookie."

"Will you make me some pancakes?"

"Absolutely."

"And a chocolate milk shake?"

"Coming right up."

"I like your positive attitude, Dot. You remind me of my granny. That's like the biggest compliment I could ever give you."

"Well, thanks, sweetie. What about your quiet friends over there? Are you two eating? Or are you just going to stare at your hands and not talk to each other while Terry eats the best pancakes of his life?"

"I'll have pancakes, too," Hunter says. "And bacon."

"Same," I say, too tired to even think about what I want to eat.

We sit there in silence, our heads turned to watch Cindy's back as she pours what looks like a cup of oil on the already greasy grill. She whistles while Terry drums off rhythm with his silverware. It's excruciating. I don't care about the pancakes. I don't even care about the bacon. I want out of here. I can't stand being so close to someone I feel so far away from.

"I have something I need to ask you, Kinsey," Hunter says severely, as if he's reading my mind, as if he too is obsessing on what has happened between us in the last few days. Part of me desperately wants to talk, to answer whatever question he's about to ask me, but part of me still wants to run.

"What?" I say, instantly tensing, readying for war.

There's a dramatic pause. Bacon sizzles and fills the diner

with its intoxicating aroma. Terry's stool squeaks as he spins around and around. I turn my head and look Hunter in the eye.

He looks at me very seriously, then finally speaks: "Was that person in the hotel office a man or a woman?"

I blink. Then he smiles. Then I smile. "I was wondering the same thing," I say.

Cindy delivers our food, two plates stacked with pancakes and bacon swimming in grease. Hunter and I thank her and start eating and I've never tasted anything so delicious and disgusting in my life.

We eat quietly for a few minutes, but the silence is not as uncomfortable as before. Something is salvageable. A chasm has been crossed between us; our lonely worlds have touched.

"What are we even fighting about?" I say after a few bites.

He takes a bite of his bacon and chews as he considers this question. "We're fighting over which one of us is the most broken."

The sad truth of this sinks in. "So which one of us is the winner?" I say.

"We both lose."

I pick at my food. I press the pancakes with my fork and watch them absorb the grease and butter and fake maple syrup like sponges.

"The way I see it," Hunter says, "we have three options. One, we can spend the rest of this trip not talking to each other. Two, we can be polite and talk bullshit small talk. Or three, we can get real."

"I'm guessing you'd prefer the third option."

"Don't you?"

I honestly don't know. I know I'm sick of our silence, but I also know I don't want to tell him the truth about Camille, the truth about how crazy I am. I don't want to talk about me.

"Okay," I say. "Fine. Let's get real. Were you trying to die when you took all that Valium?"

"No," he says automatically, then looks down at his plate. After a moment, he looks up at me. "Maybe," he says. "But not consciously. I don't remember a whole lot. I don't remember what I was thinking most of the time."

"What do you remember? What's the last thing you remember?"

"I remember knowing I had gone too far. I was sitting in the car and all I could see was black, and it felt like my world was so small, just a black box that I was never getting out of, and it kept getting smaller and smaller until I couldn't move. I remember trying to move my arms and not being able to. I tried to call to you, but I couldn't make a sound. It was getting hard to breathe. The last thing I remember thinking was, 'Oh shit, I really fucked up.'"

"I don't understand how that can happen," I say. "Unless you really want to die."

"I lost track of how much I had taken, so I kept taking more."

"But don't you feel it? Doesn't your body tell you when it's enough?"

"It's never enough," Hunter says. "That's the problem."

We sit there in silence while Cindy scrapes the grill clean and Terry tells her about everything he wants to see at Wall Drug. Somehow their being here seems to be making this conversation possible, like we trust that nothing too bad can happen with them as witnesses.

"There's no in-between, you know?" Hunter says. "There's no space between too fucked-up and not fucked-up enough. That's the place I keep looking for, the place I've always looked for, the perfect spot where everything feels just right. But it doesn't exist. And I know that. But I keep looking for it anyway."

"You were talking to her," I say. "To Camille." It hurts to say her name. "When you were half-conscious. Do you remember?"

"No."

"Did you see her? Was she there? Was she talking to you?"

He looks at me strangely, and I realize I'm acting too eager, too excited. "What? You want to know if her ghost came to welcome me to the world of the dead?"

Yes, that's exactly what I want to know. It sounds so stupid when he says it. He laughs the question off.

"Now your turn," he says.

"What?"

"You know what. On the cliff. Were *you* trying to die?"

I don't know the answer. I don't know who it was that decided to hike to the top of the quarry, who decided to step over that fence.

"I don't know," I tell him, and I know it's the exact thing he doesn't want to hear.

"Oh, come on, Kinsey. I talked."

"But it's the truth. I don't know what I was doing there."

"You were going to jump. I saw you. You were walking toward the edge. If I had gotten there ten seconds later, you'd be vulture food at the bottom of that quarry."

"I wasn't going to jump," I say, but I know it is a lie.

"Yeah, you were just looking at the view," he says, disgusted. "Cindy, can we get our bill?"

"No can do, handsome," she says. "Your friend here already paid. He's a real high-roller."

"Thanks, Terry," I say, and start to get up.

"Are you even capable of being real?" Hunter demands, grabbing my hand and forcing me back down. "Are you even aware of all the ways you're in denial?"

"Denial?" I say too loudly. "You're asking *me* about denial?"

"I'm talking about Camille. You can barely even say her

name out loud, but I know you think about her all the time. You think if you die you get to be with her again?"

I shake my head, trying to knock his words out of my ears. But no matter what I do, I can't unhear them. "No," I say, choking on the lie.

"Talk to me."

"I can't." I try to pull my hand away, but he holds on tighter.

"Yes you can. You've talked to me before."

It's true, but now he is too close. If I let him in any more, he's going to see too much. He's going to see something that's going to scare him, something that will make him go away.

"I'm tired," I say, looking away. What a cop-out. Everything I say and do anymore is a cop-out.

He sighs and drops my hand. "Yeah," he says. "I'm tired too." And I know how to complete that sentence; I know the words he thought but didn't say: *I'm tired of you, Kinsey.*

Hunter's the first to walk out the door.

Terry gives Cindy a big hug and says, "I'll never forget you, Dot," then runs out the door after Hunter. Then it's just me and Cindy and the aftermath of our conversation.

"Something else for you, honey?"

"No thanks," I say, getting up.

FOURTEEN

I thought sleeping in my sleeping bag would make me feel cleaner, but all it did was remind me how dirty my sleeping bag is. The air conditioner rattled and groaned all night long. I would have almost preferred sleeping in the car on the side of the road.

But worse was my regret. Worse was wishing I could redo our conversation in the diner, wishing I was brave enough to tell Hunter the truth. Terry fell asleep on the couch immediately, so lucky to have nothing rattling around in his strange head to keep him up at night. It took me forever to fall asleep. The three feet of floor between Hunter's and my bed wasn't enough, but it was also too much. I wanted to reach out and touch him. I wanted to crawl into his bed and wrap his arms around me. I wanted him to make me warm.

We make good on Hunter's promise and go to Wall Drug before we get on the road. I sit in the restaurant section staring at half a doughnut while Terry runs around the place like a maniac and Hunter does who knows what. I have the familiar toxic feeling in my gut, the combination of sugar for breakfast and the agonizing push and pull of wanting and fearing the same thing. And what that thing is, I can't quite define. Is it Hunter I want? Or do I just need to speak, to tell the truth to someone, anyone? Do I want a warm body? Do I just need someone to be close to, and he's the one who happens to be here?

Or maybe Hunter has nothing to do with it. Maybe Camille has nothing to do with it. Maybe I'm going crazy and it's as simple as that.

I am so sick of all these maybes.

"Hey, Kinsey!" Terry yells, and falls into the booth. He is soaking wet. His scarf looks like an animal that died by drowning.

"Why are you wet?"

"The Train Station Water Show. It's out back. You want to see it?"

"No thanks."

He holds up a handful of stuffed plastic bags. "I got souvenirs," he says proudly.

"You shouldn't waste all your money like that. It's not going to last forever. You should save it for something important."

"I'm not wasting it," he says with conviction. "These are *memories*. They *are* important." He starts pulling out his treasures and displaying them proudly on the table: a stack of postcards, a kid's picture book about gold mining, a cheap imitation turquoise necklace, a set of plastic cowboys, a huge shiny belt buckle, a handful of colorful rocks, a souvenir thimble, a couple of T-shirts, and tons and tons of candy.

"What is this?" I ask, pointing to a stuffed animal that appears to be a rabbit with antlers.

"That's a jackalope," Terry says. "Duh."

"Hey," Hunter says, sitting down next to Terry with a giant cup of coffee.

"Did you see the T. rex?" Terry says.

"Yeah."

"Did it scare you?"

"Totally."

"Are you going to eat that?" Terry says, pointing to the half doughnut in front of me.

"Nope, knock yourself out."

"Ready to go?" Hunter says.

"Wait one minute," Terry says, stuffing a piece of fudge in his mouth before he's even done chewing the doughnut. "I've asked to see the manager. Oh, goody, here he comes."

A pale girl in an apron leads a fat man with a clipboard over to the table. "Larisa said you asked to see me," the man says. "Is everything all right?" The girl named Larisa shifts on her feet, frightened.

"Hunter and Kinsey, this is Larisa. She's from Latvia." Her name tag does indeed say, "Larisa, *Latvia*."

"Do you have a complaint?" the man says, his fake smile showing the beginnings of impatience. "Was the hospitality you received from Larisa less than satisfactory?"

"No!" Terry says. "I love Larisa! I love everything about this place!"

Larisa blushes and looks around, as if for an escape route. The manager stands there blinking.

"I just wanted to tell you that," Terry says.

"Tell me what?"

"That you're doing a great job."

The manager blinks some more.

"Also, I have an idea. I met a bunch of your wonderful employees today. Larisa from Latvia, Boris from Serbia, Maria from the Philippines. I was thinking a great way to make sure your visitors get to know them a little better would be to make a game, like a scavenger hunt kind of, where you have a score-card and you have to go around and find each employee and ask them a personal question, like how do you like working at Wall Drug? Or how do you like living in America? Or what do you want to be when you grow up? What is your favorite TV show? Are you right- or left-handed? And when you get all the answers, you bring your scorecard to the gift shop and you get a prize, like a T-shirt or a coffee cup or something."

Hunter slaps Terry on the back and laughs. "I for one think that's a great idea."

"Thank you, Hunter."

"Is that all?" the manager says.

"Also, this fudge is great. And the T. rex almost made me pee my pants."

Oh, what I wouldn't give to live inside Terry's blissful, unsullied mind.

As we climb into the Black Hills, the temperature drops down to a reasonable level. With it, Hunter's and my spirits rise, and we seem to forget that we still haven't completely made up. Terry finds a radio station with cheesy old pop ballads, and we all sing along at the top of our lungs, serenading the rocky crags of South Dakota.

"I've never had my own phone," Terry says as he fiddles with Hunter's cell phone, which has been on airplane mode for days.

"Me neither," I say.

"How do I get on the Internet?"

"You have to turn airplane mode off."

"Airplane mode?" Terry says. "But we're in a car."

"Why do you want to get on the Internet?" Hunter says.

"Why *don't* I want to get on the Internet?" Terry answers. "It's the information highway, Hunter. Get with the program."

I show Terry how to turn the phone on and it immediately starts dinging with text messages.

"Do you want to read these?" Terry asks.

"Nope."

"There's like twenty messages."

"I don't care."

"What if there's something important?"

"Fine, then you read them to me."

"What if there's something private?"

"I keep no secrets from you, Terry."

"Well, I'm honored," he says. He starts scrolling through the messages. "The first one's from someone named His Majesty. Who's that?"

"My dad."

"Your dad's a king?"

"He thinks he is."

"Well, he says, 'Turn your ass around and come home right now.'" In Terry's übercheerful, Midwestern drawl, the demand sounds comical.

Hunter laughs. "No thanks, Dad."

"'I mean it.'"

"Ha."

"This is fun!" Terry says. "It's like role-playing."

"What else, Dad?"

"'Your mom's worried sick.'"

"Oh, that's a nice touch."

"Your mom probably *is* worried sick," I say, not liking where this is going, not finding this amusing at all.

"Next," is all Hunter says.

"'You've been nothing but a disappointment from the day you were born,'" Terry reads. "Oh, that's not nice at all."

Hunter stays silent.

"I don't want to read any more," Terry says.

"Keep going."

"I don't want to."

"Keep going."

I don't know what the point of this is. I don't know what he's trying to prove. Is this the way he works through things? Making himself hurt for no reason?

"'You know you're probably not even my son,'" Terry reads carefully. "'My son would never be this stupid. Ask your dumb whore of a mother.'" Then Terry starts crying.

Hunter reaches over, calmly plucks the phone out of Terry's hand, opens his window, and throws it onto the freeway.

"Oops," he says.

"Now we don't have a phone," I say.

"Now we don't have a phone," Hunter says.

"Why is your dad so *mean*?" Terry cries.

"What if we need it?" I say.

"Who are you going to call, Kinsey? Your mom?"

I don't know if he was trying to hurt me, but all I feel is numb. No, I'm not going to call my mom. Who else is there? Camille is dead. There's no one left. I'm attached to no one. The weight of that takes my breath away.

"You know what's funny?" I say.

"What?" Hunter says.

"You're probably the only one of us who actually has someone looking for you."

"That's not funny at all," says Terry.

"I'm totally alone. So are you. So is Terry. We all are."

"That's silly," Terry says. "How can we be alone if we're all sitting right here in the same car?" He reaches back and takes my hand, and for some reason I let him. His skinny long fingers wrap around mine and I don't let go. We drive like that for miles.

Signs for Mount Rushmore, a reptile zoo, a dinosaur park, and several other tourist attractions dot the highway as the desolation of southern South Dakota transforms into Rapid City. In the silence of the car, during a short lull in Terry's monologue and without the music on Hunter's phone, it hits me that I haven't seen or heard from Camille for quite a while. In all that time, I barely even noticed. I should be thrilled, relieved, something. I should feel *something*. Wasn't that the whole point of this trip? To stop the hauntings? To stop the nightmares? So why does it suddenly seem like it's about something entirely different, something that is not at all about Camille?

Where is she? Have I really outrun her? Is this too far for a ghost to travel? Is she fading the farther I get from home, the closer I get to my destination? Or maybe it has something to do with getting closer to Hunter. Maybe letting him in is pushing her out.

But she's not gone. Not completely, not yet. I can still feel her presence. I can feel her watching me, laughing silently to herself.

"FAIR!" Terry screams.

The car swerves. "Jesus, Terry," Hunter snaps. "Don't shout like that. I almost drove off the road."

Terry is beside himself, practically crawling over the back of his seat to get a better look at the sign we just passed.

"County fair!" he cries. "Right NOW." He is breathless. He is so excited he can barely speak. "Right there!" He points and we all look. In the distance are the fairgrounds, packed with tents and rides and acres of parking.

"Please, Hunter," Terry says so softly and earnestly, it pulls at my heart a little despite how ridiculous the idea is. His eyes are glassy with yearning. "The sign said there was a *rodeo*."

I can tell Hunter is trying not to laugh. We share a moment of smiling eye contact in the rearview mirror.

"Okay, Terry," he says. "If it means so much to you, we'll go to the fair."

Terry practically jumps into his lap with a hug.

The parking lot is full of trucks. Terry jumps out of the car and wraps his scarf around his neck with a swish, and I instinctively scan the area to see if anyone was looking. This is the kind of place where bad things happen to guys like Terry.

"Elephant ears!" he cries, and runs ahead to a rusty old box on wheels housing a girl and a deep fryer.

I see cowboy hats everywhere. Plaid shirts. Belt buckles. Stiff jeans. Boots. A young girl leads a tiny cow proudly through the crowd and people look on approvingly. We pass a tent that says POULTRY AND SMALL ANIMALS, where people sit around on folding chairs to watch the judging of chickens.

"You guys!" Terry runs up breathlessly, his face sticky with cinnamon and sugar, his elephant ear already half gone. "There's a rodeo happening *right now*."

"Then we better go to the rodeo," says Hunter.

We take our seats behind a family of rowdy boys high on cotton candy. As Hunter and Terry cheer and yell with the rest of the crowd, I watch the mother, beside herself, begging her sons to stop climbing on the bleachers. Her husband is no help. He sips on his giant Mountain Dew between spits of chewing tobacco, yelling various obscenities; at whom, I'm not quite sure. The rodeo rider? His horse? The calf he's trying to rope? The boys are all tiny versions of their father, in dirty sleeveless T-shirts and ragged jeans, their sinewy, frenetic arms constantly grabbing, hitting, pulling. The only thing they're missing is his collection of faded, globular tattoos. An American flag. A pinup girl. A beer can. An Aryan-looking Jesus. Their necks are all sunburned red.

I can hear my mom's voice in my head saying, "Look, they really do have red necks," with her judgmental snarl. But then I realize I was thinking the same thing. I'm no better than her. I'm no better than any of these people. And then another realization hits me—I may never hear her actual voice again. She could be in Italy right now. She may never come back. I may never see her again.

The crowd roars as the cowboy ropes up the calf's legs. A blond woman in an American flag bikini rides sidesaddle around the arena on a white horse, holding a flag with the event's sponsor's logo on it. For a moment, I picture Camille in her place. I'm sure they started out in life much the same, as pretty, horse-loving girls from small towns. And now this girl is the lucky one simply for being alive, despite the fact that she's riding around half-naked in a pit of mud and horse shit, bombarded by whistles and catcalls.

"Oh, I love this one," Terry says as the next event is announced over the loudspeaker. I can see a rider being prepped behind a metal fence. "This is the one with the bucking broncos."

A bell buzzes and the crowd erupts as the horse and rider are released. Terry gasps. The man is a real-life cowboy, with tasseled chaps and a big black hat, his right arm raised for balance while the left holds on to the reins for dear life. The horse bucks and writhes, but still he holds on, his body undulating with the horse's violent jerks. His face is stone concentration. When he's finally kicked off, he lands gracefully on his feet and glides to the fence.

"I love him," Terry says breathlessly, hands clasped at his chest.

"Terry, don't talk so loud," I whisper-shout.

He doesn't hear me. His eyes are glued to the rider being led out of the area by the bikini woman, the fence flanked by adoring fans.

"I'm starving," Hunter announces. "Let's go get some food." I have to shake Terry out of his daze and pull him to his feet.

After a lunch of corn dogs, French fries, and nachos and an unwise ride on the Tilt-A-Whirl, we lie on our backs in a grass field by the stables, trying to stop the spinning. The clouds are fluffy sculptures above us, morphing into animals, faces, entire landscapes.

"The good news is I don't think I'm going to puke anymore," Terry says.

"I'm not there yet," I groan, squeezing my eyes shut with a new wave of nausea.

"This is almost as bad as a hangover," Hunter says.

"This reminds me of being a baby," Terry says.

"You don't remember being a baby," I say.

"Sure I do. I remember lying in my crib like this, looking up at the ceiling."

"That's impossible."

"I had one of those light show things that make stars spin around in the dark."

"Sounds like a bad acid trip," Hunter says.

"Terry, what are you talking about?" I say.

"You know, those things people put in baby nurseries. Like there's a lightbulb inside a box, and the box has all these cutouts of stars or animals and stuff on the sides, and there's a motor inside that makes it spin around and the light shines through and the cutouts dance around the room. Like shadow puppets."

A bluegrass band starts playing somewhere in the distance. A woman's voice calls out bingo numbers.

"The lightbulb is like your brain, see?" Terry continues. "And the cutout patterns around it are like all the stuff your subconscious wants you to see, all your fears and self-hatred and misery and mistakes, and maybe sometimes if you refuse to see them, your brain does something to force you to. Like it turns the lightbulb on and puts on a light show so you can't ignore it anymore. It projects all the stuff around you so you'll see it, except it gets all distorted and warped and magnified as it wraps around the furniture and walls and your stuffed animals and everything, so it turns out way bigger and scarier than it really is. But the light show isn't real. All it really is is shadows."

Someone somewhere yells, "Bingo!"

"Frankly, I don't know what babies see in those things. I think they're terrifying and I'm practically a grown-up."

"Terry," Hunter says. "You have a fascinating mind."

Terry reaches over and grabs my hand. Again, I feel an uncanny, instant comfort. I turn my head and his pale blue eyes are looking right at me. He speaks to me directly when he says, "If you're lonely enough, even a ghost will keep you company."

I shiver as Terry's eyes bore into me. I have to look away.

"I think you need to stay off the sugar for a while," Hunter says.

My heart pounds in my chest. For a moment, I feel weightless, airborne, as if I've been picked up and thrown. Terry is still looking at me, his eyes warm and somehow ancient. His hand squeezes mine, and for some reason that's the thing that breaks me. Just that simple gesture and my eyes are waterfalls. Tears pool in my ears. If I stay on the ground like this, I will drown. The sadness will wash me away.

"I need to walk," I say. I sit up too fast and am instantly dizzy.

"Good idea," Hunter says. I wipe my face clean before he has a chance to notice the tears.

"I'm going to the stables," Terry says. "I'm going to see if I can get that cowboy's autograph."

"Are you sure?" I say, feeling a fierce need to protect him, to wrap him up and keep him safe. But there's also another feeling, like all the rules I'm used to have been turned upside down—maybe his presence is making *me* safe.

"I am always sure of everything I do," Terry says proudly. "Grandma said I was born without the self-doubt gene."

"I'm not sure if that's a blessing or a curse," Hunter says.

Terry shrugs, then leans over and kisses me on the forehead. "You'll be just fine," he says, then skips away.

Hunter and I walk around the rides, the air light with laughter and the smell of popcorn. I worry for Terry. I worry about his enthusiasm, his confidence, his hope. We live in a world that eats people like him. How can he not know that? How can he think he is safe among all these people who will never understand him? I don't feel safe, and I've been playing their game perfectly my entire life.

The paint on the rides is peeling. The metal creaks with years of travel, of being dismantled and put together again, city after city. Are there inspections? How do these people know the rides are safe? How can they trust their children to these rickety contraptions run by strangers?

"Kinsey, what's going on with you?" Hunter asks me as we pass the merry-go-round, all the smiling, unassuming kids who have no idea how dangerous the world is.

"Nothing."

"I thought we agreed you were going to stop with that shit."

I sigh. "Just something Terry said."

Hunter laughs. "Everything that comes out of that kid's mouth is nonsense. What could he possibly have said that upset you so much?"

"He's said things," I say carefully. "Things I don't think you heard." I search Hunter's face for signs he thinks I'm crazy, for a signal that I should either stop now or continue, but he's barely listening. He's looking at the row of carnival games. He doesn't want to hear my crazy theory that Terry is psychic, that he knows things about Camille. About me.

"Hey, let's play a game," Hunter says, pulling me in their direction.

"Those games are expensive."

"It'll be worth it, I swear."

"But they're all rigged."

"Oh, Kinsey, where's your sense of adventure?"

Hunter takes me to a booth with a bunch of balloons stuck to the wall, manned by a pockmarked guy with stringy red hair and a stained Confederate flag T-shirt. "Five dollars for three tries," the guy says without enthusiasm. "If you get all three, you get one of the prizes on the first level here." He points to the smallest row of cheap stuffed animals that probably cost a penny to make in China.

"You may not know this," Hunter says to me as he hands the guy his money and collects his three darts, "but I am quite the dart champion. Eli had a dartboard in his basement. I could get a bull's-eye even after a six-pack and a couple of joints."

"That's really something to be proud of."

"So," Hunter says, ignoring my sarcasm. "Let's make a bet. You decide what I have to do if I lose."

"Drive the rest of the way to San Francisco."

"Really, that's the best you got?"

I shrug. I'm obviously not finding this as amusing as he is. "And if you win?"

He smiles. "If I win, I quit drinking. For good."

I search his face for a sign that he's kidding, that he's just screwing with me. But his smile is genuine.

"Really?"

"Yes, really."

"You could just lose on purpose."

"That's true. I could."

The game attendant yawns. He has no idea how important his stupid dart game is right now.

Hunter takes a dart in his fingers, aims, and throws. He pops a blue balloon.

"Good job," the attendant says. He could not be any less excited.

Hunter aims again. A red balloon explodes.

"The moment of truth," Hunter says. "Pick a color."

"Yellow," I say.

He makes a big production about aiming, repositioning himself several times. "Yellow, you say?" He rocks back and forth on his feet. He turns around. Turns around again.

"Come on!"

He smiles, aims, and pops a yellow balloon.

"Congratulations," the attendant says in a dreary monotone. "Take your pick of these wonderful prizes or play again for the next row up."

"What do you think, Kins? Should I try again?"

"Let's quit while we're ahead."

"Then pick the prize," Hunter says, throwing his arm around my shoulders. "Will it be the rubber snake, the inflatable beer can, or this blue bear-looking thing?"

"The bear," I say. "The one with the pink nose."

The attendant hands it to me and I can't help but smile. This is the best five-dollar piece of crap I've ever gotten.

"You should name him," Hunter says.

"How about Terry Junior?"

He laughs and squeezes me against him. We walk like that back to the grassy patch to meet Terry, Hunter's arm around my shoulders like we could be any happy couple at the fair. Hunter could be any boy who won his girl a prize. I could be that girl.

We find Terry sitting on the grassy patch with his backpack on. Even from several yards away, I can see him bouncing on his seat, unable to sit still; he's practically vibrating. He jumps up when he sees us, as if there are springs under him.

"Look what Hunter won," I say, holding out the cheap blue bear. "We named him after you."

"I'm honored," Terry gasps.

"What's with the backpack?" Hunter asks.

"Oh!" he cries, overcome with emotion. He grabs my shoulder for balance. "You won't believe it! Dreams do come true. This is a magical place. I knew it the second I saw the sign on the freeway."

I have no idea what he's talking about, but I look at Terry Junior in my hands and have to agree.

"I got a job! With the rodeo! I start *right now!*" Terry says, grabbing both our hands.

"Did I leave the car unlocked?" Hunter says.

"I'm a stable boy!" he exclaims. "Doesn't that sound *sexy?*"

"Wait, you're leaving us?" I say. I'm shocked by how sad this makes me. Wasn't it just a few hours ago that I couldn't stand Terry?

"Was our stuff okay?" Hunter says.

"I get to help take care of the horses and the cows and feed them and brush them and go on the road and hang out with the cowboys," he says as he unwinds his scarf from around his neck. "With *my* cowboy. Jimmy. His name is Jimmy." Terry is breathless, love struck. "I met him. He *likes* me."

"How did all this happen in less than an hour?" I say.

"I told you this place is magic," he says. He holds out the slightly moist pile of scarf. Without it wrapped around his thin neck, he is suddenly transformed, an ugly duck turned into a swan, almost beautiful. His black hair makes his pale skin porcelain. His glasses enhance his long curled lashes and bright blue eyes. His long neck makes him regal, elegant.

He dumps the scarf in my hands, makes a nest, and plops Terry Junior in the middle.

"I want you and Terry Junior to have this."

"Terry, I can't. It's from your grandma."

"She'd want you to have it." Something tells me not to object. "It's a good luck scarf. I got my wish. Now it's your turn."

I throw my arms around him and squeeze him tight. He's so thin, but not fragile like I first thought, not brittle like a bird.

"There he is!" Terry cries when I let go. I turn around and see the handsome rodeo cowboy, riding toward us on a big black horse. He waves and Terry bounces over to Hunter for a hug good-bye. Hunter looks confused, half his mind still worried about the car, not comprehending the surreal scene in front of us: the cowboy offering his hand and pulling Terry onto the horse, Terry wrapping his arm around his waist, the cowboy tipping his hat to us, Terry waving like a beauty queen in a parade as the horse takes them into the sunset, the sky an explosion of orange neon behind them, their entwined figures receding into its flashy brilliance until all that's left is the romantic afterglow.

"Did that just really happen?" Hunter says.

"I'm not sure." I look at the cheap blue bear nestled in the homely scarf in my hands, and I don't think I've ever held anything so valuable.

My heart aches a little as I realize I'll miss Terry. But maybe that's okay. Maybe he was supposed to touch my life in exactly this way, bless it with his special magic, then move on to share it with someone else.

Maybe Terry found his cowboy. Maybe they really did just ride off into the sunset together. Maybe I was wrong and the world isn't as cruel as I think it is. Maybe there are happy endings, even for kids like Terry. Even for Hunter, and even for me.

The next five hours are too quiet without Terry. There are no decent radio stations in the middle of nowhere and neither Hunter nor I want to talk. It's not an unpleasant silence, but it seems heavy with meaning, full of things that need to be said. I can't stop thinking about what Terry said on the grass. I can't stop wondering if what he said was more than nonsense, if loneliness alone can make somebody crazy.

Terry Junior sits on the dashboard facing us, his calm smile unchanging, watching over us with his shiny black plastic eyes.

Wyoming is rugged in a way Michigan is not, even the Upper Peninsula. Everywhere we've been so far—Wisconsin, Illinois, Iowa, Nebraska, even South Dakota—seems so tame in comparison. It feels like an entry to somewhere wild and primal. The farther we drive into the harsh scrub, the farther from civilization I feel, the farther from everything familiar. The huge sky surrounds us on all sides and there is no turning back.

We camp for the night in a place whose sign said it was an RV park and campground, but it is really just a big, empty, dusty parking lot. A few broken-down RVs seem to have set up camp a few years ago and aren't going anywhere. One is wheel-less and up on blocks. Another has pots of faded fake flowers outside the door. An old dog is chained up to a fence and is too depressed to even bark at us as we park on our designated concrete slab. The night is lit by the blinking light of televisions inside the RVs.

Hunter makes a fire and gets dinner ready while I set up the tent. After all these stops, we've finally developed a good system for setting up camp. But it barely matters now. We're only two states away from the end. Our trip is almost over.

We cook hot dogs on sticks over the fire. "I can't believe I'm saying this, but I miss Terry," I say.

"I miss him too," Hunter says. "Crazy bastard."

We sit in silence for a while, watching the hot dogs turn brown and bubbly. As the sky darkens and we finish dinner, Hunter suddenly jumps up and starts running in place.

"What are you doing?"

He stops running, clenches his fists, and makes a sound like a pained growl. "I feel itchy."

"I have some calamine lotion. It works pretty well on mosquito bites."

"No," he says, stretching his arms above his head. "Like itchy *inside*. Like I've been sitting in a car too long. Like I need a drink."

My heart drops and I say nothing. What am I supposed to say? Am I supposed to forbid it like I'm his mother? Am I supposed to beg him not to?

He runs over to the car and opens the trunk, where the box of remaining bottles has been waiting like a loaded gun these fragile days he's been sober. I can't watch this. I can't just sit here while he does this. I stand up, but I don't have the anger to storm off. I'm just sad. Deflated.

"Watch this," he says. Watch what? Watch you destroy yourself? Watch you turn into a drooling, puking fool? For a moment, I think of running over to the car and getting Terry Junior and throwing him into the fire to make a point.

Hunter pulls a bottle out of the box, unscrews the cap, and pours it into the fire.

Red light blinds me as the fire explodes. My face burns.

Glass breaks and car tires squeal and I am lost and alone on a road in the night.

No. I open my eyes and the fire has returned to normal. There is no glass and no car and no road, just the air tinged with the sweet acid smell of burning alcohol. Hunter stands beside me. He pulls another bottle out of the box and hands it to me. "You try."

The bottle is cool and so solid in my hands. I pour it in slowly and the fire sputters.

"You have to do it with more pizzazz," Hunter says. He waves a bottle around, the splashes of liquor making little bursts of pyrotechnics.

We drain the rest of the bottles like that, cackling into the night like mad witches, pouring our potions into the fire and making magic. The fire grabs at Hunter with its red hands; it lights his face, burns its reflection into his eyes. But Hunter is its master tonight, scars and all. The fire cannot hurt him now.

And then all we have left is a cardboard box and empty bottles. We sit on a log, staring at the fire that looks like any old fire, not one that just burned and evaporated so much poison.

"It's all gone," Hunter says.

"How does it feel?"

"Kind of awesome. Kind of scary," he says. Then after a pause, "Really scary."

I reach over and hold his hand. The people in the RVs have turned off their TVs and gone to bed. The night is black around us, but the fire bathes us in warm light. We are surrounded by the unknown, but I feel safer than I have in a long time. And what's the point of safety but to make us brave enough to do something that will scare us again?

Hunter did something that scared him. He took back the fire. He tamed the thing that scarred him. Now it is my turn.

I take a deep breath. "What did Camille say about me?" I say.

He looks at me, his face throbbing with firelight.

"Tell me. I can handle it."

"She said you were best friends since you were four." He's trying to make his voice light, casual, as if this is going to be a light conversation. "She loved you very much."

"You're patronizing me."

"No I'm not."

"Tell me the hard stuff."

"Really?"

"All of it."

Hunter takes a deep breath and squeezes my hand. "She said you were too attached to your plans."

"Yeah, she always teases me about that," I say. "I mean, teased."

"She said you were too attached to her." He looks at me to see if he should go further. He cannot see my heart torn to shreds. "It drove her crazy. She said you treated her like you were both still ten years old. You refused to accept that she was changing. She said she tried to talk to you but you refused to hear her. You couldn't let go of the way things used to be, the way she used to be."

The memories don't quite surface, but I know that they're there. I know Camille had tried to break through my fantasy, but I hadn't let her. I can feel the memory of her pulling away, the tug on my heart as the distance between us increased and I refused to believe it.

"She was worried about you being roommates," Hunter continues. "She was afraid you wouldn't make any of your own friends, that you'd rely on her forever."

The fire suddenly seems too bright. It is exposing too

much. I want to tell Hunter to shut up. I want to tell him things Camille said about him that would hurt him. But I have nothing to tell him. She told me nothing. He was one of so many of her new secrets.

"She didn't want to move to San Francisco with you after college," he says. "She wanted to sign up for the Peace Corps or Teach for America. She wanted to do something on her own. Something away from you."

San Francisco. What a stupid destination. One of the most sophisticated and expensive cities in the world to live in, and we were two country girls with no money and no skills. And now I am one country girl, alone, on my way to a place that I imagined as ours. But it never was, and it never will be. She wanted to be somewhere else, somewhere far away from me. And now she is.

Camille would never choose to stick around as a ghost, would never have the kind of troubled soul that tethers itself to the world it's supposed to leave behind. Camille is not the one holding on to a long-gone past. Terry was right—if you're lonely enough, even a ghost will keep you company.

"Are you okay?" Hunter says softly.

"Yeah," I say, but I'm not sure if I mean it. I'm not sure if I even know what okay feels like.

We sit on the log and watch the fire die out. There is no more need to talk; enough has been said for tonight. Coyotes or wolves howl and they sound closer than they should be. They could eat us in the night. We could be killed before we even knew what was happening. The fire turns to embers and we go silently to bed. Hunter falls asleep quickly, but I can't. I feel so on edge, so shaky, so close to shattering. I need something, someone, to help hold me together.

I know I shouldn't, but the night is so big and empty, the wolves are so close and hungry, my arms need to be around someone warm and solid, and Hunter is so close. He fits so perfectly in my arms. My body curls around his. His warmth is my warmth. He is asleep, so it doesn't matter that I'm crying, that my sobs are mixing with howls of the wolves and turning the night even blacker.

But his arms wrap around me and squeeze back. The night is black and the world is empty, but he is here and I am not alone.

We hold on to each other as the wolves take over the night. But we are safe from them in here. This is the solid place. Everything else drifts away, leaving only us, holding on, curling into each other. I listen to him breathe as sleep falls over me. I let myself feel the dull pain grinding inside my chest, but I also let myself feel Hunter's warmth around me. I let myself feel held and safe, even in the midst of so much pain.

FIFTEEN

Hunter and I didn't even kiss last night, but when I wake up in his arms I feel like we did much more. When I open my eyes, his are right in front of me, inches away, blinking away sleep just like mine. For a brief moment, I panic—did something else happen? But no, we are still in our own sleeping bags. Our clothes are still on.

"Good morning," he says, a little unsurely.

"Good morning," I say, discomfort starting to spread through me. My body stiffens and he lets go, scoots a few inches away so I can no longer feel him against me.

We're both a little embarrassed as we pack up, a little too polite and careful with each other. As we drive away, Hunter leans over; I think he's going to kiss me, and my body tenses in anticipation. His face is close and I can smell the toothpaste on his breath. My lips part a little—to say something or kiss him back, I'm not sure which. But he just smiles, reaches over, and pulls a twig out of my hair.

"Make a wish," he says, holding the twig in front of me.

"On that?" I laugh, still giddy from the almost-kiss.

"Sure, why not? It's like making a wish on an eyelash. It's a tree's eyelash."

"Okay," I say, and scrunch my face into a caricature of serious thinking. But even though this is a joke, it somehow seems important. I really do need to make a wish. But what do I even want?

I close my eyes and send my wish to God or the universe or whatever's out there listening: *I want to know what I want.*

I open my eyes and blow on the twig in Hunter's fingers. He flicks it out the window. "What'd you wish for?" he asks.

"It's a secret," I tell him.

"You and your secrets, Kinsey Cole."

The mountains of northern Wyoming turn to rolling hills as we go south. The landscape is yellow with dried grass, dotted with mountains of straw bound in swirls like giant cinnamon rolls.

"Look at those things," I say. "They must weigh at least a ton."

"Let's find out," Hunter says, and jerks the car to the side of the freeway.

"What are you doing?"

"I have to go check out this straw."

"Why?"

"Just because."

"Because why?"

"Not everything you do has to have a reason." He grins. He leans over and gives me a quick peck on the cheek. Before it has a chance to register, he's out of the car and running around the field.

So I follow. I feel the rush of cars on the freeway as I make my way over the embankment and into the field. The rolls are massive, at least twice my height. I walk in and out of them, calling for Hunter. The wind plays with his voice, makes it come from all directions, and I feel like I'm going in the circles trying to follow it. "Where are you?" I call.

"Here!" he says, but I don't know where here is. I run and weave, chasing his voice. The straw towers above me and I can't see the car anymore; I don't even know which direction the freeway is. I'm lost in a maze of yellow. The paths from here are infinite. I look up and the blue sky towers above me.

But it doesn't feel heavy; it feels expansive, limitless. Amid all this unknown, I don't feel scared. Maybe being lost isn't such a bad thing.

Arms grab me from behind and I scream. Hunter wraps me in a bear hug. "Where are we?" I say.

"I was hoping you knew." His breath is warm on the back of my ear. We stand for a while like that, looking up at the sky. In this moment, everything feels so simple, so perfect. There is only us; there is only here. It doesn't matter that we are lost.

Somehow we find our way back to the car. As soon as I see the freeway, see the cars rushing to their destinations, feel the harsh wind of their speed, my bliss is joined by an uneasy doubt. Is *this* the real world—this freeway with its hostile speed, this straight, hard path? What I felt out there in the maze, was that real too? Or was it just the result of chasing a beautiful boy, of having his arms around me?

This trip will soon be over. Whatever this is brewing between Hunter and me will end. Or will it? My plans for the future never included him, not like this. Maybe once I thought we could be friends, but now do I want him to be something more? How could that be possible while working full-time and going to school? How would I make room in my life for something like a relationship?

Is that even what I want? Do I want to be in a relationship with him? I care about Hunter, I know that. I feel alive when I'm with him. But does that automatically need to translate into something long-term? Am I supposed to re-envision my path as something in tandem, something defined by "us" instead of me? Should we aspire to become like Eli and Shelby? Should we make a home together? Should we plan on forever?

Hunter hums as he starts the car and gets back on the freeway. How can he be so calm at a time like this? How can he not be terrified? I must do something. I must say something.

"Did you love Camille?" is what comes out of my mouth.

I feel the car jerk a little. "Whoa, where the hell did that come from?" he says. I have no idea. Probably my instinct to say the exact wrong thing at the exact wrong time.

"It's an obvious question."

He doesn't say anything.

"If you were me, wouldn't you want to know?"

Silence.

"Well?" I say after a few unbearable moments.

"I don't know," he finally answers.

"'I don't know'? Isn't that what I'm not allowed to say? That's not an answer."

"It's my answer."

"But it's not an answer."

"My answer is 'I don't know,'" Hunter says softly after a long silence. "That's my honest answer." I hold my breath, waiting for him to say more, waiting for something definitive. But he just says the same thing again: "I don't know if I loved her. I'm sorry if that's not the answer you wanted."

I don't know what I'm supposed to say. Am I supposed to tell him it's okay, as if it's my place to give him permission for his feelings?

"I think I loved lots of things about her," he says, and I'm surprised to feel a squeeze in my chest. Is that jealousy? "Her laugh," he says. "Her enthusiasm. The way she always saw the positive in something. The way she saw the positive in people. In me."

"I loved her hope," I say, but the last word gets tangled in my throat. Heat rushes to my face, and my eyes well with tears and I have to clench on tight to keep my heart from bursting.

Hunter looks at me briefly from the driver's seat. "Yeah. Exactly. It felt good to be around her. I loved how she made me feel. We had a lot of fun. But I don't know if that's love. I think love has to be something more than that."

"So what is it then?"

He doesn't even pause to think. "Someone knowing every piece of you, from the top all the way to the very bottom. All the light and all the dark." He says this with such confidence, as if he's absolutely certain. "And they love it all, even the shitty stuff. And you let them, even though it's the scariest thing you've ever done. And you want to keep doing it forever."

"Wow," is all I can think to say.

"Wow, what?"

"You've thought about it a lot."

"Not really. I don't know. I guess I'm secretly emo."

"Not so secret," I say.

He laughs a little, and it lightens the car just enough. "What about you?" he says then. "Have you ever been in love?"

Does he want me to say yes? Does he want me to say I'm in love with him? I look at his face and realize no, that's not what we are. I don't know how to define what we're doing, who we are to each other, but I know that whatever it is it doesn't include these one-word definitions, these standard labels, any of the bullshit dating games, those half-truths and slow reveals, all those fears of letting someone in bit by bit, the lying to keep them interested. We are beyond all that. Maybe because we were thrown together by a tragedy. Maybe because we are two people who would never have crossed paths otherwise. Maybe because we never planned this.

Or maybe because we know it's only temporary, because we know it's going nowhere. Maybe that's what frees us—we can tell the truth only because we have no future.

So I answer truthfully. Have I ever been in love? "No."

There is no sign of hurt on Hunter's face. He doesn't want me to be in love with him. "But you've had boyfriends?"

"Yeah, a couple. It was fun for a while. Then it wasn't."

He chuckles. "How romantic."

"Yep, that's me. Miss Romance."

"Are you a virgin?"

"Oh my god! That is so none of your business."

"Oh, come on," he teases. "I'm sure Camille told you way more about our sex life than I'm comfortable with."

"Not really."

"Oh."

"She hardly told me anything." The truth of this is too big for this moment, too big for me. I suddenly feel so lonely, but it's a loneliness that goes back in time and erases my denial, erases Camille from my memories of all the times I told myself that things were fine, that *we* were fine, back all the way to the beginning of when she started pulling away and I refused to see it, refused to let her change, refused to let her go. Truth erases Camille until all that's left is me, standing alone, with an empty space next to me where she used to be.

"No, I'm not a virgin," I say.

"You didn't have to tell me," Hunter says.

"I know," I say. "I wanted to tell you."

I'm sick of hiding. I'm sick of secrets.

I want lightness. I want truth.

Something feels off. Tilted. On the verge of spilling over.

We've barely spoken during southern Wyoming and into Utah. We are so close now. Only Nevada stands between us and California.

I am not ready. The car is suddenly suffocating. Hunter takes up too much space. It is crowded with him, with us, heavy with these new bonds that tie us together.

The suburbs are turning into desolation. We are outside of Salt Lake City, back on the 80 after avoiding it for so long. "Fuck my dad," Hunter said. "He was bluffing. He wouldn't go through the trouble to hunt down this car. He can buy a new one. And he sure as hell doesn't want me back."

My mind keeps returning to the same thought—what's going to happen when Hunter and I separate? Maybe it won't happen right away, but I know that whatever this sweetness is between us right now, it's not meant to last forever. I cannot see him in my future. I cannot see our lives in tandem. He stepped into my life and gave me something beautiful, but he will step back out when our time together is done.

Some things are not meant to last forever. Some relationships are meant to be intense and vast and life changing, but also short, also temporary. And after the person is gone, you're left with what they've done, how they've changed you. And it stays with you forever, even if they don't.

So we will touch each other's lives, we will change each other's course, and then we will move on. And then what? Who's going to protect me from my dreams? Who's going to protect me from my own loneliness? Who's going to keep me safe? Who will I be without him?

Who am I without Camille?

I turn the radio on to fill my head with something, anything besides my own thoughts. The newscaster is saying something about a forest fire in the mountains east of Salt Lake City. The sky is thick with its smoke, red and sickly as the sun makes its slow way down to the horizon. I can smell the fire in the air, the destruction, all those trees burning.

A sign says something about salt flats. There is nothing around us but white, flat nothingness, a dry, ancient seabed, too salty for life. Dead.

I reach over and turn the radio off. The only sound is the wind whipping through the open windows. Even the breeze is hot. This place could be the moon, a distant planet, and yet recognition throbs inside me, like I've been here before, like I knew I'd return. The pressure in my chest builds as we drive deeper into the sterile desert, as color drains from the world, leaving only the heavy orange of the sky and the ashy white of the salt flats. The setting sun is a huge puncture in the sky, a gaping red wound, a cotton ball collecting blood.

I can't keep living like this, living in fear, running from myself, dependent on Hunter to keep me safe. That's not what friendship is, not what love is. It's not dependence, not desperation, not falling apart the moment we're separated, not seeing ghosts because I'm so afraid of being alone. And now here I am, in the blank space between earth and sky, where the horizon is forever away, where all color but fire has been completely bled out of the world. This is the place where Camille is lost, where I am lost, the place of infinity, the place of nowhere.

"Stop the car," I say.

"What?"

"Just stop the car."

"Here?"

"Yes. Pull over."

"Why?"

"Just pull over." My voice is fire.

He doesn't question me. Before the car even comes to a complete stop, I jump out, barefoot, and start running. The air is thick and hot, the wind hard and screaming, shoving the heat like a bulldozer, huge heavy mountains of it. I jump over broken glass and garbage, all coated with the same dingy white dust, all these discarded things that used to be colorful, now just bleached trash on the side of the road. My feet find the flat white clay—sterile, empty, dry, and dead, with no rocks, no plants, no hills, nothing for as far as the eye can see. The ground is springy, like gym mats, perfect for running. I could run forever on this and never get injured. I could just keep running until the end of the world.

So I run. Somewhere in the wind, I can hear Hunter's voice calling my name, but I have crossed over, I am a ghost, I am so far away his voice just barely reaches me. I run and run until he is gone, the road is gone, the sound of cars is gone, everything but the clouds at my feet and the bloody sky darkening into night.

"Camille!" I scream into the void.

I hear her laughing.

"Camille!"

I conjure her into being.

Her footsteps padding beside me.

Her long legs and thin waist, her graceful arms pumping.

Her face, smiling. But it is not her smile.

I run as fast as I can, track team fast, star of the soccer team fast. Camille could never run as fast as me. I feel like I've been running for miles, like if I turned around I wouldn't even be able to see the road anymore. But the view in front of me hasn't changed a bit; the horizon is still forever away. There is no end to this. There is no destination. I could keep running and running forever and never get anywhere. I could run until I died, and I'd still end up here anyway, a restless ghost like Camille.

Is that what I want? To just keep running? To keep going nowhere? Even out here, in this alien place, I carry everything from home with me. I carry Camille. I carry fear and sorrow and emptiness. I carry myself. As fast as I run, I will always carry myself.

So what happens if I stop running? What happens if I stop being scared?

Take away fear, and maybe Camille will just be a memory; maybe she will stop being a ghost. Memories still hurt; they can rip you apart with loss and pain. But they're not monsters. Not things that kill.

I stop running.

Every muscle in my body burns and my lungs scream from pumping the smoky air, but I am not dying. I turn around and Camille's ghost is standing in front of me with dark nothingness behind her. The sun has set. There is no moon. The red of the sky has been replaced with black. But Camille is perfectly illuminated, dressed in the same jeans and tank top she was wearing the night she was killed, the same thing she was wearing when she led me to the top of the quarry and asked me to join her.

"This isn't you, Camille," I say.

"Who am I?" She smiles.

"It's not you."

"Who am I, Kinsey?"

She stares at me and I look deep into her eyes. I see right through them, into the blackness behind her. She is transparent. She is nothing.

"If I'm not Camille, who am I?"

All of a sudden, it's so obvious.

The image of Camille in front of me flickers. Like bad reception, like faulty wires.

It's not her. It never was.

The girl in front of me is only a hologram, projected out of my own mind. She is a shadow puppet made out of fear. There is only one person who could ever hate me this much, only one who could be capable of causing me so much pain.

"Kinsey!" the voice pleads. It crackles like radio static.

"You're not real," I say.

"Oh yeah?" The ghost laughs. "Then why are you talking to me?"

"I'm done talking to you." I start walking. I walk right through her. She is not real. She cannot hurt me.

"I'm ready to let you go," I say.

"What if I'm not?" says the voice, wavering in the darkness.

"You have no choice."

The image of Camille flashes in front of me. Her face goes in and out of focus. Her screams whip through the air with wind, but they have lost their sharpness. I close my eyes and breathe. I inhale and my chest opens to memory, to the real Camille, the one I've been trying to escape.

Images flash through my mind— Camille in her jeans and tank top; Camille in her favorite yellow bikini, with curves I will never come close to having; Camille in her prom gown, stunning and elegant; Camille at twelve, gawky and only just turning beautiful. Here we are playing dress-up as little kids; here we are staying up late and gossiping in the darkness. Here is Camille's first love; here is Camille's first heartbreak. Here I am watching her life, saving mine for later, always later. And here is her patience, her love, her loyalty, despite all my demands.

And now here she is in front of me, on the ground in a pool of blood, her face gone, her skin charred, her arm twisted in a way no arm should ever be twisted. Just the memory of a body, now ashes buried in the ground back home, dissolving back into the earth. The image fades until there is only the lifeless, flat clay of the salt flat in front of me.

No ghost, no monster. Just memory.

Just feelings that cannot be seen or measured.

Just love and loss that is infinite.

"Good-bye, Camille," I say. That is all I ever needed to say.

And then, in the darkness, two eyes shining white. The black broken by headlights, Hunter searching for me.

I walk slowly toward the light, for once not in a hurry. I look up and the sky is suddenly clear, the cloud of smoke from the forest fire pushed away by the wind. A gentle breeze now blows, cooler than the hot blasts of before, as if trying to soothe the parched earth, as if telling it *you have gone through enough*. Stars poke through the black, little twinkling beacons of hope.

The headlights get closer, shining a long, straight path to me. I hear the hum of the car's engine. I am held by the spot-light.

Hunter turns off the car and gets out. The sound of the car door closing is so sharp in the empty night. With the light in my eyes, I can make out only the barest outline of him in the black.

"Hi," I say.

"Hi," he says.

"Turn the lights off, will you?"

The world goes dark again.

"Come here," I say. I reach for his hand, pull him gently down to the ground. "Lie on your back," I say.

We are side by side, holding hands, warmed by a blanket of diamonds.

"Did you find what you were looking for?" Hunter says softly. His words float up to the heavens and mingle with the stars.

"Yeah. I think so."

"You scared me a little."

"Maybe it's not so bad to be scared."

Silence holds us. We could stay here forever.

The world is drained of color and we fill up the emptiness.

Hunter squeezes my hand. "Do you think she's up there?"

"Sure," I say. "Why not? She could be anywhere. Up there. Down here. In some other dimension we don't even know about."

"I believe in heaven," Hunter says. Like a confession, like an apology.

I do not respond. There is nothing to say to faith.

"You think I'm stupid," Hunter says.

"No I don't." I turn my head to look him in the eye, to make sure he knows I mean it. "Why would you think that?"

"You must think I'm stupid for believing. You strike me as the kind of person who would think that. No offense."

I sigh. He's right. I have been the kind of person who would think that—cynical, superior, untrusting of mystery. But that was me before this, before everything happened, before I chased a ghost across the country and convinced myself it was chasing me.

"You believe in heaven," I say. "I believe in ghosts."

"So we're both delusional."

Looking up at the sky like this, I can understand why people would think there was something up there, some kind of magical, mysterious promise, something better than down here. Even now, with all the things we know through science, the mystery is still there—we can imagine all those stars as other suns, with worlds like ours orbiting around them.

"You never thought about it?" Hunter says. "With Camille's death and everything? You never thought about where she is now?"

"I was too busy freaking out that she was still here," I say, knowing he can never fully understand what I mean. "And maybe if I let myself think about where she went, then I'd have to admit she was really gone."

We are quiet for a while. I feel my hand warm in Hunter's. And that is all I feel. There is no sense of Camille stalking behind me, no Camille hiding behind the car, no Camille in my head, no Camille hanging on to life. For once, no me hanging on to her. I don't know how I know, but I am certain she is gone for good.

I have never seen so many stars.

"Maybe I believe in something like reincarnation," I say. "Like how science has proven that matter never really dies, it just moves around as energy and eventually becomes part of something else. Maybe souls are like that too, made up of a bunch of little soul atoms that get recycled over and over again, forever. So maybe you could have atoms in you that Jesus did, or Buddha, or a whale, or a tree, or a rock, or even an alien from another galaxy."

"And maybe Camille's soul is getting blown around," Hunter says. "Getting recycled and becoming parts of new things being born."

"Like babies."

"Or algae."

"Or starfish."

"Or stars," Hunter says.

I start crying. The tears run down the side of my face and drip onto the parched earth below me. "And maybe we are breathing in pieces of her, and they get caught in our lungs and spread through our bloodstreams."

"And maybe one little piece made it into our hearts," Hunter says. "And it's just going to hang around there for a while."

"Keeping us company."

"Yeah."

Hunter lifts my hand and places it on my heart, puts his hand over it, and pushes gently. I can feel the slightest rhythm.

"You feel her?" he says.

"Yes."

"Me too," he says.

We lie there for a while, our tears turning the salt earth back into sea, feeling the tiny pieces of Camille pulse through us, watching her above us, her soul as big as the sky, turning into stars.

We are drained. We are zombies. We are colorless, powdered white with the fine dust of the salt flats.

We do not speak the half hour it takes to drive across the border into Nevada. I don't consult Hunter as I pull into the first casino/hotel I see. I know he's as ready to stop as I am.

From the blank, colorless nothingness of the salt flats, we are thrown into its exact opposite. The casino is a different kind of nightmare, where we have to find our way through a maze of ringing, blinking slot machines. We float through the smoky haze, the air heavy and poisoned with cigarette smoke illuminated by the false cheerfulness of flashing lights. Old, haggard faces are bent and distorted, glued to their slot machine screens, multicolored lights reflecting off thick bifocals. Clawlike hands grasp buckets of quarters. We are the only youth in a sea of dead eyes and loose skin.

We cannot get to our room fast enough. The elevator smells like mothballs and cigars. We do not look at each other. The only words we have spoken in the last hour were what was needed to ask the clerk at the front desk for our room.

I open the door and a blast of air-conditioning welcomes us. The room is clean enough, with a bare minimum of decor and comfort. The dust of the salt flats sticks to my skin, mixed with my sweat like a layer of concrete paste. I throw my bag on the floor and walk to the window, look out at the sad nothing of a town, the few lights in the sea of desert beyond. How did anyone decide to settle here? Why would anyone want to make a life in such an empty, dead place?

I feel Hunter's hand on my shoulder, see his reflection in the window. We are only half there, just outlines filled in with darkness. I watch him behind me as he unbuttons and takes off his shirt. There is only the black of night where his scars should be. He kicks off his shoes and unbuttons his jeans, keeping his eyes locked on mine the whole time. He turns around and walks, naked, to the bathroom. And I follow.

Our bodies fill the small shower. Dust turns into mud and pools at our feet in gray puddles. We are human colored once again. Hunter unwraps the small bar of soap and runs it up my arm, my collarbone, my neck. I close my eyes as he washes me, as his touch makes me clean.

I trace his scars with my fingers. His ravaged skin is like a map of his suffering, all the mountains and valleys the sites of historic events. I place my finger on a spot on his shoulder. "This is where we crashed," I whisper. "Right here."

He moves my finger a centimeter to the right. "This is where Camille died."

I move my finger a centimeter more. "This is where you saved me."

He takes my hand in his and holds me close. Every part of us is touching, the maps of our bodies becoming one big world.

The bed is hard and the sheets are scratchy, but it is heaven enough for us. We leave the lights on as we make love; there has already been too much darkness. It feels like dying, like being born, like it's both our first and our last night on earth. We push ourselves together, erasing the boundaries between us. But through the heat and the sweetness, it feels somehow like we're saying good-bye. This is the closest we're ever going to get. No matter what, we'll have to come apart. Tomorrow we'll be in San Francisco and this journey will be over.

* * *

We wake up early, but neither of us wants to get out of bed. We don't say it out loud, but we both know this is our last day on the road, our last morning, and we want to make it last. We splurge on room service breakfast and eat it naked. For some reason, this makes me feel more grown-up than I've ever felt in my life.

Checkout is at ten. We pack in silence. Hunter takes my hand as the door closes behind us and I squeeze it tight as we pass through the casino to get to the parking lot. I try not to look at the handful of people slumped over their slot machines, many with cocktails. Whether their drinking is a continuation of last night or a start to today, it's equally depressing. I try not to imagine how sad the rest of their lives are that this is where they'd prefer to be at ten in the morning. Have they been here all night, parked in front of the same machine, convinced that if they stay in the same place long enough, their luck will change? Don't they know that's not how luck works?

After so many days and nights and miles of tension, Hunter and I are finally relaxed. I think back to the crazy night with Mountain and Chesapeake—which seems years ago now—when Mountain asked if I was "loose" yet. Even in his inebriated state, he already knew the answer; I could tell by the smirk on his slobbery lips. Even in the middle of the forest, miles away from home, I was still the uptight girl sitting primly on the sidelines, not participating, just judging, thinking everyone so foolish for having fun. And now, finally, I feel somewhere close to the "loose" Mountain talked about, except it didn't take copious amounts of alcohol or pot brownies to get here. It didn't even take running away from home, driving almost the entire way across the country, and making love to a beautiful boy in the saddest hotel in the world. It could have happened anywhere, anytime, if I wanted it to. The key is wanting to. And then it's so simple. Then all you have to do is let go.

The sun rises and paints the desert pink. Mountains grow in the distance, waiting for us to cross them. I look over at Hunter sleeping in the passenger seat and feel so many feelings all at once—warmth, yearning, gratitude, sadness, fear, hope. Just weeks ago, I never would have believed this was possible, that I would be capable of being so human, that I would welcome it. I never would have thought that it would be Camille's death to end up teaching me how to be alive.

Hunter wakes as the sun rises higher in the sky, the heat rising with it. The car is loud with wind from the open windows. We have to yell to hear each other.

"What'd I miss?" Hunter says as he stretches his long limbs.

"Some clouds. A few cars. Trucks. Quite a lot of dirt and rocks."

"Fascinating."

"Hunter, I have to tell you something."

"Oh shit, are you pregnant?"

"Very funny."

"Did you lie about being on the pill? The condom didn't break, I swear."

"Shut up. I'm serious."

"I know. That's why I'm trying to make things not serious."

I close the windows with my controller so the car will be quiet. "Hey," Hunter protests. "We're going to bake in here."

I take a deep breath. The car is quiet, but already uncomfortably hot. "Hunter," I say. "I'm not staying in San Francisco with you. I'm going back to Michigan to go to college."

"I know." He says it so casually, I think for a second he misheard me. "I never thought you were running away for good."

"I'm sorry."

"Don't be. You're going to love college. College is going to love you. You were born to be a college girl. Now can we open the windows?" His window buzzes down and our words fly out.

"I'm going to miss you," I say, barely audible.

"Let's not have that conversation," he says, looking out the window.

"What are your plans? What are you going to—"

"Let's not have that conversation either."

"What conversation should we have?"

"Let's just be quiet for a while," he says, his head turned so I can't see any of his face. He is only his back, his shoulders.

So we are quiet. I open the rest of the windows and the wind screams in our heads, filling up the silence.

After five hours of driving, we cross into California at the peak of the Sierra Nevada mountain range. The freeway hugs the steep side of the cliff, with only a short concrete barrier protecting us from falling to our deaths. Silver rock towers above us and alpine trees grasp on for dear life. The air is crisp and pine-scented. I suck it in and feel clean, refreshed. I have never smelled air so pure.

We scale Donner Summit and begin our descent to the Pacific Ocean. "It's all downhill from here," Hunter says. We could coast all the way to San Francisco. We could ride there on inertia.

In the late afternoon, we stop for gas and snacks outside of Sacramento. Neither of us says it, but we both know this is our last stop before we get to San Francisco.

The restroom is a single, but there is no avoiding it. I must go in there alone. I must face whatever there is to face.

I enter and lock the door. I take stock of everything I see—the toilet, the sink, the garbage can, the hand dryer, all in their logical places. I am ultra-aware of every minuscule movement I make. I look in the mirror at my gaunt, tanned face, my sunburned nose. I adjust my ponytail. I take a deep breath.

I whisper to my reflection, "Camille."

I feel the heavy tugging at my insides, the empty place where I store my love. I close my eyes and wait.

All I hear is the faucet dripping and the muted sound of a cash register.

"Camille," I say again.

Nothing.

She is gone, really gone. And I am on my own.

My heart still hurts, a dull ache around the edges, and it may be that way forever—wounded, scarred by fire. But at least I know now that it is not empty. As imperfect as the filling is—Hunter, my mom and her various absences, memories of half friends, my grandmother, whatever friends and lovers the future has planned for me—I am not alone. There is a world of people yearning just like me, just as lost and lonely, just as desperate to make connections. They are living, breathing people—not ghosts, not hallucinations, not my sad, lonely brain trying to punish itself for feeling.

I splash my face with water. I take one last look in the mirror. I watch myself smile as I realize this is the first real privacy I've had in days. Peeing in a bathroom without the company of a psychopathic ghost—one of life's little pleasures.

I turn off the lights and spend a moment in the dark before opening the door.

Camille, you are gone. And it hurts. But I am going to be okay.

The 80 delivers us to Oakland at rush hour, where it's sunny and warm as we make our way along the eastern shoreline, watching sailboats fight the wind against the backdrop of Marin County's rolling hills.

"Eli has a friend who lives around here somewhere," Hunter says. "A guy he met in rehab. He said he'd give me a place to stay until I get on my feet."

"In Oakland?" I say. All I know about Oakland is its sports teams and reputation for crime.

"Apparently, it's way cooler than San Francisco now. But I guess you have to be cool to know that."

We inch across the Bay Bridge with the windows down and our arms out, San Francisco opening up in front of us with its famous skyline, the water sparkling below us. The sky is clear and everything glows with promise. Even the old prison of Alcatraz seems welcoming on its pretty little island.

I wonder how many like us have made similar journeys, have arrived here full of hope and been welcomed by this dazzling view. I wonder how many have shown up on San Francisco's doorstep with their backpacks full of history, counting on the city to give them something they could never get where they came from. All those Midwestern kids, those Bible Belt kids, those rural and suburban kids, fleeing the lives they were born into, fleeing the fear of ending up like their parents—how many of them make it? How many of them find what they're looking for? Will Hunter? Will I?

The bridge drops us in the middle of downtown San Francisco, where we have to dodge hordes of pedestrians and kamikaze bicyclists. We leave the high-rises and weave through narrow streets on what seems like an intentionally complicated route to the Golden Gate Bridge.

"Are you sure this is the way?" Hunter says.

"I checked the map like five times."

"There's seriously no freeway that goes through the city?"

"This is the freeway."

"This isn't a freeway."

"The map says it's a freeway."

"The map is a lying sack of shit."

The tires squeal as Hunter breaks abruptly. We barely miss a half-dressed man pushing a shopping cart across the street in the middle of traffic.

"Jesus!"

"City life already getting to you?"

A few minutes later, we barely avoid a fender bender. Hunter honks and curses the guy in front of us. "Are all these people high? These are the worst drivers I've ever seen in my life."

"Take a deep breath," I say. "We're almost there."

Earth lost in a sea of fog.

We are floating above it, held suspended by blood-orange bones.

The sound of water, of waves crashing. Wind howling.

Jagged land opening to ocean.

After ten hours of driving, we are finally here, just in time to see the sunset off the Golden Gate Bridge. But we can't see anything. The perfect summer day of Oakland seems so far away—a different season, a different world. I have Terry's scarf wrapped around my neck; never did I think I would actually be grateful he gave it to me.

"It's July in California," I moan, my teeth chattering. "And I'm going to freeze to death."

I can make out other tourists through the fog, huddled together in their summer shorts and tank tops, wondering what to do with their cameras.

I prop Terry Junior on top of the fence separating us from the white nothingness. He can't see anything either.

"How's our love child doing?" Hunter says.

"He's a little disappointed with the view."

We look out into the whiteness. There's a huge world out there, but we can't even see it.

"I think we need to start talking about the custody arrangement," Hunter says.

"He should stay with you. I get the scarf, you get Terry Junior."

"But a child needs his mother."

"But you need supervision. Someone to keep you accountable." I don't need to remind him that it's only Terry Junior and me who know about his promise to stay sober.

The wind changes. Fog swirls around us, the water droplets so big we can see them. They stick to our skin and our clothes until we are wet. We are drowning in a river of thick white blindness, caught in the current, suspended. The wind gusts and I have to grab onto Hunter to keep from falling. Tourists squeal and scatter.

Then one more gust. Color pushes out the white. The sky opens and gives itself to us.

The crowd utters a collective "Ahhh" as the famous view is unveiled before us. The sunset is a rainbow above the perfect cushion of white fluff that still hugs the sea, a thin strip of blue the only barrier between the fog and every hue of orange imaginable.

"We're at the end of the world," Hunter says. "What do we do now?"

I don't know the answer. In the past, this would have filled me with panic—not knowing, not having a plan, not having a direct route from A to B. But maybe it's okay to not always know the path in advance. Maybe it's okay to allow for some wandering.

I'm eighteen years old. I've barely even lived yet. How could I possibly know what I'm going to do with the rest of my life? How could I possibly know who I'm going to be in five, ten, fifty years? Maybe that's how people get stuck in lives they don't want—assuming that their decisions must be permanent, that there are no do-overs. But what if life is really a series of lives, a series of reinventions? What if the best paths are made up of detours?

"We turn around, I guess," I say.

"Can't you hang out for a while before school starts?"

I lean into him. "I'm not going to suffer the last two weeks driving across the country with you just to turn around as soon as I get here."

"Good," he says, wrapping me in his arms. His musk mixes with the smell of the sea water and I breathe it in deep. "Then I guess real life starts after that."

"Hunter," I say, kissing him lightly on the lips, the sun setting behind us like a postcard. "This is real life."